Tsukasa
Mikogami
POLITICIAN

Masato
Sanada
BUSINESSMAN

Aoi
Ichijou
SWORDMASTER

Prince Akatsuki
MAGICIAN

©Sacraneco

"Is it still all right to give this everything we've got?"

"While we're willing to help you, if we don't **hold back**, we're likely to end up accelerating your world's culture by at least **five hundred years.**"

©Sacraneco

©Sacraneco

The women... were all wearing bikinis made from nothing but leaves.

CONTENTS

RIKU MISORA
ILLUSTRATION BY SACRANECO

High School Prodigies Have It Easy Even in Another World!

High School Prodigies Have It Easy Even in Another World!

1

Riku Misora

Illustration by SACRANECO

YEN ON

NEW YORK

High School Prodigies Have It Easy Even in Another World! 1

Riku Misora

TRANSLATION BY NATHANIEL THRASHER
COVER ART BY SACRANECO

CHOUJIN KOUKOUSEI TACHI WA ISEKAI DEMO YOYU DE IKINUKU YOUDESU! vol. 1
Copyright © 2015 Riku Misora
Illustrations copyright © 2015 Sacraneco
All rights reserved.
Original Japanese edition published in 2015 by SB Creative Corp.
This English edition is published by arrangement with SB Creative Corp.,
Tokyo in care of Tuttle-Mori Agency, Inc., Tokyo.

English translation © 2020 by Yen Press, LLC

Yen On
150 West 30th Street, 19th Floor
New York, NY 10001

Visit us at yenpress.com
facebook.com/yenpress ★ twitter.com/yenpress
yenpress.tumblr.com ★ instagram.com/yenpress

First Yen On Edition: July 2020

Yen On is an imprint of Yen Press, LLC.
The Yen On name and logo are trademarks of Yen Press, LLC.

Library of Congress Cataloging-in-Publication Data
Names: Misora, Riku, author. | Sacraneco, illustrator. | Thrasher, Nathaniel Hiroshi, translator.
Title: High school prodigies have it easy even in another world! / Riku Misora ; illustration by Sacraneco ; translation by Nathaniel Hiroshi Thrasher.
Other titles: Chōjin-Kokoseitachi wa Isekai demo Yoyu de Ikinuku Yōdesu! English
Identifiers: LCCN 2020016894 | ISBN 9781975309725 (v. 1 ; trade paperback)
Subjects: CYAC: Fantasy. | Gifted persons—Fiction. | Imaginary places—Fiction | Magic—Fiction.
Classification: LCC PZ7.M6843377 Hi 2020 | DDC [Fic]—dc23
LC record available at https://lccn.loc.gov/2020016894

ISBNs: 978-1-9753-0972-5 (paperback)
978-1-9753-0973-2 (ebook)

10 9 8 7 6 5 4 3 2 1

LSC-C

Printed in the United States of America

❧ The Seven High School Prodigies ❧

In Japan, there were seven high school students whose names were known the world over.

The first was a modern-day samurai, who wielded her blade in a Middle Eastern conflict in order to protect the weak.

"Dammit! Fire, fire! Kill her already!"

"I can't! She's too fast, I can't hit— GAAAAH!"

The young woman dashed across the bullet-filled wasteland like a gust of wind, her long hair fluttering behind her.

Then she charged the line of soldiers and swung her katana. A flower of blood bloomed.

Flustered, the soldiers took aim at her, but their frantic shots only managed to hit their allies. None of their rounds even came close to her.

"Th-this can't be… She slaughtered us all…! Our entire squad, armed to the teeth…was taken out by a little girl using nothing but a sword…?!"

As the commander trembled in fear, the girl turned to him with fury in her eyes.

"You people are fiends, menacing women and children with guns and violence, and the blade of Ichijou has no mercy for brutes like you."

"Ah, ahhhhh!"

"Thus, I must cut you down—!"

—Her name was Aoi Ichijou. She was the world's greatest sword-master, even though she was still in high school.

The figure she cast as she dashed across war-torn lands, taking down foes equipped with the finest modern armaments while armed with but a single katana, was the spitting image of a heroine right out of a fairy tale.

The second was a physician who was treating refugees at a camp near Aoi's battlefield—

"AAAARGH! IT HUUUUURTS! I'M GONNA DIEEEE!"

"Ow! Hold his leg down, there!"

"Y-yes ma'am!"

"Heh-heh-heh. If you can thrash about that wildly after being hit by a bullet, you're going to be just fine. Still, if you keep on like that, I won't be able to treat you. Let's get a sedative in you so you'll behave, shall we?"

"But, Doc! Aren't we out of morphine already...?!"

"I won't need any."

And with that, the girl wearing a blood-drenched white gown grabbed a needle, stuck it in the nape of the writhing patient's neck, and gave the syringe a light flick with her finger.

Even though he'd been squirming violently, the man's expression instantly became rapturous. He promptly passed out.

"Wh-what did you...?"

"I used the needle to adjust the amount of endorphins his brain was secreting. He'll be out for eight hours on the dot... Can you all handle removing the bullet and stitching up the wound?"

"Y-yes, Doctor!"

"In that case, I'm going to go around with needles and apply this sedative to all the patients with minor wounds and leave the rest of their treatment to you. Ah, and one other thing. If you could follow Aoi and bring me some dead soldiers, that would be lovely. We need blood for transfusions and organs for transplants."

"A-are you sure, Doc? Ethically speaking, that's a little...you know..." Despite being a member of the same NGO, the man who'd asked the question had gone quite pale.

Even with all the blood spraying about and the screams echoing through the hellish refugee camp, the girl stained in crimson maintained an unbroken smile as she answered.

"Of course I'm sure. I can save far more lives than ethics ever will."

—Her name was Keine Kanzaki. She was the world's greatest doctor, even though she was still in high school.

There was no disease her treatment couldn't cure, and as far as she was concerned, the term *lifespan* was little more than a suggestion.

The third was an enigma who'd traveled to the land of the free and was currently hovering in the air beside its symbolic representative.

The mysterious figure was clad in a top hat and cloak, and his face was concealed beneath a glittering eye mask. As he floated in the air beside the Statue of Liberty, which was covered from top to bottom in a gigantic cloth, he waved his baton. The moment he did, the helicopters surrounding him lifted the cloth, but...the Statue of Liberty was nowhere to be seen.

A wave of panicked whispers passed through the assembled New York crowd.

"This is some kinda joke, right?"

"Oh my god! The Statue of Liberty's gone!"

"What a startling development! Somehow, Prince Akatsuki slipped past the US armed forces and through their military satellite net. Somehow, he was able to make off with the Statue of Liberty! Even President Obara, the man who'd challenged Akatsuki, is in shock!" As the announcer's voice boomed from the megaphone, the mysterious, floating figure gave his cape a flourish and strained his voice in an unsuccessful attempt to mask his youth.

"Bwa-ha-ha-ha! There are no tricks or contrivances behind my magic! Not even satellites or the military can stop it! How about I make the White House disappear next?"

—His name was Prince Akatsuki. He was the world's greatest magician, even though he was still in high school.

Clairvoyance, telekinesis, teleportation, levitation—as an illusionist, there was nothing he couldn't do. His illusions earned him as much as ten billion yen a night, and even other magicians couldn't figure out the secrets behind his tricks.

The fourth was a girl squirreled away in a dark laboratory.

"Ringo, Ringo!"

"Nn… What is it, Bearabbit? I'm in the middle of making the final adjustments to my living metal-cell-division program. I need to focus…"

"Now's bearly the time for that! There are only two days before the meeting! Bear in mind that you have to run the checks on the airplane, too. So you have to head down to Earth soon, or you won't make it!"

"Oh. Right. There aren't really days and nights up here, so I sort of lost track." The girl took off her large goggles and looked out the window. Outside, she could see a vast sea of stars...as well as a large blue planet.

She was in low orbit on a one-woman space station of her own design.

"Fur gosh sakes, you should really pull it together. Getting fixated on one thing and ignoring everything else is a really unbearable habit of yours. I think you should fix it if at all pawsible!"

"Hmph. Who cares? I know I have a bad habit—that's why I made you, Bearabbit, to be my management AI. If I got my act together, I could just uninstall you."

"What?! I-I-I'm expendable?! In that case, I think your laid-back nature is one of your best koalaties!"

"Hee-hee, I'm just joking... Okay, Bearabbit, can you take us down in Tanegashima?"

"Aye, aye! I've got my bearings!"

Under AI control, the space station shifted into reentry form and gradually began its descent.

"...I wonder how Tsukasa's doing..."

—Her name was Ringo Oohoshi. She was the world's greatest inventor, even though she was still in high school.

Her intellect had advanced humankind by several centuries, as she'd invented the pillars of modern technology—the pocket nuclear fission reactor, liquid metal, and the nuclear waste neutralizer, to name a few—all on her own. Her mind was so valuable that it played a role in international politics, and the countless agents from various governments trying to kidnap her were why she spent the majority of her time aboard her personal space station laboratory.

The fifth was a young man busy dining with a beautiful woman in a restaurant that offered an unbroken view of the entirety of Las Vegas.

＊　　＊　　＊

"Kelly, I must be the luckiest man alive. Your smile captured America's heart, yet here I am getting to enjoy it all to myself."

"Is that really how you feel?"

"Of course. I would never lie to someone as beautiful as you, honey."

"...If that's true, then would you mind getting off the phone?"

The young actress who'd charmed every man in America made no effort to conceal her irritation as she glared at the boy. And who could blame her? Even though the hors d'oeuvres had already arrived, there was still an array of smartphones laid out in front of him, all connected to his earpiece.

"Sorry, sorry. But you gotta cut me some slack, Kelly. Right now, the Japanese market's do-or-die. I can't take my eyes off for a min— Ah, sorry... Yeah, that's right. East Rezo is a buy. Don't worry, President Aramaki won't just abandon it. The guy's got too much honor and empathy to do that. The company-wide vote'll definitely pass— Sorry, hold that thought. I've got a call from Sarutobi coming in. Yeah, don't hang up. I'll be back in a jiffy... What's that? Huh? The financing came through?! And they added an additional ten billion yen? Ha-ha! Nice, nice! It's so *boring* when everything goes the way you thought it would, though! ...Huh? Yeah, yeah, I know. I'll pay you back by joining your project. I've got it worked into my schedule, so you don't have to worry about a thing. Later, then. —Hey, are you listening to me? Well, are you? I told you, didn't I? That should be obvious. Who the hell do you think you're talking to? Yeah. Go ahead and raise it to two thousand for now. Then... All right, I'm counting on you. Keep 'em on tenterhooks for a while."

At that point, the boy finally removed his earpiece and flashed his partner his pearly whites.

"Good news, honey! I know we were just at the Kiribati vacation home, but whaddaya think? Wanna be the first ones in the world to greet the new year? There's no place more fitting for the two of us than the world's forefront, don't you…? Huh? …Hey, waiter. I seem to have misplaced the goddess I just had with me. Do you know where she went?"

"If you're referring to Ms. Kelly, sir, I believe she said, '*This asshole cares less about my smile than he does about the Benjamins on the other side of that phone*' and left in tears."

"…Wow, that's so rude. I mean, *she's* even the one who forced *me* to make room in my schedule today."

"If I may, I think she may have been testing you."

"Testing me?"

"By asking for something unreasonable, I believe she may have been testing how deeply you loved her, Mr. Sanada."

The boy nodded in understanding, satisfied that that might well be the case.

After all, she wouldn't be the first woman he'd dated who'd tested him like that.

"Man, I thought we'd be able to see eye to eye because we're both so busy, but I guess not."

"One more thing, Mr. Sanada."

"Yeah?"

"Would you still like me to bring out both meals?"

"…You're a funny guy. Get outta here before I give you an Osaka-style comeback line with my fist."

—His name was Masato Sanada. He was the world's greatest businessman, even though he was still in high school.

After his father's death and amid a raging global financial crisis, he'd started by using his nigh-devilish foresight to succeed in both investment and construction ventures. Then, through continued successes in a myriad of other industries, he'd managed to revive the dying Sanada Group in just a few short years. It was an act of sheer genius. Nowadays, he was known as the Devil of Finance, and it was said he was involved in approximately 30 percent of all global trade.

The sixth was the boy statesmen who'd just gotten out of his car only to be met by a gun barrel.

"Long live love and kindness in Japan!"

A shot echoed through the street as blood and gray matter splattered across the asphalt.

However, it didn't belong to the boy, but rather, the man who'd pulled the gun on him.

The assailant had been stopped by the tall fellow standing at the boy's side.

As the tall man stowed his gun, he calmly barked out orders to the people around him.

"We're drawing a crowd. Get this cleaned up, now."

"Y-yes sir!"

"Good work acting so quickly, Chief Secretary Chang." The boy who'd been saved offered his companion his thanks as passing pedestrians screamed.

"I was only able to do so because you got behind me and cleared my line of fire so promptly, Mr. Prime Minister."

"You taught me well."

"You're too modest, sir. Even without me, you could have taken someone like him down on your own... Trying to make me feel useful, sir?"

"Maybe, maybe not. Who knows?" With a thin smile, the young prime minister headed into the building beside which their car had stopped, with the tall man in tow.

"It looked like he was with the fraternity party."

"That it did. They're probably upset I'm raising the national defense budget and steering the country counter to their ideals. After all, they'd rather we take a pacifist stance and dismantle the Japanese Self-Defense Force altogether. They'll probably start coming after me even harder than they did in the election two years ago."

"Stupid kids. Do they not realize they're being manipulated in bad faith?"

"Their fundamental idea, disbanding the military for the sake of peace, isn't ideologically that far off the mark. Or at least, it wouldn't be if they were trying to get something like that enacted worldwide. But because they're only demanding it of Japan, I have no way of answering their zeal... We bear a responsibility for the lives of our people. If they don't have a plan for how to protect them in a crisis, then we have nothing to talk about."

"You're absolutely right, sir."

"I mean, all I'm trying to tell them is that the price of these peaceful days of ours is far higher than they imagine. And the perpetual peace they're after would be more expensive yet. It's certainly not cheap enough that they can buy it with one Beretta and my life."

On that note, the young man turned back toward the entrance he and the tall man had just passed through and narrowed his heterochromatic eyes.

They were filled with intense compassion.

Suddenly, his personal cell phone rang. He pulled it out and looked at the caller ID. The name displayed on the screen belonged to one of the few people he called a friend.

"Hey, Shinobu. What's going on?"

—His name was Tsukasa Mikogami. He was the prime minister of Japan and a genius, even though he was still in high school.

After the changes to the Public Office Election Law, he was elected as prime minister in Japan's first popular vote for the office in an overwhelming 92 percent landslide. The country's social welfare, public order, and finances had all been in shambles due to the previous administration's misgovernance. However, despite the unprecedented economic depression, he was able to turn all of that around in just two years. Unfortunately, that miraculous achievement had earned him the hatred of many, and at the moment, there were more assassins aiming for his head than anyone else in the world.

The seventh was a girl standing atop Tokyo Skytree wearing an armband that read PRESS.

As she gazed down with her nigh-superhuman vision at the spot where the attack on the prime minister had just occurred, she spoke into the smartphone she was holding.

"Oh, nothing. You got attacked again, so I was just wondering if you were okay, y'know."

"The wind is really loud on your end... Please don't tell me you went and climbed it again."

"You can see all of Tokyo from up here, though! It's super-handy for sniffing out scoops. Like just now, for example."

"You're incorrigible... Anyhow, thanks to my talented secretary, I'm fine. There won't be any problems with your project."

"Nyeh-heh-heh. Very good, very good. That's what a girl likes to hear."

"Calculating as ever, aren't you...? I'm almost at the conference room, so I have to hang up now."

"Aight. Remember, we're meeting at Narita Airport in two days. Make sure you don't forget!"

"I'll remember."

And with that closing remark, her phone conversation with Tsukasa came to an end. Moving on to her next task, she stood up and leaped from the top of the 2,080-foot-tall building as casually as if she were diving into a pool.

"Sha-sha. ♪ Y'know, we haven't had a reunion with all of us there since middle school. This is gonna be great! ♪"

However, she never hit the ground. As she fell, she unfurled the scarf from around her neck, spread it out like a parachute, caught the wind, and soared off.

—Her name was Shinobu Sarutobi. She was the world's greatest high school journalist, even though she was a descendant of Sasuke Sarutobi, the ninja. Her information-gathering skills were so keen that she knew everything from rumors about global politics and commerce to the idlest of neighborhood gossip. There was no scandal she couldn't sniff out and no crime she couldn't expose.

—Each one of them possessed gifts far beyond those of normal high schoolers.

Out of fear and reverence for their preeminent talents, people referred to them as the Seven High School Prodigies.

One day, though, an airplane carrying the seven of them disappeared over the Pacific.

A frantic search was conducted, but it ended in vain, unable to recover so much as a piece of scrap from the plane.

But had they simply...vanished into the ocean's depths? No. That wasn't it. In fact, it was in that moment that their story was just beginning. In a far-off land, more distant than even the bottom of the Pacific—

🎏 The Boy from Earth and the Girl from Another World 🎏

Tsukasa Mikogami's awakening began with a touch. Specifically, the feel of a damp cloth wiping his hand. The sensation pulled his consciousness up from the depths of darkness. Tsukasa heeded it and slowly opened his eyelids. His heterochromatic eyes—one a frigid blue, the other a fiery red—began taking in light.

The first thing he saw…was a dull wooden ceiling. The next was a beautiful girl dazzling enough that he could make her out with perfect clarity despite his bleary vision.

Her outfit was predominantly white and light green, bearing a close resemblance to the dirndls he'd once seen in Germany. She was gently wiping his hand with a damp cloth.

"Ah…!"

Suddenly, their eyes met.

"You're awake? Oh, thank goodness."

As she spoke, a relieved smile spread across her youthful face.

How lovely…

Rather than a beauty, she'd be better described as a cutie.

Also, her ears were quite long. Perhaps it was some sort of genetic quirk.

She looks almost...like an elf. The kind you'd find in fantasy novels, thought Tsukasa.

But more importantly, who was she? She wasn't anyone he recognized. And also, what was he doing...wherever it was he was? Why was he lying down? His memories were all jumbled up.

"Wh...ere...? OW!"

But when he tried to sit up and voice his confusion, a sharp pain ran through his entire body, like his bones were cracking. His body was so hot, he felt like he was burning up.

"Oh, no, you mustn't! You're badly wounded; you need to rest!"

Badly...wounded? Ah, that's right. I was...

Upon hearing those words, Tsukasa finally remembered what had happened to him.

"I wanna write a special article on all of us High School Prodigies."

An old acquaintance of his, the journalist Shinobu Sarutobi, had invited him. So he, Shinobu, and the five others had all crossed the Pacific aboard an airplane piloted by Ringo Oohoshi's AI.

Midway through that flight, though, the plane had been abruptly engulfed by a massive thundercloud, rendering it impossible to navigate.

A shrill alarm had gone off.

Swallowed up by some sort of waterspout, they'd suffered severe turbulence. Then, as they'd watched themselves descend, a conspicuously large shock had rattled the plane.

That was everything that had happened before Tsukasa lost consciousness.

The moment he remembered, Tsukasa immediately ignored the pain burning through his body, wrenched himself up, and firmly grabbed the girl's slim shoulders.

"Hwah—"

"Please...! Oh..."

He paused for a second, not sure what language to use when conversing with this clearly non-Japanese girl, but then pressed on after remembering that she herself had spoken in Japanese just a moment ago.

"Please, tell me! There were six other people on that plane...! Did they make it out...?!" Cold sweat beaded on his forehead, and his face contorted in pain as Tsukasa asked about the well-being of the other passengers.

The girl had initially been confused at his sudden outburst, but she quickly gave him a soft smile to set his heart at ease.

"They're all fine. Including you, we found seven people. All collapsed in the same place. We brought you all here to watch over you." She glanced around the room as she answered the boy's question.

When he followed her gaze, Tsukasa saw six familiar faces all bandaged up like him and sleeping on pelt beds.

"Don't worry. They're wounded, but it looks like they're all going to make it."

"Ah... Thank you..."

Given that they'd been in a plane crash, surviving would have practically taken a miracle. Knowing that, Tsukasa had been prepared for the worst. Upon hearing that everyone else had been rescued like he had, the tension drained from his body, and he collapsed back onto the bed.

"Oh man... Thank God..."

"You seem like a very kind person." The girl gazed at him with eyes the color of lapis lazuli as she placed a cool, damp cloth on Tsukasa's sweaty forehead.

"...Any public figure worries about the safety of his people."

The cool rag helped relieve the heat and pain in his body. The sensation caused him to break out in a relaxed smile. He looked back at the girl taking care of him.

"Forgive me, I've forgotten my manners. My name is Tsukasa Mikogami. Might you do me the honor of telling me yours?"

"Who, me? I'm Lyrule."

"Well, Lyrule, it would appear we owe you and your people a great debt. I speak for all of us when I express my gratitude for your generous, diligent treatment. Thank you."

"Oh, we wouldn't have dreamed of just leaving you there. We people of the mountain look out for one another." Seemingly embarrassed at Tsukasa's earnest words of thanks, Lyrule quickly stood up after replying. "It'll take some time before your injuries are fully healed, but now that you're awake, let's see if we can get some food in you. Would you mind waiting here for a minute?"

And with that, Lyrule trotted out of the room. A few minutes later, she returned with a steaming pot in her hand.

"It's a stew made from goat milk. Here, let me cool it down a bit." She scooped up a piece of soft meat with a wooden spoon, then brought it up to her full pink lips and blew gently on it. After doing that a few times to clear the steam, she moved the spoon toward Tsukasa's mouth.

"Here you go. Say *ah*."

"It feels kinda like I'm a kid again."

It was a little embarrassing. That said, his body did crave the nourishment.

Doing as instructed, Tsukasa opened his mouth wide to accept the soft chunk of meat. But the moment he tried to chew it, it immediately tumbled out. He couldn't close his jaw well. Even with how soft the flank was, his body was too weak to bite through it.

"...My apologies. It would seem I haven't recovered enough to eat just yet."

However, Tsukasa's weak words prompted Lyrule's expression to sour slightly.

"Well, that won't do. When you're injured, you have to eat meat, or you won't get better. Here, just a moment," she said, picking up the dropped piece of goat meat with her fingers and popping it in her mouth. Then, after chewing it almost too thoroughly...

"Mmm..."

"Mph...!"

...she laid her lips over the prone Tsukasa's.

Upon feeling her soft, supple lips placed gently against his, his eyes went wide in surprise. She slid her wet tongue into his mouth. Then she pressed down on Tsukasa's teeth with the back of her tongue, opened his mouth, and poured in the masticated, mushy goat shank. Once the deed was done, she separated her mouth from his.

"This way, you'll be able to get food down...right?" she asked, averting her gaze. Her face was so red it looked like it had caught fire.

It had doubtless been a deeply embarrassing act. However, she'd pushed through her shyness in order to help Tsukasa eat. A clear testament to how dedicated she was to his recovery.

"...Thank you. I suppose you're right; that is one way I can eat." Tsukasa elected to gratefully accept Lyrule's kindness. Turning her down at this point would honestly come across as rude.

"Would it be all right if I depended on your goodwill for the time being?"

"...Why, yes. Of course. Let's fill you up so you can go ahead and get better quickly." Lyrule's mood lightened, having seen that her unusual actions hadn't given Tsukasa any strange impressions.

Her charming smile returned as she carried another spoonful of stew to her mouth. Then, just like before, she thoroughly chewed it up, and...

"Mmm—"

...brought her face close to Tsukasa's so she could feed him mouth to mouth, but...

©Sacraneco

"Lyrule! Is it true that one of the stragglers we found woke up?!"

"Pfft—!"

…promptly spat it out, startled by a woman opening the door and entering the house. As Tsukasa's face was directly in front of hers, what had been in her mouth was, naturally, sprayed all over him.

"Ahhh! Oh, Tsukasa, I'm so sorry! Here, I'll clean that up right away!"

"Oh-ho? Am I getting in the way of something?"

"Wh—? No—that's not it, Winona! That… It wasn't what you think!" Lyrule tried frantically to explain the situation as she wiped at Tsukasa.

Tsukasa looked out from under the towel being pressed haphazardly against his face to take in their visitor. It was a woman in the prime of her youth with chestnut hair and a capricious, teasing smile dancing on her lips. Unlike Lyrule, whose features were more childish, the new woman was well deserving of being described as a beauty. It was easy to tell how voluptuous her breasts were even through her loose garments, further accentuating her womanly charm.

At that moment, though…Tsukasa couldn't have cared less about that. What was monopolizing his attention was her butt—and the top of her head. The woman was sporting a pair of wolflike ears and a bushy tail.

…Are those some sort of regional accessories?

The world was a big place, after all. It wasn't beyond the realm of possibility for there to be some ethnic group that customarily wore such things.

But that wasn't important right now.

"Ma'am, I find myself unable to chew at the moment, so she was just grinding up the food for me. I would ask that you not poke fun at her for aiding me in my time of need." Tsukasa's gaze was focused straight on the woman, chiding her for teasing Lyrule. He knew that

Lyrule had put aside her embarrassment in order to devote herself to nursing him back to health. Even though he could tell by their tones that the two were close, he still couldn't let it slide.

"Tsukasa…"

"Oh dear, I've been told off. You seem awfully dependable, for a straggler…but I guess that's a good thing. With that much spunk, all that's left is to eat up, and you'll be better in no time," she said, flashing Tsukasa a pleased smile at his rebuke. She made her way over to sit down beside him.

"Call me Winona. I live in this village, just like Lyrule. Pleasure to meet you."

"I'm Tsukasa Mikogami. I heard a little bit from Lyrule, but it seems my friends and I owe you a great deal."

"Oh, don't give it a second thought. We all have to help one another out when we're down, don't we?"

"Still, a debt is a debt. Once I've returned to my country, I'll be sure to thank you properly."

"Oh my, you *do* seem dependable, especially considering you're only about as old as my boy."

"Oh, you have children my age? You look far too young for that to be the case."

Going off appearances, Tsukasa would have pegged her as early twenties. Certainly not old enough to have kids his age. Tsukasa was honestly surprised, a fact that seemed to tickle Winona pink.

"Oh, you. Someone your age shouldn't be allowed to be so smooth…" Delighted, she smiled bashfully like a young maiden. But as Tsukasa watched her, his eyes widened in surprise.

Much to his shock, her tail accessory was bobbing up and down in concert with her embarrassed smile like a dog's would when it was happy. Its movements were so lifelike it was difficult to imagine them to be the work of a machine.

"…W-wait, is your tail…real?"

"Hmm? Real? Why wouldn't it be? I am a *byuma*, you know. See?" Winona wagged her chestnut tail and patted Tsukasa's cheek with it. The boy felt the unmistakable warmth of flesh and blood as it brushed his face.

Huh… It really is real.

That fact caused Tsukasa no small amount of consternation. After all, people with animal ears and tails…didn't exist. If they did, it would turn the entire field of biology on its head. Humankind had reached the point where they were able to go up to outer space and gaze down at the Earth from on high. There was no way such an oddity could have passed unnoticed. Especially not in a culture that could communicate in Japanese. However, Tsukasa's surprises didn't end there.

"Have you really never seen a *byuma* before? That's odd; you can find us pretty much everywhere in Freyjagard."

"Their clothes were all really odd; maybe they're from a foreign country."

Frey…jagard?

"I'm not sure I follow, but we're from Japan."

"J'pan? I can't say I've ever heard of it."

The unexpected response sent Tsukasa into even more of a tizzy.

"Wh-what are you talking about? You two are speaking Japanese right now."

"???"

"What are *you* talking about? We've all been talking in Altan this whole time."

"…?!?!" He'd never even heard of that language before. At first, he thought they might be messing with him, but…

Their gazes, their breathing, their enunciation… There's no sign either of them is lying…

As a genius high student turned prime minister, Tsukasa's powers of observation were keen. However, what they were telling him only served to further his confusion.

What's going on here?

There were people with animal ears and tails talking about a language he'd never heard of. And also…there was his initial impression when he first saw Lyrule devotedly nursing him. Tsukasa's mind mixed together all the strange hints—and arrived at an unbelievable theory.

There's…no way…!

It simply wasn't possible. Not only was it unscientific, it seemed downright unreal. Surely it was just a delusion spurred on by Lyrule's and Winona's odd appearances.

Even so… *Science had never conclusively proven this nightmarish phenomenon impossible.*

I have to be sure…!

"Rgh—!"

"Wh—? No, no, you mustn't move yet! Your wounds will reopen!"

"Lyrule's absolutely right. You really need to get back in that bed."

Lyrule and Winona scolded Tsukasa as they watched him hunch over in agony. But Tsukasa refused to back down.

"Sorry, but…I'm afraid I can't do that right now. There's something urgent I need to check. Do you know where my phone went?"

"What's a *fone*?"

"It's a flat black slab. There should have been one in my pocket."

"Oh, you mean this?"

"Please, give it here!"

Tsukasa's clothes were piled up beside his bed. Lyrule retrieved the smartphone from atop them and passed it to him. Tsukasa tried to use its GPS to determine his present location, but…

"Dammit, it's not working…! It's okay, though, there's still a way…!"

Their plane had been equipped with GPS and satellite communication systems. Given that the crash hadn't been serious enough to kill them, there was a good chance those features were still intact.

"Forgive me for imposing, you two, but could you take me to the crash site...or rather, *the spot where you found us?*"

"Wh-what are you talking about?! You're in no state to be going any—"

"I'm well aware of that. But it's a politician's duty to push himself to the limit when his people are facing a crisis. If my *insane hunch* ends up being right, it'll be my responsibility to take charge of the other six. In other words, it won't do for me to end up just as alarmed as they'll be... I need to be the first to fully understand the situation. So please, I beseech you..." His words of supplication and his expression brimmed with an unshakable will. Winona tried to glare him down but eventually heaved an exasperated sigh of defeat.

"...Fine. I'll take you."

"Winona?! You can't; that's crazy!"

"Look at his eyes. If we left him to his own devices, he'd crawl there on his hands and knees. It's useless trying to stop a man with eyes like those... I don't know what it is you want to check, but it's that important to you, is it?"

"It is..." Tsukasa nodded.

"In that case...grit your teeth!" Winona slid her hand around Tsukasa's back, then hoisted him to his feet.

"Rrr—!!!!"

"Does it hurt?"

"I'm...fine...!"

"Way to be a man about it. All right, let's go. Watch your feet, now."

"W-wait! I'm coming, too!"

And thus, the two of them helped bring Tsukasa to the spot where they'd found him and the others. With him borrowing their shoulders and taking it slow, it took them about fifteen minutes to get there. Houses were scattered along their path, all made of wood and limestone. There was no concrete to be seen, nor did he spot any cars or bicycles. The ground was free of tire tracks. It was like a mountain village straight out of the Middle Ages.

Several villagers came and talked to the three of them as they walked, but despite ostensibly looking human, they all had animal ears, tails, or both, like Winona. The absurdity of the scene made Tsukasa increasingly concerned that his impossible, illogical theory was on the mark. Then, when they reached a crag overlooking a valley near the village—Tsukasa gaped at what he saw.

"This here's where we found you. Four days ago, there was a big sound in the middle of the night, like a landslide. We all rushed over and found that big birdlike frame shooting out fire with the seven of you collapsed beside it."

"………"

Sure enough, he could make out the wreckage of a familiar airplane down at the bottom of the red valley Winona was pointing at.

The *wreckage*.

The nose of the plane had been crushed and had sunk into the exposed red clay of the valley's side. The flames had done a number on it—all that was left were the frame and the destroyed passenger cabin. The wings and tail were torn clear off and their pieces scattered about. Tsukasa could tell in a single glance that the GPS and satellite comm systems were unsalvageable.

What truly worried the boy had little to do with the status of the plane's navigational devices, however. It was the state of the crash site as a whole.

There's no way we made it out of there…

The plane had been designed by Ringo Oohoshi, a genius inventor and member of the High School Prodigies. Up until now, Tsukasa had assumed they'd survived thanks to some subsystem designed to protect the passengers in the event of a crash.

However, that clearly hadn't been the case.

It was physically impossible for anyone inside an airplane in that condition to have survived. The very fact that Tsukasa and the others were alive at all was an unnatural occurrence bordering on the inconceivable. Each new detail the boy was confronted with defied comprehension.

What in the world had happened to the seven of them?

At a loss, Tsukasa turned his gaze to the sky, and that's when he saw it.

"————........"

A massive figure descended from the clouds. Tsukasa had already encountered many surprises that day, but this was the first that left him completely dumbstruck.

Up in the sky…soared a winged lizard the size of a mountain, swimming through the air.

"Oh. We get smaller ones all the time, but it's not often you see a dragon that big."

"It isn't, is it? We should pray for everyone's safe recovery."

"........"

Lyrule clasped her hands and began praying to the flying dragon. Winona appeared pleased, happily smiling at having been able to see something so seemingly rare. It was their reactions to that utterly unearthly sight that made Tsukasa finally realize his insane theory… actually matched his current situation.

"Man… I guess I just have to accept it, huh…"

"What do you mean, you have to 'accept it'?" Lyrule tilted her head to the side, confused.

Rather than offering an excuse for his words, the boy answered quite honestly.

"Well, it would appear that my compatriots and I have arrived in a world entirely different from our own."

And there they had it—the world Tsukasa and the others now found themselves lost in existed in a different dimension and had developed along a different path from Earth.

⚜ Banquet and Hostilities ⚜

Although the seven high school students had come from Earth, they'd crash-landed on another world, in a country called Freyjagard.

They'd all been wounded in the crash, but the diligent care they'd received from the villagers of a small mountain village called Elm had restored them to full health. Their emotions were on the mend, too. Although they'd initially been confused and overwhelmed by their strange predicament, their interactions with the villagers and the staunch leadership of Tsukasa Mikogami—the high school politician who'd gone on ahead and been the first to confirm the situation—had largely set their minds at ease.

A month later, on the day they all finished their recovery, the villagers threw them a celebratory banquet.

"Ahem! Now, then! A toast to the full recovery of our stragglers from another world!"

""""Cheers!!!!""""

The one who'd given the toast was an older man with wolf ears, a matching tail, and an impressive beard and sideburns. His name was Ulgar; he was the mayor of Elm Village and Winona's father. The forty-odd other villagers and the guests of honor—Tsukasa and his six companions from Earth—all followed his example.

Having raised their beer steins into the air, the assemblage began helping themselves to the feast laid out on the floor of Mayor Ulgar's house, which doubled as the local mayor's office.

The main course was a freshly hunted wild boar roasted with herbs, but that wasn't all. There were steamed potatoes with butter, as well as apples, pears, plums, and other fruits in honey that the villagers had bought from the city just for the occasion. Also, each person got their own serving of fresh-baked bread, a boiled egg, and two slices of goat cheese that had been made right in the village. Finally, there was the usual offal stew and sauerkraut.

The fruits proved especially popular, with adults and children alike rushing to grab them up. The region was largely populated with coniferous trees, so they rarely got to eat anything so sweet.

"Bwa-ha-ha-ha! I thought your clothes looked strange, but I never would have guessed that you lot were from a whole other world! Now there's a shock!" Ulgar downed his stein in a single gulp, wiped the beer froth from his beard, and let out a stereotypically hearty woodsman's laugh.

Masato Sanada, the genius businessman, responded with a sigh.

"If it was a shock for you guys, imagine how bad it was for us. When we woke up, not only were we being tended to by people with wolf ears and tails, Tsukasa goes and tells us that we aren't even on Earth anymore. I'd always figured that nothing could make that guy lose his head, so hearing him say that scared the shit out of me."

"Nya-ha-ha. True that. The first time I saw one of the villagers other than Lyrule, I was afraid I'd gone crazy or something." Shinobu Sarutobi, the prodigious journalist, popped a plum in her mouth as she agreed with Masato.

"Oh yes, your reactions when you saw our ears and tails for the first time were hilarious. Tsukasa managed to keep a straight face, but the rest of you were all great. After a couple of you woke up, we started having fun with it. A bunch of us all got together and brainstormed about the best way to startle you."

"A-and like I told you, telling an injured person who just woke up 'I'm gonna gobble you up!' is too much, even for a joke! Their situation is hard enough as it is!" Lyrule gave her frank opinion of the tasteless prank Winona and the others had been plotting.

Today, her scolding stopped there, but back when they'd actually been planning to play the prank, Lyrule had been quite indignant. She'd dragged Winona and the rest of the immature adults to the middle of the village, forced them to kneel on the ground, and lectured them like a magistrate judging the wicked until tears welled up in their eyes. Given that one of the adults in question was Mayor Ulgar, it was quite possible that the most powerful person in the village was secretly Lyrule.

"Nah, I think that mischievous side of Winona's is kinda hot."

"Oh my, Masato, was it? I see you've got quite the eye for women."

"Good grief..." After a sidelong glance at Winona getting all full of herself off Masato's flattery, Lyrule sighed and turned around to face Keine Kanzaki, the expert doctor.

"By the way, how are you doing? Are you starting to get used to life here in the village?"

"Yes, thank you," Keine replied with a mature nod. Other than when she'd awoken, her smile had never broken during her tenure in the village. "It has been a whole month, after all. I've gotten used to life here, and I've come to terms with the fact that we're in a different world. Now that I think about it, it might have been a good thing we got injured. If we'd been able to move about freely, some of us might have panicked and done something rash... That said, it appears one of us still seems rather distressed." With that, Keine turned to look at the one person who hadn't joined the banquet and was instead facing the wall. Prince Akatsuki, the brilliant magician, sat cradling his legs in his arms.

"This isn't happening, this isn't happening, this isn't happening. This is all just a dream. I'm just having a nightmare."

They'd all been confused at first, but unlike the other six, who'd acclimated to the impossibility of it all over the past month, he was the only one who still refused to accept their situation. As a magician, perhaps the idea that conjuring "impossibilities" was his job was what made it so hard for him to come to grips with things.

However, the fact that Akatsuki kept cowering—

""""Grah! We're gonna eat you all up!"""""

"AHHHHHHH!!!! CAT EARS!!!! DOG EARS!"

—made him an excellent toy for the more mischievous kids of the village.

"I'm not looking! I'm not looking at it! This is all just a trick! It has to be! That morning TV station director must have set this all up! That asshole always comes up with crazy-elaborate plans to mess with me! This is just another one of their high-budget pranks; I'm sure of iiiit!!!!"

"Ha-ha-ha-ha!"

"Miss, you're funny!"

"Wh-wh-what, no, that's wrong! I'm a guy! It's 'mister'!" Upon being called *miss*, Akatsuki finally stopped screaming long enough to correct one of the kids.

Indeed, his facial features were too pretty for a guy. Between that, his short stature, and his low muscle mass, he was often mistaken for a girl. So much so, in fact, that he'd developed a complex over it. It was so easy to get Akatsuki's gender wrong that, in all his life, the only person who'd gotten it right on the first try had been the preeminently observant Tsukasa. And the people of the village were no different. Lyrule and the others all look shocked.

"Wait, Akatsuki, you're a boy?!"

"Huh. For a boy, his face is pretty darn cute... Wait, hmm? But Lyrule, I dealt with the boys' bedpans, and I left you to deal with the girls', right? How did you not notice, then?"

"I assumed his chest was just on the flatter side... Nothing seemed particularly off, so I guess I just never realized..."

"Oh? So does that mean that *it* was just so small you couldn't even see—?"

"Stoooooop! I'm gonna cryyyyyy!"

""""Graaah—!""""

"WAAAAAAAAAAAHHHHHH!!!" He actually started crying.

"...Poor Akatsuki..." Master inventor Ringo Oohoshi unconsciously let out a sympathetic murmur at seeing the small boy so thoroughly mocked.

When Masato heard her, he quipped: "Hey, the kids are happy. What more could an entertainer ask for?"

"Hweh?!"

Not having expected to be heard, Ringo leaped in her seat, went as red as an apple, looked down, squirmed, and finally elected to immerse herself in her food. Due to her inherent disposition and limited opportunities for human interaction, she tended to be shy and anxious around others.

"Seeing how surprised he looks, I guess you all really did come from a world without *byuma*, huh?" Winona remarked.

"Back in our world, the prevailing theory is that humans evolved from monkeys."

"So, Tsukasa, you're saying that this *Urth* of yours only had *hyuma*?"

"Wait a minute, wait a minute. What's this about *hyuma* and *byuma*?" asked Shinobu.

"Oh, that's right. You hadn't woken up yet when we talked about this last time, had you? Basically, *byuma* have animal features, like the people from this village, whereas *hyuma* are apparently people like you and me who don't," replied Tsukasa.

"There are a few differences besides our appearances, too. *Byuma* tend to be stronger, but there are some rare *hyuma* who can use a strange power called magic."

"Whoa! This place sounded like a fantasy world from the get-go, but you've even got magic here?"

"My, my, how surprising. Incidentally, what kinds of things can this magic do?" asked Keine.

"Well, they say that you can talk to spirits and control things like wind and fire… But I'm sorry, all I know is what I've heard from Winona's husband," replied Lyrule. "I've never actually seen magic myself or met anyone who can use it. It's extremely rare, after all. But because there are so few with the gift, even commoners who can use it are respected among nobles."

"Ah, I do remember him mentioning something about that…"

"…At any rate, it sounds like magic is something we'll need to look into at some point," Tsukasa murmured to himself.

During his life in the village over the past month, he'd come to learn that most of the civilization in this world roughly corresponded to life on Earth back before the Age of Discovery. However, he still knew almost nothing about magic. At some point, that lack of knowledge was liable to hinder their search for a way to get back home. And more importantly…

…It might hold the key to whatever fantastical phenomenon got us here in the first place.

Someone might have used magic to summon them. It sounded like a story straight out of pop fiction, but it was still the most plausible explanation. At that point in the conversation, Winona suddenly clapped her hands together.

"Ah, that's it!" She then went on to say something *truly outrageous.* "You know, when you guys said you came from another world, I thought it sounded familiar, but I only just remembered where I'd heard it before. It was a story he told me back before we'd even gotten married. *A tale about seven heroes who came from another world.*"

""""_____?!"""""

Everyone, even Akatsuki, who'd been plugging his ears and covering his eyes, turned to her in shock. It was a natural reaction. After all, the story she was talking about bore a striking resemblance to their current situation. It wasn't something they could just ignore. They all started rushing toward Winona with questions.

Tsukasa, sensing that, raised his arm to cut the other six off. Having everyone pile on her at once would have been terribly poor manners. It was a politician's job to keep his friends in line. Immediately realizing what he was doing, they swallowed their questions and plopped their butts back down on the ground. After making sure they were going to stay put, Tsukasa turned his attention back toward Winona, presenting himself as the group's representative.

"Forgive us. Would you be so kind as to elaborate?"

However, Winona's response wasn't quite what they'd hoped for.

She leaned back and replied apologetically, "…Sorry, but I don't know any of the specifics. My husband was a peddler who traveled the whole of Freyjagard, from up north around Elm Village to all the way down south. When he was working down there, he heard a story that began *'Long ago, seven heroes arrived from another world and saved the continent from an evil dragon's rule'*...or something like that. But I'm afraid that's about all I know."

"Is your husband around here somewhere?"

"...He got caught up in the war and passed away three years ago."

Tsukasa found himself at a loss for words.

"...I'm so sorry; I shouldn't have."

"Oh, don't worry about it. It sounded like an important clue toward getting you back to your world. I can hardly blame you for being eager about it. In fact, I'm the one who should be apologizing for not being able to help more." An awkward silence hung over their banquet after Winona finished.

The reticence was suddenly shattered by a young man's outburst.

"This is horseshit!" A biting shout suddenly cut through the room. Its source was a boy about Tsukasa's and Lyrule's age who'd been drinking beer alone and off to the side. He slammed his stein onto the table with a *bang*. Although they'd never personally talked, Tsukasa knew who he was. The boy's name was Elch, Ulgar's grandson and Winona's son.

"What's wrong, Elch?"

Elch responded to the mayor's question in a tone dripping with irritation. "What's wrong? Ha! Everything's wrong, that's what—you and Mom and Lyrule and everyone else in the village! These guys are all 'Golly gee, we flew in from another world on an iron bird,' and you're taking them seriously! You guys actually buy this nonsense?! And also, the village's coffers were running low because of how bad the harvest was this year, and you're all throwing them a *feast*?! Now we're flat broke and heading into winter! How do you expect us to make it till spring?! We're certainly in no position to be taking in seven deadbeats!"

"What's the harm? It's a happy occasion."

"As the village treasurer, it sure isn't happy for me! We should have just left them there to die!"

"*Elch.* Watch your mouth. A mountain man of Elm should never say something so cowardly."

"Rrr..." Elch winced after being scolded by his mother, Winona. His confidence quickly returned, however.

"A-anyway! You guys are all better now, so hurry up and get out of here! This village doesn't have food for con artists like you!" Still making no efforts to conceal his animosity, he stormed out of the banquet hall with his shoulders squared. Shinobu grinned bitterly as she watched him go.

"Nya-ha-ha. He tells us to get out, then goes and leaves himself..."

"I'm so sorry about that. He knows his numbers and letters and is a natural with a bow, but...his character needs some work."

"Don't worry about what the kid said. You got thrown here out of the blue from another world, so you don't have anywhere to go, right? You're more than welcome to stay until you figure out a way home."

"Yeah, yeah."

"There's no rush, after all."

"I'm sure you guys'll figure something out eventually."

The villagers all nodded in agreement, offering encouragement.

Help and support everyone, no matter who they are. A philosophy indispensable in these barren, conifer-filled mountains.

"We thank you for your kindness, good people of Elm," Tsukasa said, bowing, grateful for their hospitality. The seven of them were in a completely unfamiliar world. Without this kind of home base, they might not even have been able to survive the night. As a result, Elm Village's goodwill was a sorely needed blessing. That said…

"Still, Elch has a valid point. The soil around here is white, hard, and too infertile to grow even wheat. All you have are small fields of potato and other roots. I hear your feudal lord also collects taxes on the meat and pelts from the animals you hunt, leaving you with nothing but offal and scraps. I can't imagine your lives are luxurious… And even if you did have a small surplus, asking a village of fifty-odd residents to take in seven new people and care for them for a whole month borders on insane."

After all, that was a population increase of over 10 percent. Furthermore, the newcomers had been too injured to work. All they'd done was consume resources without giving anything back.

"…I can see that we've caused you quite a bit of inconvenience. We're healthy enough to move around now, so please, let us help around the village starting tomorrow. If we're going to live here, we need to at least earn our keep."

Masato piped up to add on to Tsukasa's declaration. "At *least*. I've got a policy of repaying both my debts and my grievances twice over."

Ulgar seemed to take a liking to their assertiveness, as a broad smile spread across his face. "Ha-ha! I'll take you up on that! All right, then, another toast for the new members of our village family!"

And with that, the villagers greeted their new residents by letting out another cheer.

"Cheers!"

The air was filled with beer steins and happy laughter. Amid the hustle and bustle, Lyrule scooted nimbly over to Tsukasa without standing up. She was holding a stein and making an adorably bashful smile.

"…I look forward to spending more time with you, Tsukasa."

"Likewise, with you." A quiet *clink* sounded out as they gently tapped their steins together.

And thus, the Seven High School Prodigies became members of Elm Village.

❦ Unity and Orders ❧

With the banquet over, the Seven Prodigies headed back to the house they'd been given, tossed some logs on the hearth, and warmed themselves beside it as they brushed their teeth with salt. Then, once they'd finished their evening routine, Tsukasa made a proposal to the group.

"All right, I think everyone's stomachs have probably settled by now. It would be prudent to hold a meeting about the peculiar situation we're in—the fact that we're stranded in another world—and how best to deal with it."

Five of the others nodded as one.

"We can move around now, and we've got a decent handle on what this world's like. Seems as good a time as any."

"I quite agree."

However, one member of their number declined to join the conversation, instead remaining balled up under his fur bedding. The boy in question was the brilliant magician member of the Prodigies, Prince Akatsuki. Shinobu, never one to miss a beat, yanked the blanket off.

"C'mon out here already, Akatsuki!"

When she did, Akatsuki stood up, unable to bear it anymore, and let loose a flurry of complaints, choking back tears all the while.

"I don't wanna, I don't wanna, I don't wanna! How are you guys all taking this in stride?! You go to one party, and now everything's sunshine and rainbows?! This isn't even Earth, remember?! There're people with dog ears! Cat ears! There's even one lady who looks like an elf! A-all that stuff's impossible!"

"But it clearly *is* possible. We're here, aren't we?" replied Shinobu.

"And besides, it was never even impossible in the first place," noted Masato. "Nobody's ever disproven the existence of alternate worlds, y'know."

Tsukasa was the last to chime in. "I respect that you're shaken up, but you need to pull it together. If you keep insisting that stuff's impossible, you're going to miss what's right before your eyes. Besides, Akatsuki, you saw that crash site. If anything's impossible, it's the fact that we're even still alive."

"But…"

"Now is no time to be closing our eyes and plugging our ears. We have to survive in this strange world however we can while searching for a way home. Right?"

"That's…" After hearing so many logical arguments thrown at him one after another, Akatsuki's mood deflated. Shinobu patted him on the shoulder.

"It's gonna be okay, Akatsuki. It's not like you're here alone, remember? We're all in this together. Working together, I'm sure we'll figure something out!" Perhaps her words cheered him up; he seemed ready to come to terms with their situation at last.

"…Yeah, you're right." With that, the boy joined the circle and straightened his posture. With Akatsuki now engaged, Tsukasa reopened the discussion.

"Now, to the main topic… Like Shinobu just said, we'll need all seven of us if we want to get through this. Given how little we know about this world, working independently would be too inefficient. Furthermore, I propose that we proceed as a team acting more or less under my command. Does anyone have any objections?"

"Thinking isn't my strong suit, so I have no problem following your lead."

Keine followed Aoi's assent with her own. "I have no objections, either."

"I mean, you're clearly the right one for the job." After Masato voiced his approval as well, Tsukasa moved the conversation along.

"I appreciate it. Now, as far as our fundamental approach goes, I suggest we remain in this village for the time being."

Akatsuki yelped in surprise at the suggestion.

"Wh—? But why?! Shouldn't we be trying to figure out how to get back as soon as possible?!"

Masato quickly offered a rebuttal. "Nah, Prince, I don't think that's the play. First, there's no guarantee that the people everywhere else'll be as welcoming as Winona and the others. More importantly, there's just too much about this world we don't know. We'd have no destination, no intel, and nowhere to sleep. Wandering aimlessly around a foreign land with nothing but the clothes on our backs is all risk, no reward."

"Quite right," agreed Keine. "As far as what we currently know goes...the culture is similar to Earth's Middle Ages, but that's just about it."

"And even if we come up with points of reference from our world, that's really all they are. There are sure to be loads of differences. I mean, this place has dragons and magic. That's not a lot to go off."

"It really isn't. But hey, at least they have toilets, right?" remarked Shinobu.

"Preach."

"I second the sentiment."

"Although, I suppose a warm bath would have been too much to ask for...," Aoi added wistfully.

"...And there you have it. While I certainly understand your impatience, I think it would be best if we limit our search to Elm Village for now. Do you understand where I'm coming from, Akatsuki?"

"Y-yeah. I'm with you."

"Good. Now, within that plan, we should lay out our agenda. As I see it, there are three major points:

"The first is gathering information.

"As our favorite merchant just said, there's too much about this world we don't know. What kind of country is Freyjagard? What laws does it operate under? What kind of currency does it use, and how much do common goods cost? What religions exist, and what topics are considered taboo among its people? Also…what exactly is this magic Lyrule mentioned earlier? We're going to start by using Elm Village as our base to gather information on things like that.

"The second major point, of course, is figuring out how to get back to Earth."

"The only sorta-clue we've got on that front is the Seven Heroes story Winona told us about, right?"

"Pretty much. We should be able to look into that as we're researching the other things from point one. Then, once we've learned more about this world, we can start actively prioritizing it.

"Finally…point three—and the most pressing matter of the bunch. Mending the village's finances."

Everyone nodded deeply in agreement.

"For sure. We can't just screw up their lives and then go 'Thanks for everything, see ya.'"

"Indeed! A meal and a roof beget debt enough, and they've given us that many times over! Failing to repay them would be a stain on our collective honor, that it would!"

"Well put. The point of the matter is: All three of these tasks are essential, so I was going to assign each of you a job that fits your skills. Does anyone have objections thus far?" Their resounding silence gave

Tsukasa his answer. "In that case, I have individual orders for each of you. First, Aoi."

"Me?"

"You're the most skilled in combat out of all of us, so you could accompany the hunters without slowing them down. Could you join the village men and help bolster their stores?"

"Understood. In a stroke of good fortune, my trusty katana—Hoozukimaru—survived the crash. With it at my side, I can hunt even lions and tigers, that I can."

"Well, I haven't seen any lions lurking in the grass, but...according to the mayor, there's a sixteen-foot-tall bear around these parts called the Lord of the Woods."

"Yikes. What's that, some kinda monster from an RPG?"

"Well, this world does have dragons. It wouldn't be odd for it to have a monster or two, as well. I'm sure I don't need to tell you this, Aoi, but be careful. Now, Ringo, you're up next."

"........."

The next one he addressed was Ringo Oohoshi, the genius inventor. Hearing her name, the girl twitched and stiffened.

"I want you to set us up with a comm system. We all have smartphones, but this world doesn't have any Wi-Fi or 4G. As things stand, it'll be hard for us to exchange information when we're apart, and that won't do. If possible, I'd like you to modify our existing phones so we can use them here. Can you do it?"

At Tsukasa's question, Ringo's gaze wandered hesitantly from one member of their group to another. Even though she'd known everyone there since middle school, Ringo was so shy that the only one she could even talk to was Tsukasa. She'd trusted him completely ever since a certain incident in middle school.

Sensing her trepidation, Tsukasa added, "If you don't want to talk in front of everyone, you can come whisper your answer in my ear."

©Sacraneco

Visibly relieved, she inched her butt right up next to his and brought her petite lips to his earlobe so that only he could hear.

"…Um…I…can do it. My laptop…survived…so if I take some materials from the plane…I should be able to manage…somehow."

"Are you good for tools?"

Ringo nodded, then clapped her hands together.

In a flash, countless spiderlike manipulator arms extended out from her backpack, which had been lying inert by the wall.

"Wh-wh-whoa! Didn't see that one coming!"

"Damn, that's handy. Those arms have all sorts of tools on 'em."

Masato was right. With just that one backpack, Ringo had access not just to normal tools, like drills and pliers, but also equipment for welding, lathing, laser machining, and pretty much every other type of manufacturing imaginable. She was definitely set when it came to equipment. That said…

"But whatcha gonna do for power? We're a little short on outlets."

Ringo responded to Shinobu's concerns by whispering "That's… okay" in Tsukasa's ear. "I checked…the crash site…and I…didn't detect any radiation."

"The plane ran off one of your pocket nuclear fission reactors, so if that had been damaged, there would have been a radiation leak. Because there's no radiation, we can infer that the reactor's still functioning. Is that what you mean?"

"Yeah… The refined uranium won't last forever…but we should be fine on power…for now."

"Well, that's good to hear. Could you go ahead and get started on that tomorrow?"

"…Y— Yeah…"

Hmm?

Ringo had agreed to his request, but she'd hesitated for a moment.

"What's the matter? It sounds like you have something you want to say."

"…!" Ringo's shoulders twitched. Apparently, Tsukasa had hit the nail on the head.

There was something else she wanted to do, too. However, afraid that she'd end up upsetting Tsukasa somehow, she hadn't been able to bring it up. The boy prime minister, however, was observant enough to pick up on even her subtlest tells. And because he knew she was the type to think too hard about other people's moods and opinions, he knew just the way to get her to speak her mind.

"If you have an idea, by all means, let me know. I'm the one giving instructions, so it'd be a big help."

It'd be a big help.

Hearing those words made Ringo relax a little. She leaned into Tsukasa's ear again and said falteringly, "…Um, well, see? When I went to the crash site…I saw the red valley where the plane's nose was…and I had a hunch. So I used these…to check."

When she said "these," she pointed at the work goggles affixed to her hat. Just like her backpack, they were one of her many inventions. They were equipped with a multitude of features, such as the ability to zoom in when doing precise work, to scan a machine and see its insides through its frame, and to analyze objects and gases to check their chemical compositions. After pointing at the goggles, she told Tsukasa about her surprising discovery.

"Oh, wow. That's…"

"What'd she say?"

"Apparently, there's a deposit of bauxite ore at the crash site."

The unforeseen development caused Masato and Shinobu to ooh and aah as well.

Akatsuki, the only one who didn't quite follow, turned to Masato and said, "Hey, Masato, could you remind me what bauxite is? It sounds familiar."

"It's the base ingredient for aluminum. It forms in warm, humid climates, but it's not like biomes stay the same way forever. Depending on how far down you go, you can end up excavating it in cold places, too."

"…I want…to use the bauxite here…and make aluminum. Without easy-to-craft metal…I'm not…very useful."

"What's she gonna do for a refinery, though?"

"She said, '*I've got the blueprint for one in my head, so it'll only take me three days to build.*'" Tsukasa recited the words his friend had whispered in his ear.

"…Damn." Masato was struck speechless.

One would expect nothing less of the genius who'd advanced human civilization by centuries.

"One problem. The pocket nuclear fission reactor will cover her power needs, but apparently, the scrap from the plane won't be enough to make some 'reduction pot' she'll need to process the aluminum."

Hearing that last tidbit, Masato said "Heh" and flashed his pearly whites.

"Sounds like a job for me."

"I'm glad you're quick on the uptake. I heard that Elch, the treasurer, is going into the city next week to sell handicrafts the village women made. He's going to use the proceeds to buy food for the winter. Merchant, your mission is to accompany him and figure out how to rake in some cash. Then, once you've bought enough to fill the village stores, use what you have left to buy as many of the materials Ringo needs as you can."

"Sounds like a straightforward enough plan, but 'rake in some cash'? Really? Couldn't you have come up with a nicer way of putting it? Like 'help Elch out of the goodness of your heart' or something?"

"I have never in my life seen you help someone out of the goodness of your heart."

"...Dammit, you know me too well. Guess I shouldn't be surprised since we go back so far," Masato said as his shoulders swayed gleefully. "As it long as it exists in this world, I'll get it for ya, whether it's for sale in that city or not... Although, that asshole kid doesn't seem to have inherited any of Winona's cuteness, so getting him to let me tag along is probably gonna be a struggle."

"As far as that goes, I'll discuss it with the mayor directly. Leave it to me."

"Then, hey, it'll be smooth sailing on my end."

Tsukasa nodded at Masato's response, then turned his gaze to Akatsuki and Keine.

"Now then, Akatsuki and Keine. You two are going to stay here in the village with me and lend Lyrule and the other village women a hand. If you don't know what to do, just ask them. And if they don't have work for you, you can help Ringo out with her project."

"Very well."

"Hey, I like these orders! Safe jobs are the best!"

"I...appreciate the honesty. And finally, Shinobu."

"That's me, Cap'n! What should I do nyeow?"

"I want you to go to the city with Merchant and collect as much information as you can on this world."

"What should I focus on?"

"Everything. History, politics, culture, magic... Anything you can get your hands on. Even better would be if you could get details on the Seven Heroes story Winona mentioned. Just don't do anything crazy."

"Sha-sha. ♪ Leave it to me! Why have legs if not to pound pavement, that's what I say!" As a journalist, there was hardly a better job one could think of for Shinobu. She took on the work with pleasure.

"I'm counting on you… Oh, and one other side mission for everyone except Merchant and Shinobu. Whenever you have downtime, I want you to learn these," Tsukasa said, pulling a notepad from his breast pocket and handing it to Akatsuki.

When Akatsuki opened it, he was greeted by a script that could only be described as drunk earthworms wriggling about. The text was laid out next to some Japanese.

"Wait, is this the local language?"

"Altan, it's called. Lyrule helped me put this together while I was recuperating. It's a textbook on commonly used Altan words and grammar. Merchant and Shinobu are going to be interacting with language a lot, so I already had them learn it, but I want the rest of you to do the same. Being able to read and write will vastly increase our options going forward."

"Aw, man… I hate studying. It's weird, though. Why can they understand Japanese even though the writing is so different?"

Akatsuki's question earned nothing more than a shake of the head from Tsukasa.

"Who knows? Maybe some astronomical coincidence happened and all the pronunciations and definitions just happened to line up. There could also be some *supernatural power* at work… Either way, we're unlikely to figure out the answer anytime soon. At this point, throwing another bizarre anomaly or two on the pile isn't going to make much of a difference."

"Indeed. We should be thankful for our luck, that we should."

"Also, even if we knew, it's not like it'd help us get back home, so honestly, who really cares?"

"…You guys are really good at adjusting to all this," Akatsuki remarked.

"Nya-ha-ha. We just figure there's no point worrying about the unknowable, that's all."

"Shinobu sums it up succinctly. Now, then… You all have your orders. Any questions?"

Their silence was as good a response as any. Thus, the first course of action for the Seven High School Prodigies was set. Starting the next day, they'd begin working in earnest to get back to Earth. Tsukasa took a look at the group gathered around the hearth…and made one last speech.

"Everyone, I know we've been thrust into a thoroughly ridiculous situation with no warning or pretext, and I know you're all probably worried about whether we'll even be able to get home. Given that we don't have any firm leads, I don't blame you. But we have nothing to fear. Think back. How many countless times have we overcome the impossible, the futile, the unthinkable, the unrealistic? Besides, they call us High School Prodigies for a reason, and there are *seven* of us here. What obstacle could possibly stop us? In fact, I'd say we have *too much* to work with."

"Heh-heh. I daresay you're right."

"You said it. Hell, if anything, I'm more worried we're gonna run the tables on this quaint little place."

"Right? So let's try to take things nice and easy. If we go all out, we're liable to break this world."

Hearing Tsukasa's confidence, the other six grinned fearlessly.

""""Yeah!!!!"""" The cheer marked their vow to one another—a vow to return to Earth.

CHAPTER 1

❦ Mayonnaise and the Minor Turmoil ❦

Now that their wounds had healed, Tsukasa and the others started taking on their share of the village chores. Tsukasa had lived alone back on Earth, so he was quite good at cooking. His job was to help Lyrule prepare the meals.

Elm Village didn't have individual kitchens in each house. Instead, all the food was stored in a nearby cave, and everyone ate their meals together at either the mayor's house *slash* local office or in the village square.

Because of that, Tsukasa and the other cooks had to wake up early. The village had little in the way of seasoning, meaning the menu was depressingly consistent, but the sheer volume of food required to feed everyone meant that cooking was still quite an undertaking.

The sun hadn't even risen yet, but Tsukasa, Lyrule, and the three other cooks were already hard at work, diligently preparing breakfast. Tsukasa peeled the vegetables, then passed them to Lyrule so she could cut them into bite-size pieces.

"Mmrn…" Midway through, Lyrule let out an adorable little moan.

"What's wrong, Lyrule?"

"Why is it that I always cry when I'm cutting onions?"

"Ha-ha. Well, that's just how onions are."

"I hate it… Mmrn… And I can't just close my eyes when I'm cutting them; that wouldn't be safe."

"You could try pouring some water from that bucket onto your knife first. When you cut onions, they emit something called allyl sulfide into the air. That's what makes you tear up. But the water from your knife should dilute it and reduce the effect."

"Really?" Lyrule followed his instructions. After wetting her knife, she cut into the onions again. Tsukasa's words proved true. It didn't sting quite as badly.

"Wow! This is so much better than before! You know so much, Tsukasa!"

"Onions tormented humankind back on our world, too."

The two of them continued chatting away as they skillfully prepared the food.

Even with the village's paucity of ingredients, the culinary skills Tsukasa had gained from living alone quickly earned him a good deal of popularity among the villagers.

Lyrule had been particularly impressed and remarked, "It's so nice that you skin the vegetables properly, unlike Winona."

Winona's rebuttal had been *"There might be nutrients in those skins; you don't know! See, I was keeping that in mind and* intentionally *not peeling them!"*

However, given how many people she'd poisoned in the past by forgetting to remove potato sprouts, no one came to her defense.

Then, a few days after Tsukasa joined the food prep team…

"Hmm. What to do, what to do."

It was early in the morning, and when Tsukasa showed up at the storehouse to pick up the ingredients, he found Lyrule there with her arms crossed and a vexed expression.

"What's on your mind?"

"...At dinner yesterday, Lucca and the other little ones were complaining."

Tsukasa thought back to the previous evening. In the village, there were a number of children even younger than Lyrule and Elch. Lucca was, of course, one of them.

"Right, they were complaining about being sick of potatoes and stew. I remember their parents getting really cross with them."

"Yes, that. But I doubt the children are the only ones tired of eating the same thing day in and day out. Everyone else is just too polite to say it... That's why I was hoping I could think of something different to make with just the ingredients we already have."

"Hmm. If only we had some sugar and pepper. That would open up all sorts of options for us."

"W-we could never afford something so luxurious, though!"

"Ah, I see. So sugar and pepper are luxury items here?"

Now that she mentioned it, Tsukasa hadn't seen either since coming to this world. Honey was basically it as far as sweeteners went. Sugar must have been scarce, just like during the Earth's Middle Ages.

"Hmm... I really can't think of anything, though."

"It's hardly your fault. With us in the mix, cooking for sixty-odd people is no easy task. Your lack of options when it comes to ingredients and seasonings aside, your main problem is that there's simply no time to spend coming up with ideas."

"...I suppose you're right. It is a shame, though..."

"Ah, so this is where you two were. I couldn't find you anywhere," a third voice said, suddenly interrupting their idle conversation.

The voice belonged to Sogno, a housewife and another member of the cooking staff. She was also Lucca's mother. Although she was supposedly from the same generation as Winona, the stress of raising three children made her look much more her age.

"What're you two doing, chatting in a gloomy storehouse like this? Having a secret date?"

"N-no, no, it's not that at all! We were just trying to think of some new dishes we could make."

"Oh, did what my kid say yesterday get to you? You really don't need to spoil the little ones. We're lucky we have enough to eat at all. Before Winona's husband, Adel, brought potatoes up from the south, just feeding ourselves each day was a struggle."

"Still, I was hoping I could think of something that would change things up a little."

"Well, if it's that easy, then I'm all for it. Do you have any ideas?"

Silence was the only answer Lyrule could muster.

"Well, if not, could you hurry it up with the ingredients? We don't exactly have all day, you know." Sogno rocked the basket she was carrying. Inside, there was a heap of elliptical white orbs...specifically, hen eggs.

"Oh, wow, that's a good harvest."

"Yeah, we lucked out. There'll be enough for everyone to have two today."

Not only were eggs nutritious, their supply was relatively stable.

Tsukasa knew they'd been expensive back in Earth's Middle Ages, but poultry farming had developed faster in this world, making eggs one of Elm Village's staple foods.

Normally, they just stuck them straight in a pot and ate them boiled.

After all, it would take forever to prepare enough scrambled or fried eggs for everyone with the cookware the village had access to. The plan was probably to toss them in a pot and boil them up today as usual. However...

Eggs... Aha. Now there's a thought.

Seeing the mountain of eggs sent a bolt of inspiration through Tsukasa's mind. He had an idea. With the tools and ingredients in the village, they could easily re-create the condiment that took Earth's eighteenth century culinary world by storm.

"With that many eggs, we could try making mayonnaise."

"Mayo—?"

"—naise? What's that?"

"A condiment used back in our world. All you need are eggs—specifically egg yolks, salt, vinegar, and oil. It's easy to make and really tasty. It's particularly delicious on boiled potatoes, eggs, and fresh vegetables, but in a pinch, you can put it on anything."

"Oh my! It sounds too good to be true!"

"The village does have all those ingredients you listed, but is it really as delicious as all that?"

"You have my word on it. In fact, it's so tasty that there are some people back on our world called Mayo Freaks who can't enjoy a meal that doesn't have mayonnaise on it. Some of them get so bad that they start eating it straight."

"That...sounds really bad."

"Is... Is this stuff really safe to eat?"

Seeing their alarm, Tsukasa gave a broad grin and nodded.

"As with all things, moderation is key. So what do you think? Want me to tell you how to make it?"

After thinking for a little bit, Sogno gave him her answer.

"Well, only using the yolks seems like a bit of a waste, but we did get a lot of eggs today. All right, go ahead. Show us how it's done."

"Hooray! Oh, thank you, Sogno."

"In that case, let's head over to the kitchen. And, Sogno, your children are outside, right? Would you mind calling them over and asking them to give us a hand?"

"My kids tend to run a little wild. I'm not sure they'll be much help."

"Don't worry, it's nothing too complicated. Pretty much all they'll be doing is stirring. And besides, everything tastes better when you help make it yourself, right?"

Leaving dinner prep to Sogno and the other members of the cooking group, Tsukasa and Lyrule headed to the kitchen, accompanied by the kids and their babysitter, Akatsuki.

"All right, now I'm going to teach you how to make mayonnaise."

"I'm looking forward to it."

""""Yaaay!""""

Lyrule and the kids responded enthusiastically. Akatsuki, on the other hand, seemed miffed.

"Man, cooking isn't even my job. Why should I have to?"

It wasn't so much that the boy was an uncooperative slacker. Rather, it was that he was a magician. His very livelihood depended on his fine control over his fingertips. In other words, his aversion to cooking stemmed from the chance that he'd hurt his fingers on a sharp object or a hot metal. His magic raked in ten billion yen a night, so if he hurt his hands and couldn't perform, the losses would be considerable.

Tsukasa had, of course, taken this into account.

"You want to increase the village's culinary repertoire, too, don't you? We won't be using any knives or hot pans, so can I count on you to help?" By demonstrating that he respected Akatsuki's dedication to his profession, he was able to quell the magician's fears.

Akatsuki grinned wryly at Tsukasa's carefully chosen words.

"There you go again…showing people how much you care about their feelings while cutting off their escape routes."

"It comes with the job." Tsukasa gave a nihilistic smile in response, then began the instructions.

"Okay, so the first step is to crack your egg and pour just the yolk into a separate bowl."

"We're splitting them up?"

"Yup. Mayonnaise only uses the yolks."

"That feels like such a waste…"

"Don't worry about it. We can put the leftover whites into the stew; that way they'll still go to good use. Also, when you're separating out the yolks, it's easier to wash your hands and pick them up with your palms than to scoop them up with a spoon. We'd have to worry about microorganisms if we were planning on storing it, but it's fine to ignore that for now because I doubt any of it'll survive the evening."

"Ah, I see."

Lyrule had been a member of the food prep team for a while now, and it showed in the way she handled the eggs. As she separated the yolks from the whites, she managed to avoid breaking a single one.

Akatsuki got to show off his nimble fingers, too. Cooking may not have been his forte, but he was king when it came to manual dexterity.

The kids, however, didn't catch on quite as quickly. Unable to control their strength well when cracking the eggs, they often ended up crushing the yolks between their fingers.

"Oh no, I smooshed it…"

"Ah-ha-ha! Lucca, you suck at this!"

"I'm sorry…"

"Don't worry about it. It's not like the egg is ruined; we can still put it in the stew like the whites. Next time, make sure you crack it carefully so the yolk doesn't break."

"O-okay!"

Lucca and the other kids smiled happily at Tsukasa's encouragement, then got back to work. Seeing his tolerance for mistakes eased their nervousness. All the kids messed it up at first, but they got the hang of it soon enough.

"I did it! Miss Lyrule, look! I did it!"

"Me, too! I only broke one of 'em!"

"That's very impressive. You're all doing great."

Lyrule's praise made kids adorably bashful. Noticing that the children were still smiling, Tsukasa continued the lesson.

"Next, we're going to be adding the flavor. First, mix the salt and vinegar into the egg yolks and thoroughly stir it up. Then do the same with the olive oil."

The kids looked at Tsukasa like he'd grown a second head.

"We-we're gonna put *olive oil* in our *food*?!"

"Ew, gross!"

"...Can you even eat that stuff?"

Elm Village made its living off of hunting, but although tallow featured prominently in their culture, they had yet to come up with the idea of using olive oil in food. As far as they were concerned, it was just something they bought from the city to wash their hair, ears, and tails with. In Earth terms, it would be like having a recipe that called for shampoo. Their shock was perfectly understandable. Tsukasa was going to have to explain.

"You guys don't cook with it here, but back in our world, that was actually the main thing it was used for. It's actually better for you than tallow."

"Oh, really? I've never left this village, so I had no idea..."

Lyrule and the others did as they were told, pouring olive oil into their yolk-and-vinegar mixture and churning it.

They seemed hesitant, but that was to be expected. The boy prime minister continued his instructions undeterred, knowing that they'd be singing a different tune once they tried some.

"Once it's thoroughly mixed, replenish the oil little by little and keep churning. When it's mixed again, repeat the process and keep doing that until you've used up your share of olive oil. Once you run out, you're done."

"Huh? That's all?"

"Wow, that's easy-peasy!"

"Right? At the end of the day, mayonnaise is just water-soluble vinegar and oil with some egg yolk to hold it together."

It didn't require any special tools or techniques. All you needed was enough stamina to mix and mix and mix. As far as everyone was doing on that front, Lyrule had clearly grown up in the mountains without modern conveniences. She breezed through it. The three kids, for their part, took turns to split up the load. Akatsuki got tuckered out midway through, but Tsukasa stepped in to cover for him. Ten minutes or so later, their first batch of mayonnaise, quite possibly the first batch on this world, was finished.

Lyrule and the others all gazed gingerly at the mayonnaise sitting in the bowl.

"So this is…a condiment from your world?"

"I-it looks kinda gross…"

"It's all goopy and sticky… Hey, mister, are you sure this is gonna be tasty?"

"I thought you might ask that, so I steamed some potatoes in preparation." Tsukasa went and retrieved the potatoes he'd been cooking in the kitchen's fireplace, then placed them in front of Lyrule and the others. "Go on, try putting some mayonnaise on top."

Lyrule and the kids seemed trepidatious at first, but up in the mountains, the children didn't get to eat treats often. Furthermore, they had the healthy appetites of growing boys and girls. They weren't about to turn down a free snack.

The four of them split the two potatoes among themselves, smeared mayonnaise on them with a wooden spatula, and dug in.

"Foo, foo… Haumph!"

Their eyes all went wide.

"…!"

"Wow!"

"It's so yummy! It's so good!"

"This is way better than just eating them with salt!"

Their eyes glittered as they let out joyous cries about how tasty it was. But who could blame them? After all, mayonnaise had the soft acidity of vinegar and the richness of egg, all wrapped up in an oily coating. To a tongue that had never tasted seasoning beyond salt and vinegar, the flavor must have been downright revolutionary. The magic that had won the entire Earth over in a single short century wasn't just for show.

"This is… This is the first time I've ever had something so gently sour!"

"I don't doubt it. It's hard to find acidity quite like this outside of mayonnaise."

"Wow, man, they weren't kidding. Did mayonnaise always taste this good?"

"It's probably because of how fresh the eggs were, Akatsuki. The sweetness of the eggs is what lets the sourness and saltiness harmonize so well and why mayo doesn't need any sugar or pepper to accentuate its flavor. And because ours didn't have any additives in it, it didn't have any of that unpleasant lingering bitterness, either. In fact, it came out amazingly well."

It was wholly unlike the kind of mass-produced mayonnaise you could buy in stores. The thick richness blended perfectly with the sourness and saltiness, like in cheese. You couldn't get quality like this unless you made it yourself.

"Seconds! Can I have seconds?!"

"I wanna keep eating it, too!"

The children seemed to have taken a liking to it, as they immediately started asking for more.

But Lyrule, the senior of the group, kept them in check.

"No, no, no. If you eat any more, you'll spoil your dinners."

"Maaan…"

"Okay…"

"And also, don't you all have something to say to Tsukasa?"

The children leaped at Lyrule's reminder, then turned to Tsukasa.

""""Thank you, Mr. Tsukasa!"""" they cheered in unison, each beaming as bright and wide as sunflowers.

"I'm just glad you all enjoyed it."

Having received the best kind of thanks possible, Tsukasa started cleaning up the spatulas and eggshells they'd used.

"Oh, let me help you with that," offered Lyrule as she went over to his side.

Then, with a smile as big as the kids', she whispered, "I think you made them very happy."

"Yeah, and I'm happy, too, that my knowledge was of some use to you all."

"At any rate, between this and the onions, I'm surprised by how much you know about cooking. And I would never have expected a man like you to be so adept with your hands."

"I started helping my mother in the kitchen when I was around Lucca's age, you see."

"Oh, is that why? I'm impressed. You don't see many boys helping their mothers like that."

"I liked spending time with her. You could say I was a bit of a mama's boy. After I started living on my own, I had plenty of opportunities to polish my talents. Nowadays, it's one of my few useful skills."

"You stopped living with your mother?"

Lyrule had intended it as a casual question. She was basically just making small talk. She'd noticed something interesting in their conversation, so she'd asked about it, nothing more. That was why—

"…No. She abandoned me."

"Huh?"

—the unexpected answer made her face freeze.

"She had her reasons. After all, I did something horrible to her. Something unforgivable, and it wounded her deeply."

"Th-that's— I'm…"

But before Lyrule could ask more questions—

"What do you people want?!?!"

"""…?!"""

—Winona's uncharacteristically furious voice echoed through the kitchen.

Tsukasa left his cleaning duties and rushed outside as soon as he heard the shouting. He looked toward where it had come from: the entrance to the village. There, he saw a plain carriage with four men standing beside it. Each wore a sword at his waist. Winona was standing in front of them, eyes narrowed. Tsukasa turned to Masato, who'd been quietly watching the scene play out from beside the mayor's house.

"What's going on, Merchant?"

"They're soldiers on patrol."

"…Soldiers, huh. That means they're members of whatever

administrative body runs this world. But it doesn't exactly look like they come in peace, does it?"

Shinobu, who'd been standing next to Masato, answered that one. "They waited for the men to go out hunting, then barged in demanding beer and food."

"Ah, and that's why Winona's angry."

These were the first soldiers Tsukasa had seen, so he took a good, long look at them. Of the four, three of them all had the same equipment. Their helmets and breastplates were made of metal…it looked to be bronze. However, their arms and legs seemed more or less unprotected. As far as armor went, it was pretty light. At a glance, it all looked fairly cheap. Those guys were probably low-ranked grunts. Then there was the arrogant man standing behind the others wearing a cloak and bronze armor covering his entire body. Given his equipment and demeanor, he was likely their commander.

"Lyrule, be sure you hide, like the other times. If they found someone as cute as you living here, things could turn ugly."

"G-got it!"

Responding to one of the village's middle-aged women's stern warning, the blond-haired girl quickly scurried behind the door to the mayor's house. Winona and the others continued arguing as Lyrule made her escape.

"I'm telling you, we don't got any beer for you to drink or meat for you to eat! We give it all as tribute to the lord we serve! If you want booze, why don't you go ask him for some?!"

"Hey, lady, you'd better watch that mouth of yours. This here's Scido, an Imperial Knight! Peasants like you shouldn't be talkin' so familiar-like with him."

"Yeah, and we're tellin' you that out of the goodness of our hearts! You guys heard about that house that got attacked by bandits down in Papad Village at the base of the mountain, didn't you? All the women and children inside got killed. Even these parts're gettin' dangerous these days. I'm sayin' we'll protect you when your men are away. No bandits'd dare come here when Lord Findolph's soldiers are around."

"That's right… But if you run us outta here? Y'know, I hear these bandits don't just got swords, they even got armor. What're a bunch of women and kids gonna do against people like that, huh?"

"You people… Are you saying…?" Sensing something in the soldiers' eyes, Winona's gaze hardened.

The soldiers' grins deepened. The man with the flashy armor and self-assured demeanor, who up until now had been content to listen, approached Winona.

"Hey now, don't look so scared. We're here as knights who uphold peace in the empire 'cause we're *worried* about you. We're here to protect you. We're just askin' for a little hospitality in return, that's all… Besides, I bet you're all pent-up 'cause your husband bit it, ain'tcha? Why don't you lemme show you some pity up close and personal?" As he spoke, the knight named Scido reached toward Winona's chest. It was all too obvious where those open palms of his were heading. The sheer crassness of his actions and vulgarity of his words made Winona's face flush scarlet with rage.

However—

"Trying to lay a hand on a woman's breasts without permission? I see what you mean—these parts *are* swarming with low-life bandits."

—before Winona's fury could erupt, Tsukasa stepped in and stopped the soldier.

"Tsu-Tsukasa…!"

Tsukasa grabbed the soldier's arm as he positioned himself in front of Winona to protect her.

Masato, watching his friend from a distance, muttered, "Figured he'd do that," with a faint smile. The soldiers, however, were hardly amused. Their eyes widened in anger as they yelled in unison, "Who the hell d'ya think you are?!"

Tsukasa responded, "I'm a guest in this village and have been living here the past month. My good soldiers, we appreciate the offer but ask that you kindly leave. As you can see, the village is already under my protection. As long as I'm here, it'll remain safe. Even if, say… four bandits were to show up dressed as soldiers." The prime minister glared coldly at the shouting soldiers and released their leader's arm. Then he waved his hands at them to shoo them away. "Now, if you would please leave. Although, if you remain insistent that we feed you, I'm sure we have some potatoes we could rustle up."

Scido rose up, his body visibly shaking with rage.

"You little… You commoner, you beast that crawls on the ground! You would take that tone with me, when I hold the title of Bronze Knight? Sounds like someone doesn't know his place…!" Scido drew his overly well-maintained sword, then shouted, "An affront against a Bronze Knight is an affront against the Freyjagard Empire! An affront against His Majesty, the Emperor, himself! Men! Strike him down for his insolence!"

""""Hraaaaagh!!!!"""" On Scido's orders, his men drew their swords and charged at Tsukasa.

Winona went pale and shouted, "Tsukasa! Run!"

However—

"Oh, brother…"

—Tsukasa did no such thing.

In fact, he strode *toward* the armed men rushing at him.

"—Ur…gh?!"

The closest one was first.

After sliding past the man's sword, which had been aimed at his throat, Tsukasa casually passed him by and unleashed a knife-hand strike.

With one blow to the medulla oblongata, the soldier dropped to the ground.

Then, without missing a beat, Tsukasa turned toward the sword bearing down on him from above.

"Hah!"

Instead of dodging the attack, Tsukasa stepped into it, grabbed the soldier's arm, and performed a one-arm shoulder throw. His target was, of course, the third soldier.

"Argh!" "Urf!"

Having now dealt with those two, Tsukasa took the sword he'd snatched with his free hand while throwing one of his assailants. Bronze Knight Scido was frozen in place, utterly stunned and gaping at Tsukasa's display of martial prowess. Tsukasa seized the moment and shoved the sword in Scido's defenseless mouth.

"Ack—"

Feeling the flat of the blade touch his molars, the Bronze Knight stiffened in fear.

Frigid light burned in Tsukasa's heterochromatic eyes. "You're a worm, a parasite who preys on order. It looks like subtlety's wasted on you, so let me put this bluntly—if you value your lives, run."

Scido trembled. His rattling teeth clinked against the sword. Now he understood. Bronze Knight was the lowest rank of nobility, but it was a noble rank nonetheless. However, it meant little to the commoner before him, who clearly wouldn't hesitate to take his life.

"Y-yeeep!"

"W-wait for us, Commander!"

"Dammit! Th-this isn't over, you hear!"

Their retreat was swift. They scrambled over one another to get on their carriage, then fled the village atop it. The villagers cheered as they watched the soldiers make their pathetic flight into the distance. Townsfolk dashed over to Tsukasa, eyes glittering and cheeks flush.

"Wow! That was amazing, mister!"

"That was so cool!"

"You threw a guy that big with those skinny arms?! You might not look it, but you're buff!"

"That was just some basic self-defense. My world isn't exactly peaceful, either."

Besides, in Tsukasa's profession, he often found himself making enemies of powerful people. It had gotten so bad that he'd stopped keeping track of how many assassins had been sent after him. The fingers on both hands weren't enough to count how many he'd had to stop himself. Tsukasa might not have been as brawny as the men of the village, but when it came to surviving life-and-death experiences, he was something of an expert.

Recently, he'd had a skilled bodyguard named Chang who took care of most of that stuff for him, but Chang himself had started as an assassin after Tsukasa's life. Tsukasa'd turned the tables on him and won him to his side, so the boy was by no means weak.

"Even if they're armed, guys of that caliber pose no threat to me."

"Still, that was dangerous! You can't just go in empty-handed against men with swords!" Amid the cheers, Lyrule alone was scolding Tsukasa with a tense expression. When he looked, Tsukasa saw tears welling up in the corners of her eyes. His sudden act of barbarity must have given her quite an unpleasant shock.

Sensing that, Tsukasa offered her an earnest apology.

"…I'm sorry for worrying you, but I couldn't just stand by and watch one of my saviors be assaulted like that. I hope you can find it in you to forgive me."

"Tsukasa…" Hearing that, not even Lyrule could continue scolding him.

"At any rate, what a lovely group they were. They didn't even hesitate to attack an unarmed opponent. Is that kind of thing common in this world?"

"...Nobles can kill commoners like us without it even being a crime."

"Right, he did say he was striking me down for my insolence. Come to think of it, we used to have a law like that in Japan, too... I don't like any of this."

"Hey, don't we have a problem? Those guys may have been thugs, but they were still soldiers. If we turn 'em loose and they report back to their lord, isn't it gonna get messy?"

Masato's concerns were valid, but...Tsukasa had already thought of that.

"Don't worry. I've already taken steps to prevent that."

Elsewhere, fleeing had done little to quell the anger of the soldiers. Their faces were contorted in expressions of humiliation and fury as their carriage barreled toward the castle.

"Animals, the lot of 'em! Those barbarians, they'll see! Once we get back to the castle, we'll give a full report to our lord. That'll teach 'em not to mess with us!"

"There's no way he'll let an insult to a Bronze Knight like that slide, Commander!"

"Of course not! He'll have every *byuma* in that damn village up on a pike, even the women and children!" But no sooner had Scido spat the words than an auspicious answer came.

"Well, I can't exactly let that slide."

A sudden voice rang out from overhead.

"Wh-who was that?!"

They stopped the carriage and looked around. Then…

"AHHHH!" One of the soldiers looked *toward the sky* and let out a shrill scream.

Alarmed, Scido and the others looked up as well. And what they saw…was the High School Prodigy Prince Akatsuki clad in his stage outfit—top hat, cloak, and eye mask—floating in the fair autumn sky.

"Th-there's someone floating?!"

"N-no way…! L-levitation?! Is that a mage?!"

"That's right! My name's Prince Akatsuki, and I'm the grand mage who protects Elm *Village!*"

Akatsuki gazed down at the soldiers. The boy overemphasized the ends of his sentences, as he often did for his shows. He'd also introduced himself under a false title.

The magician was following the instructions Tsukasa had given him beforehand. Tsukasa's hypothesis had been that because mages were so valuable and respected, pretending to be one would serve as a deterrent. By all accounts, his guess had been right on the money.

The moment they heard the word *mage*, Scido and the other soldiers' faces went all the way past pale and turned a ghostly shade of white.

"But that can't be…! Only Prime Mages are supposed to be able to use levitation…! Why's there a Prime Mage in a shitty little village like that…?!"

"Heh-heh-heh. They found me collapsed in the mountains and rescued me. I owe them a great debt. Now, perhaps I can repay that debt by saving them! You threatened their lives and livelihoods, so I have but to erase you from this *world!*" And with that ringing declaration, Akatsuki grabbed his cloak and hurled it. The cape floated gently through the air, eventually landing atop the horse that had been pulling their carriage.

The soldiers had been flabbergasted seeing someone floating in the air but regained their senses quickly enough.

©Sacraneco

"I-idiots! What're you doing?! Quick, get the horse movin'! We're gettin' out of here!"

"G-got it! A-argh! This stupid cloth's in the way!"

Agitated, the soldiers pulled the cloak off the horse. But then, quite abruptly...

""""AHHH!"""""

With a jolt, the carriage pitched forward. The sudden shift and impact had made Scido and his subordinates shut their eyes in reflexive fear, but they opened them after a moment to see what was going on.

"...Huh?"

Something unbelievable had happened before the four men. There had definitely been a horse pulling their carriage a moment ago, but now it was gone. Vanished, without a trace. All that remained was the bridle that had hitched the horse to its load.

"E-eeeeeek! Th-the horse! The horse is goooone!!"

Having just witnessed something that defied all logic, Scido and the others screamed as they collapsed in shock.

Akatsuki landed and walked slowly toward them.

"I told you I'd *erase you from the world*, didn't I? Mwa-ha-ha. All right, now it's your turn. Just like that poor horse, I'll use my grand magic to get rid of you, leaving neither hide nor *hair*!"

"No, no..." By that point, Scido and the others had long since lost their will to fight.

Writhing on the ground and pissing themselves, they begged for their lives.

"P-p-please, spare us! Spare us! I won't say a word! I won't tell the lord what happened here!"

"M-me, neither! I swear to God! Please don't erase meeeee!"

"Nooooo! I don't wanna die! I don't wanna die!"

"Eeeeeeek!"

"—Pfft."

Seeing their pathetic, over-the-top reactions almost made Akatsuki burst out laughing. After all, he was nothing but a stage magician. None of his so-called grand magic had been anything more than magnificent acts of sleight of hand and illusion. All of them were based on tricks and contrivances. There was no way he could actually make them disappear, of course. That was why he found their exaggerated astonishment so funny.

Sounds like it's time to start wrapping this up.

"…Heh. It appears you understand just how terrifying Prince Akatsuki can be. Very well! If you swear not to say anything to your lord, I'm prepared to spare your lives just this once. However! If you ever *break* that promise—"

Akatsuki paused for a second, then unveiled his final trick. With a *thump*, something collapsed onto the ground and rolled toward the soldiers: Akatsuki's own head. Severed from his neck…

"—your heads will fall off, then and there." The head flashed them a malevolent grin.

That was enough to seal the deal.

"………"

Frothing at the mouth, the soldiers passed out.

"Phew! Welp, that's that."

Having finished his mission, Akatsuki sighed. His head was back on his neck as if it had never left. It made sense. After all, people couldn't talk their heads detached from their necks. After double-checking to make sure the soldiers were unconscious, he pulled out his smartphone and called Tsukasa. Thanks to the efforts of Ringo Oohoshi, their phones worked again. Tsukasa must have been waiting for him, as the call connected immediately.

"This is Tsukasa. How'd it go?"

"I did everything exactly like you told me. They bought it pretty hard, so I don't think they'll be telling anyone… But man, you're amazing. Picking a fight like that against four guys with swords?"

"Swords are only as scary as the persons wielding them… If anything, you're the amazing one. How'd you manage to pull off your magic without any of your tools or equipment?"

Akatsuki gave his tongue an affected click, then replied chidingly, "C'mon, Tsukasa, you know better than that. A magician never reveals his secrets."

Whatever the case, their enemies' wills had been broken. Thanks to Tsukasa's quick thinking and Akatsuki's magic, the seeds of turmoil that had visited the village had been successfully nipped in the bud.

The Too-Young Prime Minister and the Broken Family

The mayonnaise Tsukasa and the others had made was a big hit at dinner that evening. The villagers were something of a given, as they'd never tasted such a condiment before, but even Team Earth was excited, getting their first taste of home in a month.

Mayonnaise would no doubt go on to become a vital part of Elm Village's palate.

It had been an exciting day all around for Elm, but every day comes to an end. However, even though she knew she had to be up early in the morning to prepare breakfast, Lyrule couldn't sleep. She lay under her blankets, unable to drift off. Her mind refused to stop turning. What preoccupied her thoughts more than anything was what Tsukasa had said so nonchalantly earlier that day.

"My mother abandoned me. She had her reasons. After all, I did something horrible to her. Something unforgivable—and it wounded her deeply."

Tsukasa had hurt his mother. Enough to sever the bond between parent and child. Lyrule had only known the boy for a month, but that was more than enough to recognize his kindness and devotion to justice. The day's turmoil had only served to further illustrate that.

That was why Lyrule just couldn't believe it. How could Tsukasa have wounded his mother so badly she'd go and abandon him?

...What happened?

That question was keeping her up. Suddenly, she heard something. Someone was walking on the gravel outside. Wondering who it could be at that late hour, Lyrule peered out her latticed window.

"Tsukasa..."

The prime minister of Japan cut through the slumbering village and made his way to the crash site. Then he walked all the way up to the edge of the cliff overlooking the valley. Below, he could see the remnants of the airplane. Ringo had stripped it for parts, and the wreckage was growing more bleached by the day.

The young man looked up and was greeted by a blanket of stars. Even without streetlights, the world was awash in gentle light. It was thanks to that light that he'd made it to his destination without tripping or getting lost.

Tsukasa sat down and gazed up at the foreign sky. After a little while, he heard footsteps coming up behind him. He turned to see a familiar long-eared girl.

"...Hello, Lyrule."

"Nights are cold up here in the mountains. You're dressed so lightly, I was afraid you'd catch a cold." Lyrule handed him the blanket she'd brought.

"Oh, you didn't have to do that. Thank you."

"What were you doing up here, if you don't mind me asking?"

"I was looking at the stars. You can't see them nearly this clearly back in my country."

It had rained the previous day, so the starry sky was especially resplendent. Its glimmer was what had called him there. However, Tsukasa could tell at a glance that wasn't the reason Lyrule had come all this way.

"Judging from appearances, I doubt you just came here to bring me a blanket... Did you have something you needed to talk to me about?"

"H-how can you tell?"

"I'm pretty good at reading people's faces."

Her expression was ever-so-slightly languid, and although her blond hair shone as radiantly as gold dust in the moonlight, she also had a bit of bedhead. She'd probably been lying down but hadn't been able to sleep. Given that she'd come here, specifically, Tsukasa inferred it had something to do with him. Hence the question.

"If there's something on your mind, feel free to say it. I can't think of many things I'd need to hide from you."

Seeing how badly she'd been found out, Lyrule went ahead and cut to the chase.

"...I don't know if I'd go so far as to say I 'needed' to, but...it's about today."

"Today? You mean the incident with the soldiers?"

"No, no. Before that. It's... It's about how you said your mother abandoned you after you did something horrible to her."

"Ah, that."

"Tsukasa...I can tell you're a really good person. From the very moment you woke up in this world, your first concern was the people who were with you, and even today, you worked so hard to make a condiment for the kids and saved Winona. I... I just can't see you as someone who would hurt his own mother. I don't believe it... So I've just been wondering what exactly could have happened. But…I'm—I'm sorry. I really don't mean to pry…"

"Oh, no, no. It's my fault for being careless and letting something so ominous-sounding slip," Tsukasa answered as Lyrule averted her eyes in apology. Telling her not to worry about it would have been pointless.

And besides, Lyrule's…

Tsukasa and the others had heard from Mayor Ulgar that Lyrule… was an orphan Ulgar had found. She'd been abandoned in the forest before she was even old enough to walk. It was the reason she was the only one in the village without animal ears or a tail—she had no relatives in the village.

Tsukasa reasoned that, because of the way she'd grown up, the subject of his mother must have struck a nerve. This wasn't just idle curiosity. Knowing that…it would have been inhumane to insist the matter was private and brush her off. Besides, he was the one who'd rashly invoked the topic in the first place.

Taking all that into account, the young man decided to tell her what he'd done to his mother before arriving in this world…how he'd betrayed her.

"I was telling the truth when I said I hurt my mother deeply and that she abandoned me. But she had her reasons. After all, I took the most important person in her life from her."

"You…*took*…them?"

"That's right… I killed my own father, you see."

Tsukasa Mikogami was born to Mitsuhide Mikogami, Japan's vice minister of finance, and to the third-generation Prime Minister Genpachirou Fuyou's daughter, Shizuka.

Soon after Tsukasa was born, Mitsuhide took over as prime minister on Genpachirou's recommendation. Between his powerful father and his loving mother, young Tsukasa never wanted for anything.

—However, those happy days didn't last long.

Young as he was, Tsukasa's wisdom and powers of perception made him realize that their happiness had been built on the foundation of his father's misdeeds—misdeeds that ran so deep, they made Tsukasa wish for nothing more than to turn a blind eye.

Mitsuhide had done a staggering amount of embezzling and had accepted countless bribes, committing numerous violations of the Public Offices Election Act. To top it all off, he'd even had a number of political opponents, industrial detractors, and journalists who'd uncovered his improprieties assassinated.

Yet, despite all this, Tsukasa's father was utterly beyond reproach.

Mitsuhide had spent a long time as the vice minister of finance, and because of the mountains of dirt he'd gathered on the police, the business world, and the mass media, nobody could lay a finger on him for fear of retribution. Mitsuhide Mikogami ruled over Japan as an untouchable emperor of politics and business alike. However…that situation gave rise to a tragedy.

It happened in October, the year Tsukasa entered middle school.

A domestic airliner had crashed, killing the passengers and crew. It was no mere accident, though. One of the passengers on that plane had been Mitsuhide's old secretary, and the unscrupulous man had pulled some strings to get rid of his former aide under the guise of an act of terrorism.

In that moment, the rift between Tsukasa and his father became irreparable.

Tsukasa, who'd wanted to be an important politician like his father ever since he was a kid…could no longer tolerate his father's misdeeds.

So he went after him.

With the help of two childhood friends—Masato Sanada, who'd already made a name for himself in the business world, and Shinobu Sarutobi, who'd sold sufficient scoops to newspapers and magazines to establish herself as a skilled journalist—Tsukasa exposed all of his father's and his father's accomplices' wrongdoings. The ruling party was eradicated, and Tsukasa's father was ousted from politics.

Afterward, at his trial for inciting homicide and instigating foreign aggression, Mitsuhide was given the death penalty. Seeing Tsukasa's willingness to fight evil, even though it took the form of his own father, inspired joy in people and instilled them with trust for him, but…his mother never forgave him.

Tsukasa could still clearly recall the pain when she'd slapped him with her emaciated hands, withered by anxiety—

"You killed your own father for 'the people'? For complete strangers? You're insane!"

—and the words she'd spat at him like a curse.

"…From then on, she never met me again. I haven't heard from her, either."

"That's horrible…"

"I don't particularly resent her for it. It just goes to show how strongly she loved my father. He had to face judgment for his crimes, of course, but not her. It's no sin to love someone. And she has every right to hate and resent me. I can't deny her that."

"…Can't the two of you make up?"

"I doubt it… If I regretted my actions, that would be one thing, but…I don't regret driving my father to his death even a little. After all, the things he did were unforgivable.

"People have all kinds of desires. Desire for money. Desire for success. Desire for fame… They're important because they motivate people to change the world. Without desire, there can be no progress.

"However, I believe that in democracies, politicians need to set aside their selfishness. I believe that because they're given the 'power' to so easily change the lives of others. If someone like that acts selfishly and wields that power for their own benefit, it only drags the nation down.

"'Politicians are people, too. Abandoning selfishness is impossible.'

"Some people make excuses like that, but that's unacceptable.

"When other people entrust you with 'power' greater than that of a single man, you have to stop being a man altogether. *—In short, politicians have to become saints.*"

Tsukasa believed they at least had to try. Otherwise, countless people would be destroyed under the weight of their influence.

"History bears that out. It's not a job you can take with selfish intentions." Upon reaching that point in his impassioned speech, Tsukasa realized he'd said more than necessary.

"Forgive me. Seeing those soldiers abuse their power this afternoon must have put me on edge. I got more heated there than I needed to. I'm sorry for making you listen to such a boring rant… Let's head back. You were right, it really is cold up here."

As he apologized, Tsukasa stood and turned to face Lyrule, who was standing behind him. Then…his eyes widened in surprise.

"…Why are you crying?"

Tears were rolling down Lyrule's cheeks as she sobbed.

"*Hic…* I'm so sorry… But when I thought about how you must feel… It made me…so sad…" She wiped and wiped, but the tears just kept coming.

Making assumptions about people's emotions like that was nothing but egotistic sentimentalism. She knew that, but despite it all, Lyrule couldn't make the tears stop.

After all, she could tell.

She could tell just how happy he must have been when he cooked with his mother. In fact…Tsukasa probably even loved his immoral father, too. Yet he'd destroyed all that. His kindness and strength prevented any alternative. When she thought about that and about how it must have made him feel, her heart ached as if it might break.

"Bwaaaah…!" She couldn't contain the sorrow welling up inside her.

Seeing the girl in such a state…Tsukasa placed a hand on her shoulder.

"…Tsukasa?"

"You have a good heart, Lyrule," he said, pulling her into a soft embrace as he voiced his appreciation. "Thank you for shedding tears for me… I feel a little better now."

In truth, Lyrule's thoughtfulness had warmed his heart. He continued gently holding her close until she'd settled down.

Those warm feelings…

Directed at him alone…

Those warm tears…

Shed for him alone…

They filled him with a sort of serenity.

For a number of the days that followed in Elm Village, they put mayonnaise on everything—bread, vegetables, even in stew. It became something of a problem for the Seven Prodigies, but that's another story altogether.

CHAPTER 2

⚜ The Devil of Finance and the Slave Girl ⚜

In northern Freyjagard, the Findolph domain, in the Port District of the city of Dormundt—

"Pant...! Pant...!"

A dark-skinned girl wearing tattered rags crouched behind a pile of crates. Her breath was labored. A rugged sailor with a wide, square jaw and eyes goggling out of his head like those of a fish was searching for her.

"Shit! Where'd that brat go?!"

He was holding a knife, and his eyes bulged as he looked around. Then he started walking toward the crates behind which the girl had hidden.

"Over here?"

"_____"

She could hear him getting closer. Her lungs tightened as fear welled up inside her. But before he could reach her, he stopped. The reason being—

"Hey, you! Quit slackin' off! Get over here and unload the cargo!"

—his boss, a sailor with similar facial features, started shouting at him.

"S-sorry! One of the slaves we brought up from the south ran off, so I..."

"What?! Which one?"

"O-one of the *byuma* girls. The one with red hair..."

"Dumbass!"

"Eep!"

"It'd be one thing if it was one of the men, but girls don't sell for shit! You can deal with that later! Finish unloading the cargo first, you dope!"

"Y-yes sir!"

The girl heard the man run off.

"...Haff..." Having survived her narrow brush with death, she breathed a deep sigh of relief. Though the immediate danger had passed, that didn't mean she could just stay where she was forever.

Her legs were trembling from both fear and exhaustion, but she managed to struggle to her feet by leaning against a crate.

Have...to run...somewhere far away...

She vanished into the back alleys. En route, though, she stopped and looked up at the sliver of blue sky visible between the buildings.

But...what then...?

The world was too vast. Too big. And she was too small. Too weak. Where could she go? What could she do? She had no idea.

At the foot of the mountain down the trail from Elm Village, there was a large castle with tall ramparts surrounded by vast fields of wheat. The castle belonged to Marquis Findolph, the region's feudal lord.

Everything up to the structure's outer walls was painted white. The castle's towering roofs, on the other hand, were all coated in solid gold. It wasn't hard to deduce what kind of person its owner was.

That day, the gate to the citadel surrounding the castle's outer walls was open. This was because it was the late-autumn tax-collection day. Wagons from the surrounding villages came rolling into the courtyard one after another to pay their dues, either in the form of crops, handicrafts, or hard currency. Of course, it went without saying that Elm Village had a wagon there, too.

"Oh, it's you. You people, always reeking of wild beasts…"

"Ha-ha, you said it. Feels like my nose is gonna fall off."

The tax collector made a cruel jeer, and the knight clad in bronze who accompanied him piled on without reservation. However, as the village's usual representative, Elch was well accustomed to it by now. Instead of blowing up at them, he just ignored it and unloaded the tax from his wagon.

"…Here are our fall taxes. You can go ahead and store them."

"What, pelts and picked game again? You are *allowed* to pay in gold, you know."

"Those savages spend all their time chasing boar around in the mountains. Where are they gonna get gold?"

"Heh, too true. Besides, gold's too good for bumpkins like them."

"………"

Masato Sanada sighed as he watched the exchange from beside the horse.

"Thank goodness Tsukasa isn't around to hear this."

If he had been there, they likely would've had a repeat performance of the other day.

When someone bad-mouths him, he doesn't so much as flinch. Even though all the stress from it is what turned his hair white. But as soon as it's about someone else, the guy flips out.

As Masato mused on that fact, Elch returned.

"Welcome back. I gotta say, those tax dudes rubbed me the wrong way."

©Sacraneco

Elch frowned for a moment at Masato's friendly tone. His grandfather, the village mayor, had made him take Masato along, but Elch still hadn't warmed to these seven sudden intruders.

"Pretty much all the nobles are like that. C'mon, quit making small talk so we can head back. I'm worried about *the cargo*." With that, Elch got onto the wagon and grabbed the reins.

Shrugging at the cold shoulder he'd just received, Masato hopped back in the cargo bed.

Then, a little while after they left the castle—

"Heya! Welcome back, you two."

—they spotted Shinobu Sarutobi waving at them from beneath a tree by the side of the road. She was surrounded by the rest of the goods they'd brought down from the village...as well as three seedy-looking men collapsed on the ground.

"Who're those guys?"

"Pickup artists, maybe? I am a bona fide cutie, you know. ☆ Still, it was super-rude how they led with '*Give us a piece of that cargo you're workin' with.*'"

"Y'know, normally we call those *bandits*."

"Wait, you beat all of them on your own?"

"Yes sirree!" Shinobu puffed out her chest with pride.

Elch had known that if they went into the castle with more cargo than they needed to pay their taxes, the collectors would be all too eager to take more than their due. Consequently, they'd left Shinobu in charge of watching the excess they were planning on taking into the city to sell later that day.

Elch had balked at the idea of leaving a single girl to watch their stuff, even for a short while.

"See, I told you. You didn't have anything to be worried about. Shinobu's not gonna lose to any of the guys around here."

"It was a piece of cake. Sha-sha!"

This was the same attitude the two of them had expressed when they'd overruled Elch's concerns. The three bandits now twitching on the ground served to retroactively prove their point.

"Still, she was barely alone for a minute before getting attacked. Guess these parts are pretty rough."

"...Things weren't this bad before the old lord got sick and died... But this new lord's a real piece of work. Ever since he took over, not only have things gone to shit, but the taxes have tripled, too."

"Well, that's messed up."

"He couldn't care less about our livelihoods or how safe the roads are. The knights, the lord...all the nobles treat us like wild dogs," Elch spat in disgust, then turned and looked to the sky.

Masato followed his gaze, and his eyes caught the golden rooftops shining radiantly in the sunlight. The more wealth that castle of avarice sucked up from the masses, the more it glittered.

Staring at its infuriating splendor, Elch continued, "If... If it was just money, that'd be one thing. But that bastard even went and instituted the First Night Right."

"Huh? Whazzat?"

"When any woman in the domain gets married, she has to give him her virginity before she can sleep with her husband."

"What?! That's nuts! That's, like, abuse of authority taken to the nines! I can't believe it!"

"...I guess being in a different world doesn't change the ways assholes abuse their power."

"He's a massive deviant. That's why we keep Lyrule *hidden*. You don't see many people that attractive around these parts. No good could come of that lecher learning about her."

"Oh. Smart thinking! See, I knew you Elm guys were nice!"

Elch frowned at Shinobu's giddy display.

"Don't talk about it like it's someone else's problem. You're, I mean, you're relatively pretty, so you're in danger, too."

"Oh? Oh-ho-ho. ♪ What, are you worried about little old me?"

"D-don't take it the wrong way! Who'd worry about a bunch of weirdos like you guys?!" Elch's face went red, and he looked away.

He might not have taken to Tsukasa and the others, but he was still Winona's son and a resident of Elm Village. His heart was in the right place.

Having gotten a glimpse at Elch's true nature, Shinobu flashed him a friendly grin.

"Hee-hee. Thanks. But don't worry—they won't catch me that easily."

"…If you say so."

"Besides, Shinobu, you aren't even a virgin any— Hey, wait, my elbow doesn't bend that wa— OW-OW-OW!"

"Hmm? Did you say something? I'm sorry, I didn't quite catch that. ☆"

"…Don't break his arm; we need him to be able to help. Now, c'mon, let's load this stuff back on. Dormundt's still half a day away by wagon."

After a few hours rocking along with the wagon and asking Elch about the village, Freyjagard, and the world as a whole—

"…!"

Masato abruptly rose to his feet and looked toward the setting sun.

"What's up, Massy?" asked Shinobu.

"I know that smell. That's the smell of money…!"

Soon thereafter, the three of them crested the hill, and a massive city surrounded by ramparts came into view.

It was their destination: the city of Dormundt.

"That's one weird sense of smell you got…"

"Yeah, that's creepy."

Ignoring the other two, both of whom were looking at him less with less amazement than exasperation, Masato gazed down at the stone metropolis dyed in the oranges and reds of the sunset.

"Man, that's one nice town. Is the entire thing walled off?"

"Yeah. Dormundt is the biggest trade hub in all of Marquis Findolph's lands. Almost all the goods in the domain come through here. It's also the only port, so merchants from New World colonies and other regions all stop here, too. Because it's so important, there are lots of people who live and work here. You could even call it the heart of the Findolph domain."

"How big's the population?"

"I don't know for sure, but from what my old man told me, there're about a hundred thousand residents. But that's not counting all the people like us who come in from smaller towns and villages or who arrive by ship from foreign lands."

"I like the sound of that. All right, let's make a killing so I can bring back a nice present for Winona!"

"…Wait, you're into my mom?"

"Of course! She's so charming—yet has a mature, womanly spirit. How could I *not* be into her?"

"Massy's got a thing for older women, y'know."

"Is it a crime to like strong, beautiful, independent women?"

"Man, I don't get it. Especially the part about her spirit or whatever. She should be settling down at her age, not running around like a lunatic. Besides, do you have any idea how *much* older than you she is? I doubt she'd even go for it."

"Hey, that's fine, too. I spend money so I can see beautiful women smile. That's motivation enough for me."

To that, Elch replied, "You're weird, dude," and sighed.

This was an age where people were far more worried about where the next day's meal was coming from. Romance as a pastime was something reserved for nobles. As far as commoners were concerned, it was just a prelude to marriage and childrearing. It was a duty one performed so the village could endure. Elch and Masato were from different worlds; their values were too fundamentally different. Romance was a point on which they were unlikely to see eye to eye.

"...Well, if you wanna try to get closer to Mom, then that's your problem. But you should give up on the souvenir. We don't have money to waste on stuff like that."

"It's fine; I'll just drum up some cash by making some slick deals."

"...You're gonna run into a big problem there."

"Huh?"

Elch's words were pregnant with significance, but Masato tilted his head to the side, unable to deduce their meaning.

"...You'll figure out what I'm talking about pretty fast once we get into town."

And sure enough, once they'd passed into the city, Masato quickly learned what Elch had meant.

By the time their wagon made it through Dormundt customs and into the city proper, the sun had worked well into its descent below the horizon.

After heading down the unpaved road that stretched past the gate, they eventually reached a wide, open area. Throngs of people were hustling about. It was virtually the spitting image of the Shibuya Scramble Crossing.

"Whoa! That's a city with a six-figure population all right! It's so crowded! It didn't really hit me while we were in Elm Village, but this world's actually got loads of people in it!"

"Yeah, and the ladies are all hotties. It's hard to pass on Winona's plain, pastoral appeal, but women dressed to the nines are great, too! Hey there, gorgeous!"

"…What, so one's as good as the next to you?" Elch sighed in exasperation watching Masato wave at every attractive woman he spotted in the crowd.

"Hey, I get why Massy's so pumped. It's been so long since we've been anywhere this lively, I'm starting to get excited, too."

"It's only natural that it's bustling here. This here's the heart of the city, the central plaza. Dormundt's split into four big sections in the northeast, northwest, southeast, and southwest, but you end up passing through here to get to pretty much any of 'em. The foot traffic's always nuts."

"Makes sense, makes sense."

"Huh. There's no marketplace here, even though the location's so great?" Masato asked, not missing a beat despite his flirting.

A hint of surprise crossed Elch's face upon realizing that Masato had actually been listening, and he replied in the affirmative.

"There used to be one, but now it's down in the southwest Port District… We'll be coming up on it soon."

Sure enough, a little while after they escaped the central plaza crowds and made their way to the Port District, the roadsides became lined with stalls. Scores of people, many of them probably residents, were out shopping. It was about time to start buying ingredients for dinner, after all, so there was a decent crowd. But for all the people, the variety of goods for sale was even more impressive.

There were vegetables like cabbages and tomatoes. Luxury items like honey-pickled apples, oranges, and casks of wine. Dried meats and fish—all sorts of stuff. And it wasn't just food, either. The stalls featured farming implements, tools, cookware, and fancy clothes that were likely hand-me-downs from nobles.

"Whoa! That shirt is so cute! And that hair accessory, too! Just looking at this stuff is a blast!"

Window-shopping was getting Shinobu amped. However—

"There are a lotta people here, but I'm not feeling any excitement in the air."

—something about the market seemed off to Masato.

There were plenty of people, and the wares for sale were breathtakingly diverse. Impressive as it was, though, it all seemed kind of tepid to him. None of the shopkeepers were calling out to people on the street, and he couldn't hear anyone haggling. The dirty homeless people lurking in the small alleyways and glaring at the market only served to amplify the depressing impression the market gave off. Masato tilted his head to the side, curious as to the reason for it all.

"All this is because of the trade company we're headed for," Elch muttered.

"How do you mean?"

"…You need a license from Dormundt's mayor, Count Heiseraat, to do any trade in the city, but…the only ones who have one, and the only people who have enough money to run a market anyway, are those in the Neutzeland Trading Company."

"What? For real? They have a monopoly on the entire city?"

"Yeah. There was another one up until a couple years ago, though… The Orion Company. My old man used to work for them. Trade was booming when the two companies were fighting over the marketplace. But one of Orion's investments in the New World went south, and Neutzeland took them over. Ever since then, Neutzeland's had complete control over Dormundt."

"I see. There's no energy 'cause there's no need to compete, huh…

So that's what you meant earlier when you said I'd run into a big problem."

"Uh-huh. I dunno how good you are with words or whatever, but there's no way you'll be able to mark your stuff up when there's only one place you can sell it."

"Man...no wonder everyone looks like they're half asleep."

"We're almost there. That there's the Neutzeland Trading Company."

On Elch's cue, Masato turned his attention away from the road-side markets. Standing before them was a building that looked less like a company and more like a temple. Erected before the structure's entrance was a massive statue of a fat man carved from malachite.

"What's up with that ugly-ass statue?"

"That's Jaccoy, the manager there."

Shinobu frowned, mumbled, "Yikes, how tasteless," and leaped off the wagon.

"Hey, wait! Where're you going?!"

"Sorry, Elch, but I gotta go. I've got things to do and places to be. Later, Massy. Tacky places like this aren't my style, so I'm gonna go get started on my research."

"Sounds good. Go do your thing, Shinobu."

"Sha-sha. ♪ Do it, I shall! If you find something you want me to look into, just give me a holler on your cell." With one last "Later!" she vanished into the crowd like smoke.

Even with how out of place her clothes were, it was impossible to see where she'd gone. Her lineage as a ninja wasn't just for show. After looking in the direction the girl had vanished for a moment, Masato turned back to Elch.

"The reason we brought her along is so she could look for info on the world and hopefully figure out a way for us to get home. Don't worry, though. You'll be fine with just me here."

Elch scrunched up his face at the remark.

"Ha. I'd do fine without you, too. Nobody asked you to come."

"Oof. That's cold, man."

"Hmm, hmm… Ten rook for the leather boots. Sixty rook is the going rate for winter coats. As for the charcoal…well, I can do two rook a briquette at most. Then…"

The Neutzeland Trading Company had two counters where you could sell goods. One was installed over by the port, designed to be used by merchants who'd come via the sea. The other was at the far end of the marketplace. It was a small building that resembled a stable, built into Neutzeland's main office. That was the counter for merchants who'd come from the local towns and villages.

After waiting their turn in line, Elch and Masato drove their wagon up and had their goods appraised by a gloomy-looking trader with a thin frame and narrow eyes. The result:

"In total…it comes out to fifty gold and fifty-three rook."

Elch went pale at the result of the appraisal.

"Th-that's all?"

"That's the best I can do. I'm already cutting you some slack because you're a regular client, you know. The countryside may be one thing, but here in the city, meager foods like potatoes are difficult to sell. Yet I'm offering you a fifth of a rook each on them. If anything, you should be grateful."

"Gah…"

As Masato stole a glance at Elch's pained expression, he thought back on the info he'd drummed into his head regarding the world's currency system.

In Freyjagard, money came in two denominations. The first was a copper coin called a rook. There was the smaller copper coin with a hole in it worth one rook and a larger coin with no hole that was worth ten. Because they weren't worth much, people tended to use them for most of their day-to-day purchases.

The other type was gold. Those came in silver coins worth one gold and golden coins worth ten. They were primarily used for larger business transactions, and one gold was worth a hundred rook.

According to Elch, an adult man could live modestly for about a month on a single gold. As for the number that could survive the four harsh winter months on fifty gold...

"Huh? If I remember correctly, the village has fifty people in it."

"...Close to sixty if we count you punks."

"I mean, either way, that's nowhere near enough, right?"

"Shut up, I don't need you telling me that!" Elch's frustration was palpable.

It was only natural.

Between the forest and the farmland, Elm Village was more or less self-sufficient most of the year. But winter was a different beast. The heavy snowfall left Elm practically buried, and it went without saying that the fields were useless. An attempt to hunt deep in the woods under those conditions was tantamount to suicide.

That was precisely why Elm Village went and sold all the leather goods their twenty-odd women made at once right before the winter, when demand spiked. They needed to buy enough food to weather the cold season. Although they made regular trips to sell lumber, charcoal, and jerky, that didn't provide much income. The money they made from leather goods was their literal lifeline. Surviving the long winter with only fifty gold was utterly impossible.

What can I do? Elch's forehead broke into a cold sweat as he thought. Beside him, Masato posed a question.

"Elch, how much does it normally take for the village to make it through the winter?"

"I told you to shut up, didn't I?"

"Just tell me."

"…Tch. Eighty gold, usually."

"So you can normally make that much?"

"Yeah. But our yield from the forest this year was pretty bad. I hate to admit it, but we came up short on pelts and meat. And because you guys showed up, we're burning through food even faster. The village is basically out of reserves."

"I am sorry about that, you know…"

"If you're really sorry, then shut up already… Hey, mister, can't you sweeten the pot a bit? With so little money, we're gonna starve to death this winter."

"I'm afraid that your circumstances aren't the responsibility of our establishment."

"Isn't there something we can…?" Even faced with a brick wall of a trading partner, Elch kept pushing. But then—

"Now, what seems to be the problem over here? You're holding up the line, you know."

With a *creak*, the door between the appraisement hut and the main building swung open, revealing a middle-aged man with a potbelly, the spitting image of the large statue out front.

His outfit was so colorful it was almost vomit-inducing, and his bracelets and necklace were all adorned with gold, silver, and gems. The radiant sheen of his expensive accessories was outdone only by that of the fat on his face and his pudgy nose. This was Jaccoy, Neutzeland's manager.

"Ah, Mr. Jaccoy. These obstinate customers were complaining about our quote."

"Oh, my friends, that won't do. You aren't children; throwing a tantrum won't get you... Oh?" The manager had been glaring at Elch, but after a moment, his eyes widened with surprise. He'd recognized him.

"My oh my, I thought you looked familiar. Adel was Orion's finest star, and here we have his son! Out running errands for the village, are we? It's about time to start hunkering down for winter, after all."

"...Well, yeah."

Elch's father, Adel, had been the finest peddler in Orion, a competing trade company that once operated out of Dormundt. Apparently, Adel was so skilled that even now he lingered in the memory of his rival company and Jaccoy, its manager. This wasn't the first time Jaccoy and Elch had met, either.

Back when Elch's father was still alive, the two of them would exchange greetings whenever Elch came the city. That wasn't to say they were on good terms, however.

"I see, I see. So what did you bring us to sell today?"

"Here's their list, sir."

"Pfft." Jaccoy let out a disparaging snort after the assessor handed him the itemized list.

"Most of this is just trash, is it not? It's sad, seeing the son of such an accomplished man reduced to hawking such garbage. It was the same with Adel, you know. If he hadn't stupidly insisted on staying a peddler and just become our accountant like we'd asked, he wouldn't have gotten caught in the cross fire of the war. Being pathetic must run in the family."

"...My old man has nothing to do with this."

"He certainly doesn't. Just like we have nothing to do with what'll happen to you people this winter. Oh, and we have no obligation to buy your trash, so don't go grumbling about what we offer you for it. If you don't like our prices, feel free to take your business somewhere else… Of course, we're the only company that has the mayor's permission to operate in Dormundt. And even if you find some tiny company out in the sticks, they'll just end up coming to Dormundt and selling to us anyway, so they can't offer more money than we do. If you want better prices, you'll have to cross the Le Luk Mountain Range and try selling outside the domain."

"Ha-ha-ha. You're a cruel man, Mr. Jaccoy. If they tried to cross Le Luk at this time of year, they'd just be going to their deaths. Besides, Lord Findolph would never issue a travel pass to village commoners like them."

"Hee-hee-hee. Too true, too true."

Both Jaccoy and the assessor gave nasty sneers.

"We're your only option, so just do as we say" was the vibe these two were giving off.

I don't like this one bit.

Masato narrowed his eyes at them. As they'd been passing through the market on their way to the trade company, Masato had actually been memorizing the prices on all the goods for sale. By his calculation, Elm's cargo was actually worth approximately two hundred gold.

It was fairly standard for wholesale suppliers to get less than market rates for their merchandise, but Neutzeland was turning around and selling the goods just a few hundred yards from where they were buying them. That was nowhere near enough to justify taking a 75 percent margin. They were abusing the fact that *they were the only game in town.*

These guys aren't merchants.

Rather, they were more like the mob. Masato wasn't about to let guys like that get their way. So he made a choice.

"Izzat so? Welp, looks like there's no agreement to be reached. We're done here, Elch." The Devil of Finance quickly hopped back on the wagon, took the reins, and began steering it out.

"Huh? ...WHAT?!" Elch was taken aback at the sudden development, but...

"Hey! Hey, hey, hey! Wait up! Wait up, I said!" The young *byuma* raced after the wagon, leaped onto it, and grabbed Masato by the collar.

"What's up? That's a scary-ass look you've got on your face."

"What the hell do you think you're doing?! Turn the wagon around!"

But Masato wasn't having it.

"Screw that. I'm fine with taking advantage of people, but getting taken advantage of myself? No *thanks*. Besides, fifty measly gold isn't gonna get you through the winter, right? That means there's no point selling to those guys."

"Y-you're right, but I just told you, remember?! There's only one company in Dormundt! No matter how little they give us, we don't have a choice!"

"All right, then how're you gonna survive?"

"W-we... We can use the village's savings..."

"Oh? And how much are those savings, by the way? Given how pissed you sounded at the banquet, I can't imagine there's much."

"...There's...about eight gold."

"Y'know, Elch, we have a saying for that back where I come from. It's called 'a drop in the bucket.'"

"...! Fine, then we men'll figure something out! The forest has pretty much nothing but wolves during the winter, but...still, we'll just eat those!"

"You guys get crazy-heavy snow, don't you? It's already started falling. And once we get into winter for real, it's really gonna start piling up in the mountains. You might have wolf ears and a wolf tail, but you still only have two legs. The snow's gonna mess with your mobility something fierce… Do you really think Elm's hunters will come out unscathed against wolves in conditions like that?"

Elch furrowed his brow and sunk into silence. He was a hunter himself, so he knew full well how dangerous hunting wolves in the winter was.

Masato twisted the knife deeper, his voice turning ever harsher.

"Elch, I think you're misunderstanding what a trade is in a big way."

"Wh-what do you mean?"

"Trading isn't about buying and selling stuff. It's just a means to some end. Our goal is to get Elm Village through the winter safely by buying supplies. Any trade we make that doesn't succeed in achieving that is out of the question as a means. —Besides, look."

Masato jabbed a finger at the shops lining the street.

"Check out that store's leather boots. They're pretty much the same as Elm's when it comes to quality. Neutzeland probably bought them for around ten rook, just like they offered to buy ours. But they're *selling* them for *forty-three* rook. They bought those fur coats for sixty rook, but they're selling them for four hundred. If they were just buying raw pelts, or if they came and picked them up or something, that might be understandable… No, even then that's too wide a margin. Look, they're making you guys handle the production, the delivery, even the customs fee when you bring the goods into the city. Instead of having a supply chain, they're just making you do everything. It's insane. Long story short, you guys are getting swindled. All of you are."

Visibly irritated, Elch wrung a rebuttal out his throat.

"…We know that. Hell, even I know that! But we don't have a choice! Neutzeland's the only company in the city with a trading license!"

"See, you're getting swindled 'cause you keep thinking like that. Lemme tell you, spending your life getting jerked around by other people is no way to live. If something's screwed up, you gotta learn to say 'Screw this.' If you don't like something, it's your job to change it. Trust me, it's way more satisfying that way... When a guy mocks you like they just did, you can't just say 'Oh well' and take it. You can't let that shit slide."

"...!" Elch's shoulders twitched as he held Masato's collar. The burning rage in Masato's eyes was beginning to cow him into submission. "W-wait, are you actually mad?"

"Damn straight I'm mad. I hate getting taken advantage of. Also, that guy made fun of the man Winona chose to marry... Hey, Elch. Let me take point on this. Let me be in charge of all the trading this time around. Gimme a week...and I won't have just made us enough cash to survive the winter; I'll have destroyed that whole shitty company."

"...Is that even possible...?"

Masato nodded without a moment's hesitation. "Of course. Just so long as you follow my instructions to the letter."

In truth, Elch had a hard time believing that. But still...the confidence burning in Masato's eyes was no bluff. They wouldn't survive the winter at this rate anyway. There was basically nothing to lose...

"...Fine. If you say you can do all that, then you're in charge." Elch released Masato. He'd made his choice. He was ready to see just how strong this man was for himself. "But remember, everything I'm putting you in charge of is the village's property. If you're all talk and no results...then I'll chop you into wolf bait myself. Consider yourself warned." The harsh glint in Elch's eyes made him the very image of a wolf. However, Masato's confidence proved unshaken by the threat.

"Heh. Don't you worry, Elch. Money loves me more than just about anyone else."

"If you say so... So how exactly are you planning on taking that company down? And in just one week, no less. Just for the record, I'm not gonna do any arson or burglary."

"That's not on the agenda, man; I'm not the damn yakuza. I'm a merchant. When a merchant says he's gonna crush another merchant, he means he's gonna do it on the open market. I'm gonna make a company even bigger than theirs, then take over their market share."

"...I already told you, remember? You can't do business in the city without a trading license from the mayor. If you try, the soldiers'll arrest you on the spot."

"All that means is I gotta go get one. Easy."

"Easy, my ass. The count's never gonna issue a license to bumpkins like us. He won't even give us an audience."

"A little sweet talk'll solve both those problems. Besides, you can't go givin' up before you even get started. You handed me the ball, remember? Now, just believe in me and help me run with it." And with that, Masato handed Elch the wagon reins. He had no idea where anything in the city was, after all. He would need his companion's help to find his way around.

"...Fine." Picking up on what the so-called merchant was saying, Elch glumly took the reins and steered them toward Count Heiseraat's mansion. Having given control of the wagon over to Elch, Masato fished his smartphone out of his pocket.

"Oh yeah, I've been wondering about those ever since we found you. What exactly are those glowing slabs you all have?"

"What, this? It's, uh...basically a magic item. It lets you talk to your friends even when they're far away."

"...For real?"

"Yup. Handy, right?" As Masato nodded, he opened the communication app Ringo had installed. The call connected instantly.

"Heya, Shinobu. Sorry for the short notice, but can you look into some stuff for me? Yeah, ASAP. First, I need a surface-level profile on the mayor. Personality, interests, résumé, that kinda stuff. Then I need—"

Masato and Elch left the market.

A young girl with light-brown skin emerged from a side alley and watched their departure. She'd lived in the New World until her region had been conquered as part of the New World Colonization Project that Freyjagard's eighteenth emperor, "Conquering King" Lindworm von Freyjagard, had spearheaded. Slavers had brought her all the way to northern Freyjagard as a slave, but she'd spotted an opening, slipped from her bonds, and fled into the alleys of the marketplace.

The cat ears protruding from her red hair had picked up Masato's speech.

"*...Spending your life getting jerked around by other people is no way to live...*"

Masato had been speaking to Elch. However, the girl happened to hear him, too. He'd spoken of a way of living unfettered by the whims of others.

He said...there's a way...

Was it true? She didn't know. But before she knew what she was doing, the girl found herself running after the wagon.

"You said you're a merchant from across the sea, but whereabouts exactly?" The aged *hyuma*, who had a mustache that looked like a large pair of wings, shot a piercing stare at his mansion's visitor. His visitor, of course, was none other than Masato Sanada, a member of the High School Prodigies.

As Masato knelt before Mayor Heiseraat, who was sitting atop the parlor's sofa, he offered the man a respectful bow.

"I hail from a land far across the eastern sea called Japan, Lord Mayor."

"Japan... I've never heard of such a country."

"We're a small island nation, so it's quite possible Freyjagard hasn't discovered us yet. I'm a businessman of some renown back in my homeland, but even my company has yet to do trade here."

"...Hmm. Well, no matter. I'm unfamiliar with this land of yours, but I don't doubt you're a foreigner. I've never seen garb like yours. The fabric is of such a high quality I can hardly believe it. And those leather shoes of yours shine like lustrous pearls. I can see that your country's culture has been refined over many moons. A mere liar could never produce such fineries."

"It's a great honor to receive such compliments." Masato bowed again, silently rejoicing at the man's powers of comprehension. The mayor's shrewd eye was going to make the conversation go much smoother than he'd anticipated.

"...So? What business do you have with me, merchant from 'Japan'?"

Masato thought back to the dossier Shinobu had sent him while he'd been waiting to get inside.

Walter von Heiseraat.

Walter was Dormundt's current mayor and a third-generation member of the Heiseraats, the family that had taken Dormundt from an undeveloped plot of land to the foremost trade city in northern Freyjagard. He also held the title of count. According to Shinobu's report, the way Freyjagard's peerage system worked was that marquises were given domains, and counts and barons were given cities within those domains to manage. Basically, counts and barons were like modern-day Japanese mayors, and marquises were like prefectural governors. It wasn't quite the same as the historical feudal systems with which Masato and the others were more familiar.

Although survival of the fittest was Freyjagard's one absolute law and nobles assaulted and even killed commoners like it was nothing, Walter was more of a moderate. He was a man well-liked by the residents of Dormundt. In his private life, though, he was quite the spendthrift who had a particular penchant for rare imported goods. In all likelihood, that proclivity of his was why Masato had been able to secure a meeting with him so easily after telling the guards that he was a merchant from overseas.

This was Masato's chosen avenue of attack.

"There's actually a very particular reason I sought an audience with you today. The thing is, I heard word of a renowned count who was a fervent collector of foreign trinkets, so I had hoped you might take a look at this piece of craftsmanship from my homeland."

"Hmph. So this is a sales pitch."

It appeared such visits to the mayor's home probably happened with some amount of frequency. Every pore on the mayor's face was shouting, "This again?!"

"Fine. But be warned, I have a discerning eye. If you show me something trifling, you won't get a single rook out of me."

Hook, line, and sinker.

"Oh, I'm quite confident you'll like it. Here's the item in question." Chuckling internally at the mayor's response, Masato showed him what he'd brought to offer. Sitting atop his palm was a gleaming golden armlet.

"...I see. A bracelet made of gold, is it? Very tasteful. I especially like the jewels set in the... Hmm? Hmmmmmm?!?!?!?!?!?! Wh-wh-wh-what's this, now?!"

"It's an accessory the people from my country wear. We call it a wristwatch, a clock you can wear on your wrist."

The wristlet Masato had handed over was, in fact, his own high-end watch.

There were notable differences, but Freyjagard's culture was largely around the level of the Earth's Middle Ages. Although Earth had mechanical clocks in the later part of that era, the technology to make small, delicate parts certainly hadn't existed yet. Back then, clocks were massive and generally installed in buildings. Wristwatches didn't come around until the nineteenth century.

In other words, it was doubtful that Freyjagard had clocks anywhere near that small. They certainly weren't common. It was an anachronism, like something straight out of science fiction. It caught Mayor Heiseraat's attention, purveyor of novelties that he was, like nothing else.

He'd completely fallen for Masato's scheme.

"A clock?! I-impossible! Nobody can make clocks this small!"

"Feel free to take a look for yourself. The back cover should be of particular interest."

"Hmm? Oh? Whaaaaaaaaaaat?! Th-this minute construction…! Bwuuuuuuh?! It's moving! There're so many tiny gears, all interlocked! I've never seen anything so precise…! But the technology to construct something so small, so accurately, it doesn't exist…!"

"Maybe that's true…*in Freyjagard*, Lord Mayor."

"—! S-so this Japan of yours really exists?! And your technical abilities are this advanced?!"

"They are indeed. In fact, we're so good at manufacturing that some of our neighbors call us a technological superpower. In Japan, wristwatches are so common that even children own them."

"I-it boggles the mind…! I can't believe it! I can't believe it, but…seeing it in my hand… I guess I don't have a choice! Oh, it's so beautiful...!" Heiseraat couldn't peel his eyes away from the watch's interior. His face was flushed, and his nostrils were flaring, like a kid who'd just gotten a new toy.

Sensing that the iron was hot, Masato took another step toward his final objective.

"I'm glad you like it. What do you say? ...If you honor my one request, the watch is all yours."

"T-truly?! What is it?! What's this request of yours?! I'll pay however much you want! P-p-p-please! Sell me this wristwatch!" Heiseraat clung desperately to his new curio. When the man said he'd pay however much Masato wanted, he was more or less being serious.

No matter how rare it was, though, at the end of the day, it was still just a single bracelet. There was a limit to how much Masato could realistically charge. There was a chance he could sell it for enough money to get Elm through the winter, but adding on Ringo's requests, the amount he'd need to ask for was dicey.

And besides, one-and-done deals like that were boring. What the young businessman Masato Sanada wanted had been locked in from the very start.

"Money isn't what I need, Lord Mayor. I'm a merchant, which means there's only one thing I want... Permission to do business in this city. It's a trading license I'm after."

"Wha...?! Rrr..."

However, hearing Masato's demand brought the previously elated mayor back down to earth. It was to be expected. After all, the reason he'd never issued new trading licenses was because of the large bribes he'd been taking from Neutzeland.

"W-well... About that..." He looked down at the watch reluctantly. Masato stepped forward and whispered in Heiseraat's ear.

"I know about your arrangement with Neutzeland, by the way."

"Wha...?!"

"It wasn't hard to figure out. Orion may have gone under, but northern Freyjagard is famed for its myriad industries—restaurants, breweries, glassblowing, even shipbuilding. There's no way the largest city in the region's gone years without a single company looking to open up shop."

"I… I have no idea what you're talking about."

"Month four of spring: 3,247 gold and twenty-three rook. Month four of summer: 2,789 gold and eighty-eight rook—"

Upon hearing Masato recite the numbers, Heiseraat blanched. After all, those numbers…were the exact sums of the bribes he'd taken.

"H-how do you…?"

Masato replied with a smile that could almost be described as exhilarated.

"My company employs a rather talented intelligence operative. She was able to snatch a glance at the secret ledger hidden in your safe in the time it took this meeting to start. Now, that money isn't being recorded as income from the market. That means Marquis Findolph doesn't know about it. If he was to catch wind of that fact, I doubt he'd be too pleased."

The mayor's forehead broke out into a nervous sweat.

This kind of illicit payoff wasn't all that surprising to Masato. In Freyjagard, the marquis was the one who controlled the domain.

Count Heiseraat ran Dormundt as its mayor, but he was little more than a glorified bureaucrat. All the revenue in the Findolph domain was supposed to go straight to Marquis Findolph. By illegally ignoring that decree, Heiseraat was committing embezzlement. If that came to light, it would be impossible for him to stay in Marquis Findolph's good graces.

As a threat, it was more than effective, and yet…

"*However*, I'm not here to criticize the way you do business. And

I'm certainly not planning on using that information to threaten you."
Suddenly, Masato changed his avenue.

"Wh...at?"

"Why would I? The Heiseraat family is the one that broke ground here and built this magnificent city from nothing in just fifty years. Your family members are heroes of the north. That being the case, it's your right to enjoy some kickbacks every now and again, no?"

"Yeah! Yeah, that's right! My ancestors *built* this town!"

"They did indeed, and that makes you Dormundt's rightful king. But why should a man like you have to curry favor with a single lowly company? Why should a man like you have to temper his desires? If those punks start complaining, if they start threatening to hold back payments, all you have to say is this: 'Quit your moaning, you mangy hyenas! If you don't want me to run you out of town, shut your stinking mouths!' That'll *shut them up good*. Everyone at Neutzeland would rather die than lose their business in the finest city in the north."

Threatening the mayor had never been Masato's plan. Doing so would have been stupid. Heiseraat may have just been a bureaucrat, but he was still the highest authority in town. Masato wanted to do business in the city. Making an enemy of its owner would've been counterproductive.

Blackmailing him had certainly been an option, but getting the license amiably was far and away the better option. That was why he'd praised the Heiseraat family while bemoaning the fact that they'd become Neutzeland's stooges.

And it was thanks to those honeyed words...

"...Yes, yes. You're absolutely right."

Masato had guided the mayor's emotions to exactly where he'd wanted them. Heiseraat, who'd been clutching the watch throughout their exchange like it was already his, gave Masato a domineering smile. Masato responded by grinning in kind, but his was no longer the customer-service smile he'd been wearing up until that point... It was the smile of a carnivore baring its fangs.

"Then we have a deal."

"And just like that, we've got ourselves a trading license under the name Elm Trading Company."

When Masato got back to Elch, who'd been waiting outside, he showed him the piece of parchment with the mayor's seal.

"Th-that's not a fake, is it?"

"I just went into the mayor's house, dude. If anything, wouldn't coming out with a fake be harder?"

"I never thought you'd actually get one..." Elch may as well have seen a ghost the way he stared at the document.

"What sorcery did you have to pull...?"

"Unfortunately, sorcery isn't in my wheelhouse. Wish it was, though. Nah, supply and demand are my tools of choice. Coming up with win-win scenarios for everyone, now *that's* business. Anyway, now we can go do business out in the open. This is good news, remember?"

Joy finally started spreading across Elch's face.

"Yeah. Yeah! You're right! C'mon, let's head over to the market right now! It's almost nightfall, but there should still be a decent number of people around! If we sell our goods for the same prices Neutzeland does, we'll be able to make four times as much!" Now that he was getting excited, the words came pouring out of Elch's mouth without stopping.

Seeing him get all ready to dash off, Masato...gave Elch's forehead a good flick.

"Hey, what was that for?!"

"Saying dumb crap like that. This license practically prints money, but after all the work we put into getting it, you wanna peace out after selling barely one wagon's worth of goods? Don't be an idiot. I told you, didn't I? I'm gonna crush Neutzeland's market share. We'll set up shop tomorrow. Today, our job is to *stock up on inventory to sell.*"

"...Huh? What are you going on about? We don't have that kind of money, man. I only have eight gold, remember?" Elch looked at Masato like *he* was the idiot. Masato rubbed his chin and started thinking.

I mean, my job here's only supposed to be fixing Elm's finances and buying the stuff Ringo asked for, but...

...merely using Elch to achieve that end was a little cold. Not only was Elch the village's treasurer, he would someday be its mayor. Maybe it was Masato's duty to teach him a thing or two.

If he molded him into a fine merchant, Elch could become the bedrock of the newly formed Elm Trading Company. Masato owed Elm Village a debt for saving his life, and if there was any way to repay it twice over, this had to be it. With his choice made, Masato posed a question to Elch.

"Elch, what's the one thing you need in order to secure product?"

"Money, duh."

"Bzzt. Zero out of a hundred. You can get inventory without money."

"Wh-what? No, you can't."

"Ah, but you can... Actually, this works out. I do owe you guys one, after all. As president of the Sanada Group, lemme teach you a good way to make money. And hold on to your socks. We might be broke now, but before long, we'll have more gold than we can carry."

"You mean it, mister?"

©Sacraneco

*   *   *

"""_____?!"""

Out of the blue, someone called out to the them.

Masato and Elch turned around and saw a small *byuma* girl dashing toward them across the darkened road. Her scarlet eyes were fixed straight on Masato.

"Roo wants it, too. More gold than she can carry." Her speech was a little sloppy, but it was clear from her tone that her resolution was firm.

"Roo...wants money. She wants to be able to make it on her own. She doesn't want to be tossed around anymore. So...please teach Roo how to make money, too!" The red-haired girl was disheveled from head to toe, wearing nothing but tattered rags. She'd been running along unpaved, exposed earth, but she wasn't even wearing shoes.

A runaway? Or perhaps a homeless girl? Or maybe—something worse. Elch and Masato could tell at a glance that she didn't come from great circumstances. Yet, still...

This kid's eyes...

Her scarlet irises felt like they pierced right through Masato. Seeing their burning light dredged something up from his memories. A dark room. A choking stench. A soiled tatami mat. And...his father's corpse hanging from the rafters.

...Ha-ha.

"Fine by me. C'mon."

Masato immediately accepted the mysterious girl's request. Elch let out a surprised yelp.

"Wait, are you serious? We don't know anything about this kid, and you're just gonna take her in?"

"Of course I'm serious. Besides, this works out great for us. I was in the market for another employee, after all. And she's a girl and a kid, *both of which are handy*. And above all else—I like her eyes."

"Her eyes…?"

"She might look like poverty incarnate, but her eyes are shining like rubies. This kid's got a hunger. A hunger for cash. And the drive to better her position in the world. Getting someone like that in your camp is never a bad thing. Avarice is power, after all."

After responding to Elch's confusion, Masato turned back to the girl.

"The name's Masato Sanada, and this here's Elch… You said your name was Roo, kid?"

"Roo is Roo." The girl nodded.

"Great! Then hop on board, Li'l Roo. I'll show you how to make more money than you can spit at!"

"Thank you, Teacher!"

"Ha! I like the sound of that. You've got promise, Li'l Roo! With a big clear voice like that, you could take over any boardroom! Now, you two aren't ready to set foot on the battlefield just yet. For now, just watch what I do. First, I'm gonna show you how you can build inventory without spending a rook. Strap in and follow along, kids! It's time to rake it in and have a blast doing it!"

And with that, Elm Trading Company began its quest to secure goods to sell the next day.

The next week promised to be the wildest seven days of Elch's and Roo's lives.

🜲 Gold and Greed 🜲

Masato Sanada had declared that he'd destroy Neutzeland. Even if one set aside whether he could actually pull that off, though, not even a businessman as brilliant as him could make money with nothing to sell.

But this was Dormundt, a city with a six-figure population. It was the beating heart of the Findolph domain. The center of its economy. What was he to do for merchandise? *Why, he was spoiled for choice of merchandise.* The only problem was how to raise the money to buy it. After all, he needed start-up capital to get the ball rolling. However, Masato had claimed he could get goods without needing any money at all.

—But how?

It was hard to imagine such a method existing. Elch and Roo certainly couldn't think of a way. However—Masato most assuredly knew one. There did indeed exist a method that wouldn't take a single rook.

Roo's shabby outfit was going to get in the way, so Masato had her change into one of the children's outfits they'd brought to sell. Then he had Elch take them to the city's entrance.

There, they saw a number of wagons barely make it in before the gates closed. Masato looked them over with a keen shrewdness, then set his sights on one set in particular. A group of three *byuma* with bearlike ears leading three wagons.

They were farmers from a rural village called Fitze with a population of around three hundred, and just like Elch, they were there to sell crops and handicrafts to buy stores for the winter. Having decided that they were who he wanted to get his goods from, Masato called out to them.

"The assessment counter's probably closed by now, right? As fellow suckers who rolled in too late, wanna go get dinner together and drink to our folly?" he asked. The farmers had been planning on getting dinner anyway, and as Masato had very deliberately made himself come across as approachable, they readily accepted.

He led them to a pub, just as he'd planned. Then, as their small talk began winding down…

"Truth be told, I've got something nifty here," Masato said, pulling out the trading license he'd gotten from the count and showing it to them. They stared at it in shock.

"Th-th-that's…!"

"That's Count Heiseraat's seal…! You've got an authentic trading license!"

"How'd you get your hands on that?!"

"The mayor issued it to me. He's a pretty reasonable man, you know."

The Fitze farmers went green with envy.

"With that, you can sell stuff wherever you want in Dormundt, right? Damn… Must be nice… That means you guys don't have to let Neutzeland rip you off."

"Sounds like you guys had it rough with them, too."

"Oh yeah, they're awful. When we came and sold them plums this summer, they fed us some line about '*the market being flooded, so they had to lower their buy prices*' and only gave us a fifth of a rook each. Summer's when the harvest is, so the market's always flooded then! Besides, they were selling the damn things at five for four rook. Can you believe it?!"

"Hey, could you guys buy our stock instead? We poor villages have to stick together, you know."

Masato shook his head apologetically, though internally he was grinning from ear to ear.

"Believe me, we'd love to, but we're just as broke as you guys. We don't have that kind of money."

"…Yeah, figures." The farmers looked crestfallen.

—It was the perfect time to strike.

A fierce light shone in Masato's eyes, like a falcon eyeing its prey. He dropped the question.

"But hey. We're just as pissed as you guys that Neutzeland is screwing everyone over and taking absurd margins. We can't just sit by and do nothing... So this is just an idea, but we're planning on setting up shop in the central plaza tomorrow. How do you guys feel about consigning your goods to our shop?"

And there it was. Masato's method for obtaining product without spending a rook.

"Consigning?"

"What's that? I've never heard of it."

However, on hearing the word *consign*, the farmers cocked their heads to the side. Elch and Roo did the same. Masato laid the concept out for everyone.

"It's simple, really. A consignment sale is basically where you guys set up a shop as part of our company, Elm Trading."

"Huh?! Wait, we can do that?! Even though we don't have a trading license?"

"Of course. There's no rule against it."

"So we'll be able to sell our goods without having to rely on those Neutzeland bastards?" The farmers rose to their feet in excitement, and Masato gave them a composed nod.

"Yes, indeed. Now, this license wasn't exactly cheap. Normally, we'd be taking twenty percent of your sales as our fee, but...y'know, you're right, we poor village people have it rough enough as it is. We gotta look out for one another. If you guys come to our shop and help sell the goods, I can cut it down to ten."

"Hey, uh, how much's ten percent?"

"I dunno; I'm not too good with numbers..."

"Wait, hold on a minute! Lemme do the math. Up until now, if we sold a hundred rook worth of wheat to Neutzeland, at best they'd give us fifty rook for it...but if we sold it ourselves, then paid Elm their ten percent, that'd leave...ninety rook!"

"Th-that's great! We'd be making almost twice as much!"

"Well, not quite, guys. If they're selling something for a hundred rook over there, we gotta go lower, or no one will buy from us. We'll have to undercut them on prices to bring in customers. But hey, even if we only sell it for eighty rook, you'll still get seventy-two for your share. That's almost one and a half times as much as you've made up till now. What do you think? Not a bad deal, huh?"

Instead of going with a calm, ingratiating smile, Masato instead elected to plant his elbows on the table, rest his cheeks on his fists, and flash them a suggestive, villainous grin. That way, he came across more confident in what he was doing. Masato was a guy who knew full well how to wield a smile. And just as he expected...

"Yeah! You're the best, man!"

"Please let us work with you!"

The Fitze farmers' eyes glittered with excitement and joy as they shook Masato's hand.

Masato's reply came without hesitation.

"I welcome you with open arms, brothers. Now then...let's take inventory of your load, shall we?"

And thus, with his secret weapon—consignment—Masato managed to add three wagons' worth of goods to their inventory without spending a single rook, just like he'd promised. After they parted ways with the Fitze men, he, Elch, and Roo were left with four fully inventoried wagons of goods.

"See? I told you we wouldn't need money."

"S-so amazing..."

"Damn, man, you really pulled it off..."

"If we were individuals looking to buy stuff, then yeah, we would've needed money just like you said. But as a business looking to acquire inventory, 'trust' is way more important than money. And in the world of business, trust just boils down to profit potential. That's the be-all and end-all. A trading license in this town is the best kind of trust there is."

A trading license was no mere scrap of paper. It was an absolute authority in Dormundt's markets.

"Also…Elch. You've dabbled in business a little, so you've probably noticed by now. What is it that makes this method so nasty?"

"It's that you don't need to spend any money, so you can assemble as much inventory as you want, right? Even if we're only making ten percent, it's basically no risk and all profit. We don't have to spend a rook, and we can make as much money as we want. And if stuff doesn't sell, well, we aren't out anything… It's almost too easy. It's so incredible, it makes me wonder why I didn't think of it."

"You get half credit for that."

"Wait, what?"

"Li'l Roo, do you remember what I made them agree to when I dropped the consignment fee from twenty percent to ten?"

"Um, um… You said they have to help at the shop!"

"Ah…!"

"That's it. And that there is everything. If all we did was get inventory, we'd hit our limit real fast. There are only three of us, after all. I mean, I can do the work of ten people, but even so, we'd be talking peanuts. This way, though…"

"Hey! Mister!"

With auspicious timing, a voice called out to them as they stood in front of the stable. It was the Fitze farmers they'd parted ways with not long ago. The farmers' lantern swayed as they rushed over and introduced Masato to an unfamiliar, well-dressed young man.

"This here's Tohr, a peddler from a rural company we do a good bit of business with. We told him about what we're doing tomorrow, and he said he wants in! What do you say, mister? This party have room for one more?"

"Would you mind if I joined your undertaking? I spent the whole day trying to negotiate with those city merchants, but they weren't having any of it. Honestly, I'm in a bit of a bind."

Masato replied, "Of course, glad to have you aboard," and shook the young man's hand.

"All right, you mind if we take a look at what you're working with?"

"Oh, of course not! —Hey! Bring the wagons over!"

In response to the young man's shout, seven wagons emerged from the dark. Elch's eyes went wide.

"That makes ten wagons…and with ours, eleven!"

"You get it now, right? This method lets us secure inventory and labor at the same time. In other words, as long as there're people who fit our criteria, there's no limit to how big our company can get. We can even get bigger than Neutzeland."

"…!"

That was the *real* nasty trick behind Masato's "consignment" method. While he was obtaining inventory, he was also taking advantage of the fact that this world hadn't developed the idea of hourly wages yet to obtain labor simultaneously. Because his workforce increased proportionately with his supplies, he effectively had no limits, either. His company would be able to grow completely unrestrained.

It was the perfect method for the job.

"Welcome, welcome, welcome! Five apples and four onions, is it? You got it!"

"That'll be forty rook in all! —Of course, absolutely!"

"Three leather coats; that comes out to a thousand rook. Gold? We absolutely take gold."

Elm Trading Company's central plaza market was hustling and bustling. And why wouldn't it be? It was a more convenient location than the port, and their prices were cheap. It would have been far more difficult *not* to draw a crowd.

The first day had been a smashing success—all eleven wagons' goods were cleaned out before noon. Rumors circulated quickly of their success, which drew hordes of merchants who practically ran one another over to sign consignment deals with Masato. By the third day, the company's wagon count had expanded into the forties, with Elm's personal profits totaling over a thousand gold, a sum far higher than they would have otherwise been able to reach. But even with all the money he'd amassed, Masato had no plans of stopping.

"Li'l Roo, you're up! C'mon over here!"

"Hweh?!"

Masato called out to Roo, who had been frantically restocking their goods as they very nearly flew off the shelves, and handed her a celery stick and a small dish filled with mayonnaise made from the eggs he'd picked up that morning. Then he had her dip the celery in the mayonnaise and eat it in front of their vegetable-stick-with-mayo stand.

It was basically a commercial. There was no better way to get someone to buy food than to show them the face of someone actually enjoying it. A smile was worth a thousand good reviews. However, someone as old as Masato or Elch shouting about how tasty something was would look too strange and risked coming across as sketchy. A young girl like Roo, on the other hand, would look adorable. That had been Masato's plan for Roo from the get-go.

Now that plan was paying off in spades. After all, Roo had never had much in the way of decent food. Though the small girl found pretty much everything delicious, the way she was enjoying that otherworldly condiment made people drool just looking at her. Her smile was like a secret spice that drew out their curiosity and appetites. Between that and the fact that they'd branded it as a "rare treat from across the sea," the snack sold as if they were giving it away. People in that era were starved for entertainment, so seeing something new and exciting piqued just about everyone's attention.

In the end, the mayonnaise sold out before nightfall, just like the consigned goods. Masato prepared even more the next day, but the buzz they'd generated drew such a crowd that it sold out that morning. Elm Trading Company's profits were so immense that even after paying out their consigners, they'd still filled two full-size crates with copper and silver coins. It wasn't just enough money for Elm to survive the winter, it was enough that no one in the village would have to work for the next decade. Elch could hardly believe it.

"_____"

That was why the *byuma* boy found it so strange. All those profits would have originally gone to Neutzeland, but they'd snatched them away. So why…?

"You look like you're wondering why Neutzeland isn't coming after us."

"…!"

Elch jumped a little at having Masato say exactly what he was thinking, but after having watched Masato work for the last few days, he'd started believing his companion was capable of anything. Instead of responding with the stubbornness he once showed the High School Prodigy, Elch just nodded.

"Roo thinks it's weird, too!" added Roo.

Masato laughed.

"It's simple, really. From their perspective, this kind of money is *nothing*."

That was the cold, hard truth.

"Nothing? All this?!"

"No way…"

"Yes way. Here, take a look at this map of the city… See, we're set up in the middle of town so we can catch all the merchants from other villages. But around these parts, the biggest fish…*don't come by land.*"

A shocked look crossed Elch's face at the sudden realization.

"Ah! The port…!"

"That's the one. They're set up by the only port in the whole domain. In other words, the iron and precious metals the Industrial District uses, as well as the jewels and other imports—all of it still goes through Neutzeland. And the prices that stuff goes for are off the charts. Plus, because they're the only port and demand is stable, all they have to do is move the goods from the Port District to the Industrial District. It's like taking candy from a baby. As long as they control that, their position's basically untouchable. I hear that Neutzeland manager guy uses a pile of gold coins for a bed. And I bet he sleeps like a baby, too," Masato said, giving the cashbox by his foot a nudge. Although it was so full that its contents didn't so much as stir, most of the coins in it were copper and silver.

If they traded it in for gold coins…it wouldn't even take a tenth of that space. That was how different the amounts were when you sold to individuals as opposed to businesses.

"They'll probably come after us in a couple days, but they don't need to make their move just yet. We're annoying them, but they probably figure we'll crash and burn on our own. Price wars are double-edged swords, so they'd rather not start one unless they have to."

"So—so if things stay like this, we can't win?"

"Nope, not a chance. Our returns come quick, but our profits are small." Masato gave Roo's question a firm answer. Then he compared his two students' expressions. The difference in their attitudes was quite apparent.

Elch…wasn't quite apathetic, but he didn't seem particularly worried. As far as he was concerned, the money they'd made was already more than enough. If they returned to the village right then and there, he'd be satisfied.

But Roo was different. Hearing Masato's explanation, her expression had gone as grave as if he'd said the very world was ending. Tears had even begun welling up in her eyes. Seeing that, Masato couldn't help but let out a laugh.

There's that greed I respect…

Masato smiled at Roo in admiration.

"Chin up, Li'l Roo. If things *stay like this*, we can't win. But do I look like a guy who just *gives up* without winning?" He looked right into Roo's eyes and flashed the young girl the same sinister grin he'd used when he was manipulating the Fitze farmers. Roo's eyes lit back up. She shook her head from side to side.

"So what, do you have some kinda plan?"

"…Here's a question for you, Elch. Didn't you think it was odd? You can't get mayonnaise around these parts, if anywhere. In other words, it should be worth as much as sugar or pepper. But here I was, dipping veggies in it and selling it so cheap that anyone could afford it. I mean, if I'd gone and found some gluttonous noble, I could've made gold so fast you'd have thought I was an alchemist."

"True, that did seem a little strange… Did you have some reason?"

"Of course. I was using it as bait. My goal wasn't to make money; my goal was to get everyone talking about us. I wanted all of Dormundt to know there was a company in town other than Neutzeland…*so I could reel a big one in from the sea.*"

A sudden sensation, a pressure, suddenly came over the two *byuma*.

""_____!""

It was like a freezing wind had just run across Elch's and Roo's

121

skin. The sensation bearing down on them was so strong, it was almost scary. But the thing was…it wasn't coming from Masato. It was coming from behind them. Masato looked more elated than he ever had in that world as his gaze turned to what stood behind them. Following his lead, they turned around—

"…!" "Eep…"

—and each let out a startled yelp.

The pressure was coming from a short *hyuma* man with soft, androgynous features. The tension in the air around him was as sharp as a knife. The man narrowed his eyes, as though he were smiling. A shrewd light burned in them as he called out to Masato.

"…Forgive me for interrupting your conversation. You represent Elm Trading, correct?"

"…Actually, this guy's the representative."

"No, I'm quite certain it's you. Or at least, you're the one running the show."

"How can you be so sure?"

"…Do I look like a man who couldn't figure out that much?"

"That you do not."

Masato radiated an aura just as acute. No, perhaps even more so. The air grew tenser still. Elch felt goose bumps run across his skin.

This was the kind of atmosphere that only veteran merchants possessed. They weren't farmers who engaged in trade to support their humble lifestyles or corrupt landlords getting rich off their property rights. They were starving wolves who lived their lives on razor-thin margins day in and day out so they could amass unfathomable fortunes.

"I like this guy's vibe. He feels like the first real businessman I've met since I came to this world." Having sensed that this visitor was of a similar mind to him, Masato rose from his chair and offered his hand.

"I'm Masato Sanada, and I do Elm Trading's books. Who is it that I have the pleasure of speaking to?"

The man shook it as he stated his name.

"Forgive me for the delayed introduction. My name is Klaus, and I lead the Sea Serpent Maritime Trading Company based out of eastern Freyjagard. I heard talk of an interesting company making a name for themselves in Dormundt, and…I had hoped to have a chat."

"What a coincidence. I've…been wanting to have a sit-down with you all day, too."

"You noticed me? Among that massive crowd?"

"Do I look like the kind of guy who wouldn't?"

"…That you do not," Klaus said with an elegant smile, letting out a little chuckle.

Masato offered him a seat, ordered beer and sausages from a nearby tavern employee…then whipped a jar of mayonnaise seemingly from nowhere and placed it atop the table.

"The thing is, I wanted you to try this, so I saved a jar just for you. Let's have a bite and talk about money, Mr. Klaus."

"We lost the Sea Serpents."

Learning that fact shook Neutzeland like a magnitude 8.0 earthquake.

"Th-that can't be! Is this true?!"

"I-it is! We're sure of it…! Mr. Klaus came and told us in person…! As we speak, the Sea Serpent sailors are carrying their cargo to a warehouse rented by Elm Trading…!"

"Rrrrrrgh!"

Neutzeland's manager, Jaccoy, had made light of the Elm Trading

Company at first. Given how small they were, he'd been sure they'd collapse in on themselves in no time. Now he was getting nervous.

After all, the Sea Serpents were the ones slated to bring all the wholesale goods Neutzeland was getting through the shipyards that month.

Jaccoy made his way to where the Sea Serpents' ship was anchored so he could give Klaus a piece of his mind. The leader of the maritime company was busy barking out instructions to the sailors transporting their cargo, so he wasn't hard to find. Neutzeland's manager shouted at the man in a furious tone.

"KLAUS!"

"Why, if it isn't Mr. Jaccoy. You seem upset. What's the matter?"

"Of course I'm upset! You're cutting us out and selling your cargo to those strange novices! Have you gone mad?!"

"Ah, so that's what this is about." Having learned what Jaccoy was cross about, Klaus's expression changed to one of exasperation. "I'm perfectly sane, thank you very much. I listened to what they had to say, then made a decision... He's an impressive man, Elm Trading's accountant. I don't know what he's been selling or where he's been selling it, but despite his youth, he's a shrewder man than you or I. During our negotiations, there were a number of moments where I felt as though I was about to be swallowed whole. Why, I had to try my damnedest just to make it out of there in one piece. Honestly, I'm a little embarrassed. I did learn quite a lot, though."

"You're overestimating them...! They don't have the capital for any sort of serious business, and the slightest upset could blow their flimsy company away..."

"Yet you're the one *about to be devoured*, aren't you?"

"Wh-what?!"

"Oh? Have you not realized your situation yet? Elm Trading isn't just gobbling up your market share on the land, they're stealing your share of the sea, as well."

"Only because you betrayed us!" Jaccoy, unamused with Klaus's less than sympathetic tone, grabbed him by the collar and screamed right in the man's face. "We always took market prices into consideration when we bought from you people, didn't we?! What could you possibly have to complain about?!"

Faced with Jaccoy's boiling rage, Klaus was as cool as a cucumber.

"Yet you always sold for far, far more, right? It's only natural for us to want a piece of that action... And one other thing. Instead of going after ludicrous profits like you, Mr. Sanada promised to sell the Industrial District their wholesale goods at affordable prices. When he does, it should help end the price-spike-induced recession they've been having these last few years. His vision has a future, you see. We do our share of buying, too, so we wanted to partner with a business willing to set aside their own profits for the good of the region as a whole." As the leader of Sea Serpent gave his answer, he grabbed the arm holding his collar.

Jaccoy yelped in pain and released his grip. Klaus's fingers had left visible marks on Jaccoy's fat arm.

"If you keep refusing to wake up, they're liable to swallow your beloved bed of gold coins whole—and you along with it. Do keep your wits about you. Now, if you'll excuse me, I have work to do." Having said his piece, Klaus returned to his work.

Jaccoy headed back down the road to Neutzeland's headquarters. Chewing his fingernails, he mumbled, "Dammit, dammit, how did this happen?"

He'd been certain that Elm Trading's consignment system would fail in no time. There was no way those uneducated peasants could keep decent ledgers, and without accurate ledgers, people would lose faith in them, and the system would break down. Then their bloated market would pop like a bubble. There was no need for him to burn his own money on a price war.

But Elm Trading simply refused to fail. How? How had they gotten so big yet still showed no signs of collapsing?

—Jaccoy didn't know it, but its sole secret to success was Masato Sanada.

One of the reasons the Sanada Group had grown so much during Masato's tenure was that he'd personally directed every single company under their umbrella. That's right—he wasn't their *president*; he was their *director*.

In other words, he attended every meeting of every company, from the biggest banks to the smallest workshops. What enabled him to do that was a rare gift Masato possessed called multi-listening. He had the ability to accurately listen to and process thirty conversations at once. It was possible for him to take on ten times that many discussions if they were comprised of simple words and numbers.

The farmers couldn't keep their own ledgers, so Masato had them instead confirm the goods and their prices out loud whenever they made a sale. Then, by picking those voices out from the noise of the market, he was able to record the transactions himself and keep an accurate account of the goods the Elm Trading Company was dealing with, even now that their stock had swelled to more than a whole ship's worth. That was how he'd earned other merchants' trust.

It was a feat bordering on superhuman ability. Not just anyone could pull something like that off. But the fact that he could was precisely why people revered him as one of the High School Prodigies.

—Not that Jaccoy knew any of that.

There was no way he could have known that Masato had been hailed as a prodigy back on a planet called Earth. And because of that…he'd underestimated him. He'd underestimated the threat the Elm Trading Company posed with Masato at its wheel. However…

"If you keep refusing to wake up, they're liable to swallow your beloved bed of gold coins whole—and you along with it."

"………"

Klaus's speech had jolted him to his senses.

The Elm Trading Company's influence would likely spread through the sea routes via the Sea Serpents. At the moment, the Sea Serpents had three ships docked at the port, and the Dagon Company had the other four.

Neutzeland and Dagon had already finished their dealings for this haul, so Elm Trading wouldn't be able to butt in on that. However, there was no way of knowing which way future ships would lean. This was no time to be sitting around idly waiting to be destroyed.

When Jaccoy returned to his company, he gathered his merchants and made an announcement.

"…Starting tomorrow, we're opening our market in the central plaza, too."

"I-in the central plaza?!"

"That's right. The only advantages they have over us are their prime location and their low prices. We're going to eliminate both."

"We're competing with this tiny company directly, sir?"

"They're meddling with our ocean trade routes, and that cannot stand. We have to crush them *while* they're small. We'll buy goods for more than them! We'll sell goods for less than them! Right now, their land-based trade is still their foundation! If we rip it up from the roots, they'll shrivel and die!"

"B-but what about our profits?"

"This is war! Until they're dead and gone, profits are of no concern! We'll take some hits, but when it comes to a brawl like this, that's not what matters. We have more money, so we can simply outlast them!

We'll defeat them with our superior resources! We'll bankrupt them! No, we'll *obliterate* them! We'll annihilate those country bumpkins!"

""""Yes sir!"""""

The merchants got to work as soon as Jaccoy finished his tirade. Watching his underlings scurry to their work, the man muttered a vow to himself.

"You people made enemies of the great Neutzeland Trading Company...and I'll make sure you regret it!"

That evening, Shinobu Sarutobi dropped by the inn that Masato and the others were using as their base. When she entered their room, her eyes gleamed at the mountain of gold coins piled up on the desk.

"Holy moly. That's so much gold! You guys are raking it in!"

"We're doing business with companies now. If we'd kept using copper coins, the floor would give out."

"So we're looking good on Ringo's requests, then?"

"Yeah, I was able to get everything she needed and more from my deal with the shipyard today. I was worried about being able to find magnesium. But apparently, they got some from a glass workshop, so I was able to get enough. I'm gonna charter a horse tomorrow and send Ringo's haul to Elm along with the winter stores."

"There was some pricey stuff on the list, like gold and silver. How'd those go?"

"I'm just gonna have her melt down some of the gold and silver coins for that."

"Oh, huh. Hadn't thought of that."

"...Just so you know, that's a serious crime."

"Elch, we have a saying back on our world: 'It's only a crime if you get caught.'"

"And if they catch you, you can just make a break for it!"

"That's horrible..." With a sigh, Elch went over to the bed and placed a damp towel on Roo's forehead.

"That's Roo, the protégé you took in off the street, right? What's wrong with her? Did she catch a cold or something? Her face is bright red."

"Nah, she just got so excited from seeing all this cash that she popped a nosebleed and fainted."

"...Well, you can't say she doesn't have promise."

"Yeah, but it'll be a while before she's actually useful. She can't even read. —Hey, Elch, there's a mistake here," Masato said, looking up from his tablet computer. Then he tapped the touch screen with his stylus and pointed something out to Elch.

"When you sell on credit, you don't list the debit on the day of as *cash*, you list it as *accounts payable*. After all, you don't actually have the money yet. If you do it like this, you'll end up putting in the 'cash' twice and causing all sorts of problems."

"Oh, I see..."

"What's going on over here? ...Oh, double-entry bookkeeping. You're teaching him?"

"Yeah. Single-entry causes *way* too much ambiguity."

"Apparently, up until recently, there were some developed countries that were using that ambiguous single-entry method to manage their public funds, you know."

"Well, sure. That ambiguity made things real convenient for them."

Double-entry bookkeeping was an accounting method that had only become popular relatively recently in Earth's history. Unlike the single-entry ledgers Elm Village had been using, which only had income and expenditures, double-entry ledgers classified incoming money based on its attributes, which allowed for a better understanding of an organization's financial structure. In short, it was difficult to make errors, which meant it was easier to earn other people's trust.

Learning how to use it was essentially all upside.

So while Masato used their downtime to teach Roo her letters and some basic math, he was also coaching Elch on how to keep double-entry ledgers.

"Now, onto the next drill. Go ahead and organize this cash flow here into the account book."

"G-got it!"

With that, Elch took the tablet (or as he called it, the magic paper that you could write and erase on however many times you liked) and stylus and began writing in the ledger displayed on its LCD screen.

While still keeping an eye on his pupil, Masato turned to Shinobu. His tone switched from small-talk mode to serious mode.

"...So given that you're here, does that mean they've made their move?"

Shinobu nodded in answer.

"Yup. Looks like they're pretty pissed you muscled in on the port. They're planning on taking the war to you tomorrow."

"Wh-what do you mean, *war*?" Having heard the frightening word, Elch looked up from the tablet, pale.

"They're gonna start buying and selling without caring about being profitable. Basically, they're planning on icing us out."

"Wait, but if they do that, won't they run out of money?"

"They've got all sorts of cash stored up over there. They're a hundred percent sure they can take us if it comes down to a head-to-head fight. And they aren't wrong. We made a good chunk of change off our deal with the Industrial District, but that's nothing compared to their reserves. If they'd taken full advantage of their material lead, they could have flattened us. Power plays are just as effective in financial wars as they are in real ones. Honestly, it's not a bad strategy."

It wasn't bad plan. However…

"Or it wouldn't have been, if they'd done it on day one."

"You're saying they're too late?"

"Yeah. They're so late it's almost makin' me yawn. What a bunch of slackers."

"So you have a counterstrategy ready?"

"I don't need one. That slugfest's never gonna happen."

With a wicked grin, Masato stood up from his chair and opened the room's window.

The sight outside made Elch's eyes go wide.

In the darkness behind the inn…were dozens of men. Their clothes were so shabby, they looked like beggars, but their eyes were filled with an ominous, fiery light.

Those guys… I've seen them hanging around the market, haven't I?

Masato rested his elbow on the windowsill and called out to the men like they were old friends.

"…It's gonna go down just like I told you yesterday. This ends tomorrow. I'm counting on you guys."

"""………""" The men nodded in unison, then vanished into the night. The entire exchange was thoroughly unsettling. Elch wanted to know what that was all about.

"Who were those men…?"

Masato's smile was downright fiendish.

"The blades I'm gonna use…to slay Neutzeland."

Slay Neutzeland.

Although the words had a sinister ring, he obviously wasn't going to actually kill anyone. He was speaking metaphorically. Though his blades were only figurative, they were a far crueler weapon than actual knives. After all, the blades he was using could gouge out a heart without causing any physical pain. By the time the victim noticed, it was already too late.

That's right. Jaccoy had already been stabbed by Masato's blades. He just hadn't noticed yet. The master of Neutzeland remained unaware even as Saturday morning rolled around. It had been ages since his employees had seen the man this fired up.

I won't let them have their way anymore.

Today, Neutzeland was going to open their market right in the central plaza. Then, by disregarding profits and selling for less and buying for more than Elm did, they were going to beat them bloody.

After all, Elm's foundation was so weak that they had to rely on an unorthodox method like consignment. They'd used their deal with the Sea Serpents to drum up some decent dough, but compared to the mountain of gold Jaccoy slept on, it was still little more than pocket change. At the end of the day, money was the backbone of a business. In a fight, it was their stamina. Money was everything.

There was absolutely no chance Neutzeland could lose in a slugfest. The competition for morning inventory had already begun.

The people over at Elm Trading were probably going pale at discovering that Neutzeland was using its overwhelming amounts of capital to buy up all the incoming merchandise. Jaccoy leaned back in his chair, his expression brimming with confidence. His bed of gold probably only served to reaffirm those thoughts.

The unease of the previous day had vanished from his thoughts without a trace. It was gone. Nowhere to be seen.

—In other words, this was the limit of Jaccoy's strategic ability. With this, he'd unknowingly proven himself incapable of escaping from atop Masato's palm…which meant he was dead. Masato's blades reached his heart. It was only half an hour after the market opened when the fat merchant finally learned of his demise.

One of his employees came running over to him, drenched in sweat.

"Mr. Jaccoy! Mr. Jaccoy!"

"What's wrong? Heh, did they already throw in the towel before the market even opened?"

"N-no sir! I-it's a disaster!"

"A disaster? What happened?"

"We haven't been able to buy a single piece of merchandise!"

"Wh...? WHAT?!?!"

Jaccoy shouted hysterically and stood up so fast his chair toppled over.

"I told you to offer better buy prices than they did, didn't I?!"

"You did, sir! We put up signboards and banners announcing our new prices, but...nobody seemed to care! They all just went to Elm..."

"?!?!"

It defied logic. The Findolph domain was at Freyjagard's northernmost point, and their winters were brutal. Impoverished farmers of the frigid region should have leaped at the opportunity to sell their goods for even a single rook more. They needed that money to buy winter stores. So why were they intentionally accepting lower prices?

Panicking over the incomprehensible actions of the farmers, Jaccoy rushed over to the market. But when he got there—

"What's the meaning of—? Huh?!"

—he saw something unbelievable.

"A-ah! I-it's you people...!"

Dozens of people and wagons were lined up in front of the Elm Trading Company's lot in the plaza. Mixed in with the rest of the rabble...were some faces Jaccoy recognized. They were—

"That's right. They're your old peddlers." Masato's heels clicked as he stepped out to face the shell-shocked Jaccoy.

"Y-you bastard…!"

"When we started digging, we found out all sorts of interesting stuff about you guys. Not only did you have a secret agreement with the mayor to monopolize the market, you were also real aggressive when it came to cost cutting. For example, you moved the market from the central plaza to the Port District so it'd be closer to your warehouses. But the biggest move you made…was laying off all your traveling peddlers."

Masato had always found it strange that Elch had to bring his wares to the city. He'd known that Elch's father had been a peddler who was often on the road, after all. There were a number of differences between this world and Earth, but the concept of traveling salesmen definitely existed here. Why should Elch have to bring Elm's goods to the city himself, then? Thanks to Shinobu's efforts, Masato discovered the answer to that question the first night after they'd started Elm Trading.

After Jaccoy secured a monopoly on distribution, he laid off not just Orion's old peddlers, but Neutzeland's, as well.

"You had sole control over Findolph's only port, so even if you didn't go out and buy inventory, goods would still naturally flow your way. That's why you fired pretty much all your peddlers and made the villagers come all the way to Dormundt to sell their goods directly. By doing so, you were able to cut personnel expenses while foisting the city's tariffs off on the villagers… It's the kind of dumbass idea that only a guy who spends all day looking at ledgers and who's forgotten what it's like to pound pavement would come up with. Human relationships are the bedrock of business, but you were willing to throw away all the goodwill the peddlers built up with the villagers just to make a couple extra rook."

Jaccoy had been like an octopus eating its own leg.

"It felt like a real waste to me, so we figured we'd take it all for ourselves."

"Y-you don't mean..." A nasty hunch barreled through Jaccoy's mind. With a sneer packed full of his contempt for Jaccoy's foolishness, Masato confirmed his fears.

"Oh, but I do. All these peddlers signed exclusive three-year contracts with me. We bought up all these goods before they even made it into the city... I don't have to explain what that means, do I? The fact that I employ all these peddlers means that today isn't a one-off thing. Tomorrow'll be the same, and the day after that, and all the days to come. In other words, not a single unspoken-for wagonload will ever make it to this plaza... You're gaping at me like a dumbass again."

"This...can't be!" The proud merchant master of Neutzeland turned as white as bone at Masato's declaration. It was an understandable reaction. His entire plan had revolved around coming to the plaza and undercutting Elm's prices.

However...Masato had gone and cut him off upstream. If the goods never made it into the city, Jaccoy's strategy was worthless. To make things worse...Neutzeland didn't have the ability to compete with them outside the city. How could they? Jaccoy's company lacked the peddlers to do so. His business had, in a sense, chewed off its own legs.

It certainly wasn't as if they couldn't hire new peddlers, but it was going to be impossible to find people who knew how to keep ledgers, negotiate, and navigate safely through the Findolph domain's bandit-infested roads...outside of the men who'd just signed on with Elm.

—In other words, Neutzeland had no way to counter Elm's play. This was no slugfest. *Neutzeland was completely powerless.*

"Rrrrrrgh!!!!"

Sweat cascaded down Jaccoy's forehead like a waterfall as he finally came to understand his despair-inducing predicament. He turned to the gathered farmers and shouted.

"He-he's tricking you! Look at those banners! We're paying far better prices than that deadbeat company ever could! It's not too late! You can still change your minds! If there's a penalty for breaking your contracts, we'll pay it all! So—!"

The response from the farmers was colder than ice.

"Sorry, but…Elm Trading told us you'd offer us more money. We sold our goods to them already knowing that."

"Wh-why?!"

"Why? It's simple. We just don't want to do business with you."

"?!?!"

"We're not greedy. All we ever wanted was enough to survive the winter…so our villages could make it to spring. Elm Trading made sure to take that into account when they set their prices."

"Besides…you're only offering better prices for now. Once your war with Elm is over, you'll go right back to ripping us off. We might be uneducated, but even we can tell that much."

"So instead, we just went with a trading partner who understands how we feel. Not just for this winter, but for every winter to come."

"N-no, wait! This is all a misunderstanding! I promise, we'll never try to rip you off again! I regret everything we've done! So—"

"Don't go bowing to us. That's not what we want. After all…even if you really were remorseful and telling us the truth from the bottom of your heart…we simply can't trust you."

"…………"

It was like Jaccoy was scratching against a wall of polished marble. That was how firm, cold, and absolute their rejection was. The villagers of Findolph had made it thoroughly clear just how fed up with Neutzeland they were.

And who could blame them?

Neutzeland had been abusing them for years. Money. Coin. It's all the company had ever cared about. But that had been wrong. Both from a moral perspective...and a business perspective. As Jaccoy reeled from the farmers' rejection, Masato spoke.

"Mr. Jaccoy, was it? You've been laboring under one big misapprehension. You probably thought the most important thing in business was money. That's why you tried so desperately to amass it. But see, money's not the most important thing... It's trust. Even if you're dead broke, as long as people trust you, you can still rebuild your company. As long as there are people who trust your business, money'll come naturally. But...no matter how much money you have, if people don't trust you...you're dead in the water. And you...took things too far."

".........." Jaccoy had nothing left to say. All he could do was gaze lifelessly at the merchant from another world standing before him. He was certain of it now.

There was no way...he could win.

The man standing there wasn't someone he could ever hope to defeat. Before long, this man would probably snatch away every major deal that went through the port. And when that happened...Neutzeland's cash flow would die.

If Neutzeland were a plant, it was like their roots were being ripped out. Even with their vast fortunes—even though their flowers bloomed far larger than Elm's—without their roots, all they could do was use up their stores of water and eventually wither away.

Filled with despair at that inevitable future, Jaccoy sank to his knees. Seeing the once high-and-mighty man sink so low left Elch and Roo speechless.

Amazing...

Masato had done it. He'd dealt Neutzeland a fatal blow in just a single week. They'd doubted he could pull it off. Now, though, they saw it with their own eyes as they stood in shocked silence.

However, the biggest shock was yet to come…

"But if I beat you and Neutzeland into the ground, then I'd be the one taking it too far."

Suddenly, Masato offered Jaccoy a hand of salvation.

"Huh?"

"Doesn't matter if it's Elm or Neutzeland, no good can come of a single company having a monopoly. Without competition, companies grow corrupt. Pretty much every time. So what say we all just have a little sit-down. Then we can talk about the future of Dormundt and, by extension, the economy and trade of the entire domain… Though, I suggest you prepare for a taste of your own medicine."

Stunned by the sudden glimpse of redemption, Jaccoy was silent for a moment, and then…

"…All right." His head sank low as he nodded.

Elm's hand was already around his throat. Coming to a settlement, even if it was a harsh one, was obviously preferable to being strangled.

And with that, the Elm Trading Company emerged victorious from the Elm versus Neutzeland war.

Night had already begun to creep over the city by the time they'd finished negotiations and left Neutzeland's offices.

The three members of the Elm Trading Company walked down the twilit port streets, making their way back toward the inn where they'd been staying.

"Damn, those Neutzeland chairs were *hard*. Sure, they looked nice, but would it have killed them to add a little padding? My back's killing me." Masato, the one complaining, was at the group's head. In his right hand, he was holding a spherical leather bag.

—They'd settled on three major points in the negotiations.

First, a prohibition on the use of bribes to interfere with the issuing of trading licenses.

Second, the revival of the peddler system and an agreement that the companies would shoulder all tariffs and the burden of transporting goods.

Third, for Neutzeland to pay reparations to the villages as an apology for their misconduct.

The first was largely a formality, so they reached an agreement on that point quickly. About half the peddlers Masato hired had expressed a desire to go back to their old jobs, so the second issue was resolved by Elm transferring their contracts to Neutzeland under the same conditions. However, the third topic caused no end of disputes. It alone ate up about 90 percent of the discussion.

Eventually, though, they did decide on sums for Neutzeland to pay the villages as compensation for making them shoulder the tariffs: two gold per person for villages from which they'd bought goods and three for people like Tohr who'd come peddling from rural companies.

Even for small villages like Elm, that came out to around a hundred gold. For larger ones like Fitze, it was closer to six hundred.

All in all, Neutzeland ended up having to pay over a hundred thousand gold. Jaccoy's beloved bed of gold was gone.

They couldn't pay it all at once, of course. Losing that kind of liquid capital would severely impede their ability to actually run their business. If Neutzeland ended up having to flee Dormundt on account of their increased expenses from the tariffs and the peddler payroll, that would put the situation right back where it started.

As a result, Masato asked the villagers to be understanding and sought a compromise wherein the payments to higher-population farm villages and towns would come gradually over the next few years. Jaccoy, who'd been thoroughly humbled by the whole process, thanked him profusely and agreed. They then drew up the agreement, at which point Jaccoy signed and affixed Neutzeland's seal to it. Once Count Heiseraat signed his name and made it official, the discussion came to a close.

Masato's leather bag currently held a hundred gold in reparations and 650 more of the coins as a finder's fee for the peddlers.

Elch gazed at the bag as he called out, "Man, you really had it out for them."

"What do you mean?"

"The thing where they tried to take advantage of us on day one."

"Oh yeah. I told you, remember? I hate getting ripped off."

Elch nodded. With all that'd happened, that conversation felt like it had been ages ago. However, Masato had said one other thing back then, too.

"I'll destroy Neutzeland." And yet—

"But for all that, you never ended up actually destroying them."

"Hey, I got you your money, didn't I? Don't go chopping me into wolf bait, now."

"I'm not gonna make you into wolf bait... I was just kinda curious. Why'd you decide to come to a settlement?"

Elch could tell. The agreement had almost no upside for Elm. The reparations and finder's fee together were nothing compared to the money they could have made by keeping the market all to themselves. And if that was the case, why'd Masato make the proposal he did? Well, Elch was about to find out.

"The thing is, if we'd refused to compromise and just crushed them, things would have gotten real messy for us."

"You think so?"

"Definitely. I said I'd destroy them at first to raise your morale, but that was never actually the plan. After all, Neutzeland and we are the only companies in Dormundt. If we got rid of them, we'd have to sustain all the trade in the whole city for a while."

Masato explained that even with the secret arrangement eliminated, it would take some time before other companies could get a foothold in the city.

"But that's just not possible. You don't have the skills to run a company that big yet, and I'm not planning on sticking around in this world for that long. My plan was only ever to fix the mess we made of Elm Village's finances and to get the stuff Ringo asked for. But there's another, even bigger reason why we couldn't truly kill Neutzeland—personnel expenses."

"Per-so-nnel expenses? What's that, Teacher?"

"It's the money you gotta pay people when they work for you. We hired all the peddlers Neutzeland laid off, but we're just a fledgling little company that hasn't even gotten a decent shipment of goods in yet. Our deal with the Sea Serpents gave us a little bit of bankroll to work with, but with that many employees, even that wouldn't last long. I only hired them in the first place to break Jaccoy's will. It was my plan from the get-go to force Neutzeland to take half of them back after the dust settled. For a finder's fee, of course."

"........." Elch gawked at how unashamed Masato was about all that.

For all the preaching he'd done to Jaccoy about trust, he himself had hired the peddlers with contracts he never intended to uphold. The nerve was downright unbelievable. Elch could hardly begin to comprehend the depths of Masato's audacity.

"...Hey, are you actually evil or something?"

Masato replied with an amused grin.

"You'd better believe I am. Back on Earth, they called me the Devil of Finance." His expression in that moment was his most villainous one yet. Elch contorted his face in revulsion. Roo, on the other hand, gazed up at Masato in admiration.

"All right, the Neutzeland problem might be out of our hair, but I still have a lot to teach you two. When we get back to the inn, we'll pick up from where we left off yesterday."

"G-got it!"

"Yes sir!"

But before they could make it back, the day's final incident reared its ugly head.

"There she is! It's her!"

"Stop right there!"

""""_____?!"""""

All of a sudden, four men with fishlike faces appeared and blocked the trio's path.

Seemingly unprovoked, a group of threatening sailors had appeared. Each was carrying a knife, and their eyes were tinged with anger and hostility.

Elch braced himself for trouble.

"Did Neutzeland send thugs after us?"

"...Nah, these guys don't look like merchants."

"Eeep..."

"Li'l Roo?" Masato suddenly caught on to what was happening.

Not only was Roo hiding behind him, she was looking at the men in abject terror. He wondered why for a moment, but the men quickly dispelled his confusion.

"You assholes think you can make money off goods that don't belong to you?"

"Goods? What are you talking about?"

"The kid! Dagon Company brought a shipment back from the New World…and she's one of our slaves!"

"Wh…?!"

"…Is that true, Li'l Roo?"

"………" Roo's shoulders flinched, and she looked away.

Judging by her reaction, it seemed the story checked out. To complicate things, it was clear there was no way the sailors were about to let them get away with making off with their slave and selling her.

The sailors clasped their knives in their sea-tempered hands.

"You assholes ready to pay the piper? Get 'em, boys!"

""""Yeah!!!!"""" The sailors charged.

Or rather, they tried to. Elch was one step faster on the draw, however. He pulled the bow off his back and loosed an arrow into the cobbled road directly in front of them.

""""Ah!""""

"…Don't come any closer, or the next one's going through your forehead."

Not only had he drawn his bow faster than the sailors could blink, but his arrow had landed right at their feet. It was no wonder that Mayor Ulgar had called Elch the best archer in the village. To an unskilled eye, it might have looked like he was just showing off, but the young man's combat prowess was actually well beyond that of the four sailors.

They'd been in their fair share of brawls, however. Their eyes were anything but novice.

"Yo, Boss... This guy's trouble."

The leader of the bunch, however, quickly barked at his cowering underlings.

"D-don't get spooked now! We're the victims here! Justice is on our side! If it comes down to it, we can just call a patrol over! These guys are the thieves, after all!"

"...!" Hearing that made Elch's face twitch.

The man was right. If they summoned a patrol, Elch and the others would have no excuse. The slave trade was just a normal part of life in this world. Even people were just another commodity to be sold. Stealing them was just as much a crime as stealing anything else.

—And it went without saying that criminals couldn't own trading licenses.

Even so...Elch didn't break his combat stance. Come what may, he was still a villager of Elm. He wasn't just about to abandon someone in their moment of need. Especially not if that someone was a person he'd been working alongside for the past week.

"I'll buy you some time! Take Roo and make a run for it!"

But as Elch readied himself to protect Roo...

"Nah, that won't be necessary," Masato said from behind.

"Huh?! What are you—?" Elch glared at Masato. He wasn't seriously planning on abandoning her, was he?

Masato didn't return Elch's look. Instead, he turned his eyes down to Roo as she hid behind him and asked her a single question.

"Li'l Roo...do you want me to save you?"

His voice was gentle.

"_____!"

Roo's wide eyes grew even wider. They were filled with joy. —No. That wasn't it. It wasn't joy. It was comprehension. She understood.

She understood what Masato had meant when he asked if she wanted him to save her.

It wasn't a question that needed to be asked. Obviously, she wanted to be saved. She was a runaway slave. If the sailors took her…she could only imagine the cruelties they'd inflict.

Simply put, Masato wasn't really asking if she wanted to be saved. He was asking how the girl wanted to live her life from here on out.

"Roo…wants money. She wants to be able to make it on her own. She doesn't want to be tossed around anymore. So…please, teach Roo how to make money, too!"

It was all because she'd come to him with that request.

…That's right…

Roo was ashamed that her first instinct had been to hide behind Masato. She wanted to be able to make it on her own. That had been her wish from the very start, the reason she'd followed Masato in the first place. But trembling and waiting to be saved was no way to accomplish that. She shouldn't have been relying on the altruism of others.

Roo's gonna became a big strong merchant like Teacher…!

She needed to seize her future with her own strength and wisdom.

"TEACHEEEEEEEEEER!"

With new resolve, she shouted at the top of her lungs, "Roo has a dream! Okay?! Roo's gonna make lots and lots and loooots of money, and then someday, someday…she's gonna buy Mommy and Daddy back!

"So, so! Roo's gonna study even harder!

"She's gonna learn her letters, her numbers, everything!

"Then she's gonna become a merchant just like, no, a merchant *even better* than you, Teacher! She's gonna make mountains of money, and then, and then…she's gonna get Mommy and Daddy back! Roo's not strong enough now, but she's gonna study and study and study until she is!

"Then, then! Roo's gonna give Teacher all the money she has left over!

"Roo promises! She won't let you regret this! So, Teacher, please…!

"Buy Roo right here and now!!!!"

She was practically screaming as she demonstrated her "value." She was pitching herself to Masato. As a merchant, she was her own product. At the moment, she was nobody, so she shouted to convey the one thing she had—a will that burned like fire.

"What's that kid babbling about?!"

"We should chop off her legs so she can't make another break for it!"

The sailors sneered at Roo and closed in on her as she conducted the first negotiation of her life. But when one of them reached out to grab her, something struck the man in the face.

"Agh!"

"The hell you think you're—?!"

The eyes of the sailors' leader bulged wide at the sudden attack. However, the rage quickly faded from his voice as he became transfixed by what had been thrown and was currently scattered across the pavement.

It was the leather bag full of gold and silver coins. Masato had quite literally thrown the money in their faces.

"That there's seven hundred and fifty gold. I wanna buy this slave from you… That's easily a hundred times what she'd go for on the open market. Do we have any problems, gentlemen?"

"Wh…?"

Now, the men were just sailors. They were nothing more than the people paid to transport goods from point A to point B.

They themselves didn't technically have any ownership over Roo. They were just in charge of making sure the slaves didn't go anywhere. In other words, they had no right to conduct this sale. However…their ethical concerns were no match for the sheer volume of coin they were being offered. That was precisely why Masato was offering so much.

"Nope! No sirree! No problems here! Just remember, all sales are final!"

"Then it sounds like we have a deal."

The lead sailor scooped up the bag, along with the stray coins that had escaped the sack when it had been thrown. He then turned to his confused men and said, "Look, let's just forget about all this," and he promptly dragged them all off.

His plan was probably to tell the owner that they couldn't track down the slave, then embezzle the cash for himself. Though Masato didn't much care what the man did with the money. After all—

"Well said, Li'l Roo."

—he'd just traded it for far more gold than could ever possibly fit in that little sack.

"Teacher…"

"Doesn't matter how savvy a businessperson someone is; doesn't matter if they're so lucky it makes you think they were touched by the hand of God—they're useless if they don't have the hunger… I was like that, back before my dad died. I spent my life just getting jerked around."

Back then, Masato had lived with no goals, no hunger, and no wants. Every day was tepid and uneventful.

"But when I saw my dad's corpse hanging there, I felt that hunger for the first time. A dark hunger for revenge against the companies that drove my father to his death. My eyes back then probably looked just like yours do now, Li'l Roo. And you've got it, too. Something you want to do. Something you *need* to do, deep down in your heart. And I can tell you're ready to put your life on the line to do it."

Even though she'd known that getting caught meant near-certain death, she'd sought Masato out anyway. Despite knowing how conspicuous being in public had made her, she'd taken in every drop of financial wisdom he'd given her.

"That courage? That willpower? That's worth a million times more than that paltry sum I tossed them." Masato knew full well that the girl's hunger would someday lead to wealth beyond measure. Compared to that, a single bag of gold was nothing.

"Those dumbasses just let a fortune slip through their hands for a song. Let's make 'em regret it," Masato said, giving Roo's red hair a rough tussle. His hand was so warm. Not only did he understand Roo better than she understood herself, he respected the way she wanted to live her life.

"Tea... Teacheeeerrrrr!"

The tears she'd been holding back, the feelings she'd been holing up in her heart, they all came out at once.

She embraced Masato and began crying loudly to express all the gratitude and joy she couldn't possibly convey in words. Masato gently rubbed her head, then turned his gaze toward Elch.

"Sorry about that, Elch. I kinda ended up spending everyone's money," he said apologetically.

Elch, however, understood what Masato's true intentions had been. He could hardly blame him for what he'd done.

"...It's fine. It's not worth worrying about, given how much else you made us." And more importantly, it felt nice spending money the way he had. "Heh. You know, I never knew spending money could feel this good."

©Sacraneco

Elch's words made Masato smile like a kid.

"Ha-ha, right? That's why I keep makin' it."

And with that, Masato Sanada's skills restored Elm's finances to the point where, as long as they didn't do anything reckless, they could live out their next couple decades with security. He'd easily made good on his promise to repay them twice over.

Furthermore, he'd successfully gotten Ringo Oohoshi all the iron and other goods she'd asked for. With the ability to manufacture aluminum, Ringo could now wield her scientific acumen to its fullest. It was certain to be a big boon in their search for a way home.

⚜ Report and Unrest ⚜

The night after things had wrapped up in Dormundt, Tsukasa received a phone call from Shinobu Sarutobi, who'd gone to the city alongside Masato and Elch.

"*Evening, Tsukes! Long time no see. How's the crew?*"

"Good. Due in no small part to the sugar and pepper Merchant sent over. Everyone's glad that our menu's expanded. And you guys?"

"*Oh, we're golden. I'm, like, in my element here. Being cooped up in the mountains is no good for a journalist like me, y'know. A reporter with no news is like a fish out of water. But here in the city, it's like I found my ocean again.*"

On the other end of the phone, Shinobu sounded downright elated.

"Well, I'm glad you're enjoying yourself… I hear things got a little hairy over there."

"*I mean, I wasn't there for most of it, but Massy did go on a bit of a* rampage. I think he was just happy to be back on the grind, like me. But hey, it's thanks to that we got all those supplies, right?"

"True… Although, I have to say, I wasn't expecting him to buy a slave."

"*Oh, you know about Roo?*"

"Yeah, Merchant sent me a picture."

"*I hear she cost him a pretty penny.*"

"That's Merchant for you. He's good at making money, but he spends it like there's no tomorrow. When it's something he really wants, that is."

"*Oh yeah, he totes has the hots for her. He can't get enough of her smooth brown kiddie skin…*"

"Try not to tease him too much. *He knows the right way to spend money. That's one of his great virtues.*"

"*Yeah, yeah, I know. C'mon, it's not like I'm totally tone-deaf over here.*"

Shinobu roared with laughter, to which Tsukasa replied, "As long as we're on the same page," before broaching the main topic.

"Now then, I'd say that's about enough catching up. Your battery's not going to last forever, after all. Let's hear what you've learned."

"*Wow, now who's the buzzkill? After all the long, cold nights I've had to spend alone over here, the least you can do is entertain me a little. Boooo.*" For all her complaints, though, Shinobu did finally start giving her report.

"*There's actually too much info to go through at once, so I'll write up all the stuff I learned about this country and its history and send that over to you later. For now, here's the TL;DR: First, as far as magic goes, I got a veteran to tell me a bit. Basically, it works about how you'd expect. This world has four types of elemental spirits—fire, water, earth, and air—and by communing with them, you can do stuff like throw fireballs and call down bolts of lightning.*"

"That sounds pretty useful, especially considering how undeveloped this world is."

"Yup. That's why anyone who can use it is respected, no matter where they come from. Now, that said, they're super-rare. Most of them live in the capital. The only one around these parts is the First-Class Mage at the lord's castle."

"First-Class?"

"Ah, sorry, sorry. First-Class Mages are the ones who serve the empire. There are also Second-Class Mages and Prime Mages. Second-Class Mages are basically like students, so they're all at the magic academy in the capital. First-Class Mages are Second-Class Mages who've graduated. It's kinda like the difference between trainees and full-time employees. Then, out of all mages in the empire, the cream of the crop get the title of Prime Mage. I've heard it goes even higher than that, though. Rumor has it that there are people who can cause natural disasters all on their own."

"Is there any kind of magic that allows the user to traverse worlds or summon someone from another world?"

"Mmm, I haven't heard of anything like that yet. Magic's rare to begin with, so info's pretty scarce. I figured the First-Class Mage in the lord's castle might know more, so I'm planning on getting in contact with him next."

"Got it. Well, even just learning that our assumptions about magic are largely on the mark is more than I could have hoped for from a one-week investigation. Thank you."

Shinobu replied with a singsong "Sha-sha. ♪ No problemo."

"…Now, as far as the Seven Heroes thing goes, I did get one big piece of info, but…long story short, I kinda hit a wall."

"How so?"

"Well, for starters…it might be related to this old, dead religion called the Seven Luminaries…but that's all I got so far. See, a couple *hundred years ago, the Freyjagard Empire wiped them out. Freyjagard operates under the law of survival of the fittest, with the feudal emperor at the top of the food chain...and the emperor didn't take too kindly to having a religion that placed God above him. It wasn't just the Seven Luminaries, either. He took every religion on the continent, burned their holy books, tore down their churches, brutally killed their followers, and ripped them up by their roots without leaving a speck behind."*

"...Religious persecution, huh." Hearing Shinobu's report set a flame of ugly hatred burning in Tsukasa's chest.

This entire country was messed up. A nation and its laws should exist to protect the people who live in it. But here, the masses were being violently oppressed to support a small privileged class. That... could hardly be called just.

Shinobu was just the messenger, though. There was no point shooting her. Tsukasa suppressed the fury in his chest and continued listening.

"I tried checking out the villages near Dormundt, too, but...there weren't any records or texts anywhere. I'm good, but even I can't find something that isn't there."

"...Hmm."

Shinobu's investigative abilities were far beyond those of the rest of the High School Prodigies. If she couldn't find something, odds were slim that any of the rest of them could, either. Even so, though—

"It's clear there aren't any leads around the village. But still, the roots faith leaves in people's hearts run deep. Violence can tear up the surface, but those roots will still be there. Any religious teachings that reached across an entire continent should have left footprints somewhere, even centuries later."

Winona's husband had probably stumbled across one such set of footprints. And if he could—

"Right now, the legend of the Seven Heroes is the one lead we have in our search for a way back to Earth... We need to follow up on it, even if it means scouring the entire continent. We need to find what's left of the Seven Luminaries."

Shinobu seemed to share his opinion, as she immediately agreed. *"...You're right. It's the only clue we've got, after all."* However, her voice quickly took on a shade of unconcealed irritation.

"...But there's one big problem there."

"There is?"

"Yeah, it's a doozy. See, what we're in right now is northern Freyjagard. That's comprised of four domains, and Marquis Findolph's domain, the one we're in, is at the northernmost point of the whole continent... But in order to leave it, they say you need the lord to give you a travel pass."

"Yeah, that's pretty standard for a civilization like this."

"Uh-huh. From what I've heard, though, this Marquis Findolph guy is a scumbag of epic proportions—"

At around the same time as Tsukasa and Shinobu's conversation, a shrill male screech echoed through Marquis Findolph's castle.

"Youuu little whore!!!!" A corpulent, middle-aged man wrung a naked woman's thin neck atop an opulent bed, his face red with rage.

"Ack, gah! P-please..."

"How dare you, how dare you, how dare you! How dare you try to deceive me! This is unforgivable! Utterly unforgivable!"

His pudgy arm could hardly be considered strong, but it was still too much for the slender woman to shake off.

"...H-help..."

Then, all of a sudden, the woman stopped clawing at the man's arm. She went limp. The light faded from her teary eyes as drool dripped from the corners of her gaping mouth. When a drop fell on the hand clutching her throat, Marquis Findolph grimaced in disgust.

"Gyeh! How foul!"

He heaved the woman's corpse aside, then grabbed the bell from beside his pillow.

"Inzaghi! Inzaghi, get in here!" he shouted, summoning his captain of the guard.

The man in question quickly opened the bedroom door and responded to the call. He was a *hyuma* with long hair, silver armor, and a gloomy countenance. The accessories on his ears and fingers were of a similar make to his armor, and he had a sly look about him. His name was Inzaghi, and he held the title of Silver Knight.

After bowing respectfully to his lord, he asked what was wrong.

"You called for me, my lord?"

"Inzaghi, clean up that trash at once!" Marquis Findolph pointed at the woman's corpse, which had rolled off the bed to slump on the floor.

"Oh my. Did the girl do something to offend you?"

"Why, I should think so! That whore wasn't a virgin! She even cut herself down there to try to trick me with a bit of blood! Not only did she rob me of my First Night Right, she plotted to deceive a noble! Do you think I ought to show mercy to this tart, Inzaghi?!"

Inzaghi shook his head almost exaggeratedly.

"Absolutely not, my lord. *All common women of Findolph must give their virginities to its lord.* Such is the law of this land. And when someone violates that law, they forfeit their right to live here. That is how justice is kept."

"Well put. Well put, Inzaghi. You know what to do, then, I hope?"

"Indeed. I shall track down this girl's family and any man she had relations with and have them executed." After giving his answer, though, Inzaghi found he still had a bit more to say. "...But if I may be so bold, my lord, I fear that punishing the transgressor after the fact does little to solve the underlying problem."

"What do you mean by that?"

"You may be being too gentle with these commoners, your lordship. While lenience is a virtue among rulers, your subjects are quick to take advantage of it. Commoners are like wild dogs roaming the fields. Without proper discipline, they'll never learn their place... My lord, might I suggest that we hold a little ceremony to teach these uneducated commoners exactly whose property they are and what Freyjagard's absolute law is?"

Marquis Findolph contemplated the suggestion for a moment.

"...Hmm. True... You're right, Inzaghi, quite right." His gold teeth glimmered as a barbaric smile crossed his face.

"It's high time these people know who owns them."

Inzaghi smiled internally at his lord's response, thinking how easily manipulated the man was. However, the Silver Knight was careful not to let any of his scorn leak out as he guided the marquis in the direction he wanted.

"If I might make a suggestion, your lordship, I heard tell of a village of greedy peasants who've recently amassed wealth beyond their status—"

It was a moment that marked the beginning of the next great trial the High School Prodigies would have to face.

CHAPTER 3

⚜ Public Bathhouse and Sudden Panic ⚜

It had been about two months now since the High School Prodigies found themselves in their new world. The freshly fallen snow crunched under Tsukasa's feet as he headed to visit Ringo. Suddenly, he heard something.

"Hyah!"

A rousing shout, loud enough to reach the very heavens. Turning to face its source, he saw Aoi Ichijou standing between the village and the woods. With each swing of her trusty katana, another massive tree fell. Tsukasa reflexively found himself applauding the nigh-inhuman feat.

"I see those thick trees are no match for your skills, Aoi."

"Tsukasa, m'lord… Mmm…" The girl turned around upon hearing Tsukasa's praise, only to immediately scrunch up her face.

"Waaaaaaah!" Tears began gushing from her eyes like waterfalls. "I would prefer you did not say such things! I—I… I am nothing but a useless good-for-nothing who gets in everyone's way, that I aaaaam!"

…She's still hung up on that?

She was crying like a baby. As for the reason…it was because Mayor Ulgar had kicked her out of the hunting group. It wasn't because she was a woman. Rather, it was because she was *too* strong. Her mere existence gave off a powerful kind of aura. Animals sensed it and would flee before the hunters could even find them.

In the end, the hunts with Aoi present had gone so poorly that the mayor had no choice but to relegate her to woodcutting duty. The hunt had gone back to normal in her absence, but Aoi herself had spent the past few weeks fretting over the trouble she'd caused.

"Waaaah! The Ichijou Rishin style even teaches us to wield our swords to protect the weak, that it does… I am beside myself over my own ineptitude!"

"It was my decision to have you join the hunt, Aoi. I'm the one who misjudged your skill set. You have nothing to be ashamed of."

"…Rgh. This is the same as saying I am of no use to this village, though. I am but a base fool, good for nothing but cutting people down… I cannot cook. I am unskilled at commerce. I lack the *wit* to entertain the children. Woodcutting is all I can do for those who saved my life, that it is…"

The girl insisted she wanted to be of true help, to be useful. She sobbed as she slumped over, dejected.

At this rate, she's liable to lose focus and get herself hurt.

That was no good. Tsukasa stepped toward Aoi and placed a hand on her shoulder.

"Don't abase yourself like that, Aoi."

"Tsukasa, m'lord…?"

"I've heard that the winters here get downright frigid. And the snow's already started piling up. Firewood is the lifeblood of anyone who lives in places like this. There's no such thing as having too much."

"…So you are saying that my blade is of use, despite cutting neither beast nor foe?"

"Absolutely. Remember breakfast this morning? We cooked that with the wood you cut and charcoal made from it. The only reason we're able to have warm meals is because you're chopping down trees out here. Your katana is doing plenty of protecting as it is, both of the village and of us. Take pride in that." Tsukasa wasn't patronizing her just for the sake of it. Everything he'd said had been true.

The boy gazed straight into her wet eyes, his voice firm and reassuring. Hearing it seemed to bolster Aoi's spirits a bit.

"I am in your debt. Thanks to you, I feel a good deal better."

"I'm glad to hear it. Now, those trees aren't going to chop themselves. And like I said, there's no such thing as too much firewood."

"Understood. Hyah!"

Aoi still wasn't at 100 percent, but the look in her eyes had recovered some of its focus and vigor. At least now she wasn't likely to hurt herself.

…*Still, that was just a stopgap. I need to think of a good follow-up at some point.*

Deep in thought, Tsukasa turned away from Aoi and continued walking.

—It had been two months since they'd come to this world.

Not just Aoi, but pretty much all of them had settled into their roles in the village. Tsukasa's cooking skills hadn't gone anywhere, so neither had he.

Akatsuki was still beloved by the children, so he was still on babysitting duty. Keine was good with her hands, so she was helping out with the sewing.

Masato had been back in the village for the last two days, but he generally spent most of his time over in the city, wheeling and dealing for the company to further support the village finances. And as for the new member of the village the Devil of Finance had picked up, she was over at Lyrule's house, busying herself with learning to read and write. Everything was going smoothly. The peaceful days were passing gently by.

In fact, things are far less stressful here than they were back on Earth...

Back there, he'd had to restore his country's failing economy while constantly fending off assassins. Tsukasa was certainly getting more sleep in this world. To him, the days he was spending in the village were downright blissful. If he wasn't careful, he might've soon found himself not wanting to leave.

...This is bad. I have to get back to Earth—and sooner rather than later.

They all had responsibilities back there.

Tsukasa quickened his pace as he made for Ringo's base. He needed to talk to her about how they were going to find a way home.

There was a river on the outskirts of the village that folks used for bathing and washing clothes. Beside it, there was an ancient ruin built into the side of the mountain. It very nearly resembled a temple. However, there were two things by its entrance that were decidedly un-templelike.

Specifically, a pair of signs: One read ELM VILLAGE NUCLEAR POWER PLANT and the other had the universal symbol for radiation on it. Yes, Ringo Oohoshi—the genius inventor—had turned the masterless ruins into a power plant *slash* laboratory.

After slipping past the entrance's now-spoiled view and continuing on through the ruins for a while, Tsukasa eventually came to a large dome-shaped hall. Originally, it had probably been used for some sort of ritual. Now, the entire hall was lit with electric lights, and there was a throng of towering machines grouped in its center. Pipes and wires snaked all along the walls and floor. The machines themselves were made from a hodgepodge of organic and inorganic materials—stone, wood, iron, and the like—giving them the countenance of a certain moving castle from an anime movie Tsukasa had seen in the theater when he was a child.

At first, there had only been the pocket nuclear fission reactor—the one that had survived the crash. But Ringo had added countless new machines since then. Things like a blast furnace and a reduction pot for making aluminum, which explained the current state of the hall.

All the machines were chugging away. The cavern was filled with the sounds of ventilators pumping out air and steam blasting from pipes.

It's been some time since I last heard the sounds of civilization.

Back on Earth, it would've just been a racket, but now the chorus of machinery sounded like home. As he basked in the nostalgia, Tsukasa searched for the room's master. It didn't take him long to find her.

The girl in question, Ringo Oohoshi, was in the middle of doing some welding at the base of the cluster of machines.

"………"

Wearing the goggles that were usually perched atop her hat, she traced the two sheets she was joining with her oversized gloves. The fingertips of the gloves glowed red-hot as she did, their heat melting the metals together.

The gloves she was using were one of her inventions, the All-Purpose Gloves. Once connected to a power source, they could serve as basic tools like pliers and hammers while also being able to weld, cut, and cleave. One pair of gloves allowed their user to perform almost any type of simple industrial work without having to constantly swap out tools, making them indispensable to any sort of craftsman. They were incredibly convenient and efficient, and their creation was estimated to have increased worldwide productivity by 20 percent. Some people referred to them as the invention of the century.

Currently, it appeared that Ringo was using them to remodel a machine.

Tsukasa chose not to call out to her. He didn't want to interrupt her work. But just as he was thinking of leaving and coming back later, a mechanical voice piped up behind him.

"Why, I can bearly believe it! It's Tsukasa!"

The boy prime minister spun around and saw Ringo's massive backpack using its manipulator arms to walk around on its own like a spider. After it scuttled over to him, its top popped open.

"I haven't seen you since the crash! It's been a bear's age!"

Then a monitor displaying a cartoon character that looked kind of like a bear crossed with a rabbit emerged and greeted him.

Tsukasa knew the character well.

Ringo was bad at conversing with others, so she'd developed an AI to talk to people in her place. Its name was Bearabbit, and it had also been in charge of piloting the Prodigies' plane.

"Did you have something you wanted to tail Ringo?"

"Yeah, but she looks busy. I'll just come back later."

"Oh, don't worry about it! She'll be pawsitively elated when she finds out you've come! Ringo, Tsukasa's here to see you!"

"Huh?! Tsu-Tsukasa…?!" Hearing Bearabbit call her name, Ringo looked up like she'd just been flicked on the head.

"Good morning…er, evening? I think?"

"Good afternoon, Ringo."

"Oh!"

The hall was artificially illuminated both night and day. Apparently, she'd been cooped up in there so long she'd forgotten what time it was. When Tsukasa corrected her, the girl's pale cheeks went as red as an apple.

"Hard work is good and all, but you should try to get some actual sunlight every now and again. No good will come of you ruining your health."

"O…kay. I'll be careful…"

"Please do." Tsukasa walked over to Ringo's side and gazed up at the machines she'd built. "I have to admit, this is all really impressive. It seems like they get bigger each time I visit."

"We have Masato to thank fur getting all the materials!"

"That's right… Masato…is amazing."

"When it comes to making money, he's the best in the business. What are you working on right now?"

"Oh, um, this newborn over here just came together. Come look!" Ringo let out a happy exclamation, seemingly pleased that Tsukasa had taken an interest in her work. She hopped over to a laptop connected via a wire to a large machine and punched in a few lines.

When she did, the machine thundered into motion. After a short delay, it spat out something hard that clanged noisily as it emerged from something resembling a rubbish chute on the machine's lower half. Upon inspection, the "something" was actually ten-odd silvery shovels.

"Are those…aluminum shovels?"

"This little one can take any material, then process it according to the design I put in."

"I can already make pretty much anything myself, but for mass production, a piece of equipment like this is beary handy."

Tsukasa found himself unable to conceal his surprise at Ringo's accomplishment.

"That's amazing. I had no idea you were already able to manufacture aluminum."

"Eh-heh-heh…" Hearing Tsukasa's admiration for her work made Ringo rock her body like she had an itch. However, she seemed happy.

"We're pawsitively surrounded by raw materials, and we're able to refine the sodium hydroxide we need for the reduction pot from salt. As long as we've got electricity, bruin up aluminum is a piece of cake."

"Oh, so that's why you asked Merchant for so much salt. That's what you were using it for. It all makes sense now."

"Yup... Now I can finally be useful to the village." Ringo picked up one of the shovels, then turned back to Tsukasa. "Will they...be happy with this, do you think?"

Ringo seemed unsure of herself, so Tsukasa nodded vigorously.

"They'll be thrilled, I'm certain of it. Up until now, the shovels they've been using have been barely better than wooden spatulas. Digging up the hard ground around here with them was a nightmare and a half. Light, sturdy shovels like these will make the farm work far easier."

"Eh-heh-heh... I'm glad... Ah..." Tsukasa's praise seemed to have drained her tension; she let out a cute little yawn.

"I-I'm so sorry! We were in the middle of talking, and I...!" Ringo frantically apologized, but Tsukasa told her not to worry about it.

"You look exhausted. Maybe you should call it a day."

"Oh...but you came because...you needed something, right?"

"While that's true...it's going to be a big job. We can't have you pushing yourself and passing out. For now, just rest up. That way, you'll be able to give the next assignment your best."

"...In that case, I think...I'll take you...up on that..." Having seemingly reached her limit—unable to stay awake any longer—the girl tottered over to the pelt at the back of the cavern and rolled herself up in it.

"You're going to sleep here? Shouldn't you turn off the machines first, at least?"

"I can't... If I stop the coolant pumps all of a sudden, the machines will break."

"Isn't it loud, though?"

"No…it's nice. This way, I can hear all the voices of my children."

"…I see."

To Tsukasa, it was just noise, but apparently, she heard it differently. Her expression had a certain kind of pride to it.

"It seems my question was rather boorish. Rest easy, now."

"…Mmm. G'night …"

As soon as their conversation finished, Tsukasa could hear Ringo breathing softly in her sleep. She must have been dead tired.

I definitely need to make sure she doesn't push herself any more than this.

Originally, he'd come because there was something he wanted her to build.

Namely—an airplane.

Given the info he'd gotten from Shinobu the other day, there appeared to be no easy way for them to pass through the checkpoints marking the edge of the domain. Travel over land wasn't a viable option. And the ports had the same checkpoints, so the sea was no better. In other words, there was only one route left: the sky.

However, if he so much as mentioned that to Ringo, she would undoubtedly ignore her fatigue and immediately turn her considerable intellect toward drawing up blueprints. And that could only end poorly.

Things aren't so urgent that we need to drive her into the ground just yet.

Ringo's scientific prowess was abnormal—even for Earth, which was centuries ahead of this world to begin with. Her skills were without question the greatest weapon in their arsenal. Right now, he needed to make sure she rested and recovered her stamina.

"What's up? If it's something time sensitive, I might be koalafied to help."

"No, it's nothing that urgent. I'll just try another time."

"In that case, I'll come with you. I want to let her hibernate peacefully for now, so I thought I'd go recharge in the sun until she wakes up."

"That sounds like an excellent plan."

Tsukasa and Bearabbit headed down the path leading outside.

"...I'm beary sorry." Bearabbit sprung a sudden apology on the boy, midway through their walk.

"I can't say I recall you having anything to apologize for. What's this about?"

"It's my fault the plane crashed... If I'd kept my bearings, we wouldn't have ended up having to live in this inconvenient new world." The AI appeared to feel responsible for their current situation. However, Tsukasa immediately refuted his claims of guilt.

"Not at all. For one thing, traveling to another world can only occur via a supernatural phenomenon. Losing control of the plane wasn't your fault. Either some unfathomable power is at work here... or we're the victims of a coincidence of cosmic proportions. One way or the other, there's nothing for you to feel guilty about. Nobody could possibly blame you for that."

"That's beary sweet of you to say..." Bearabbit's response to Tsukasa's reassurances was decidedly vague. The mere fact that he'd been the one piloting the plane still clearly weighed heavily on the AI. It was something he was going to have to come to terms with on his own, but...

Still...he wasn't wrong about how inconvenient this was.

Tsukasa thought back to the way Ringo had passed out like a light. And it wasn't just her, either. He could tell that fatigue was eating away at all of them.

It was only natural. Back on Earth, they could get potable water at the turn of a faucet and fire at the turn of a knob. They could eat whatever foods they wanted, no matter the season, and seasonings were varied and plentiful. But now they'd been set adrift in a world where they had to sweat and bleed just for a single grain of pepper. And to make matters worse, they had no idea how to get back.

The exhaustion was eroding their bodies and minds. Recently, they'd even had to start worrying about the temperature. They'd all come from Japan, a subtropical climate, so Elm's harsh winters were especially brutal on them. Each bath they took in the frigid river felt tantamount to punishment. Even Tsukasa himself had started feeling like his feet were made of lead.

...I wish there was something I could do about it.

Futile thoughts swirled around his head as he made his way out of the ruins.

"Well, Bearabbit, I'm heading back to the village, so— Hmm?" Suddenly, he noticed something peculiar. White fumes were rising from the woods out back.

"Is something on fire?"

If so, that could be real trouble. However, Bearabbit quickly put his worries to rest.

"Oh, nothing to fur. That's just steam."

"Steam? But why?"

"A lot of our machines get unbearably hot, so we draw water from the river to cool them down. The steam is coming from the used coolant."

"So that's industrial wastewater?"

"Oh, it's not nearly dirty enough to koalafy as industrial waste. All that drains there is water we used as coolant. The only thing wrong with it is that it's pawsitively boiling, so we can't pour it back in the river immediately."

"Where's the *actual* waste, then?"

"We're keeping all the contaminated water and bauxite tailings in tanks for now. It's not like we're mass-producing, so the amount is still bearable. We can't exactly dump it here, though."

"True. You'll have to ask Merchant to take it out to sea for you."

But that aside, boiling water...

Tsukasa gazed up at the pillar of steam as the gears in his mind began turning.

It's not something we strictly need, but it certainly isn't useless. Also...given the state those two are in, the timing works out nicely.

After considering every aspect, every pro and con, Tsukasa made his choice.

"If you're not busy, Bearabbit, would you mind lending me a hand?"

"With what?"

"I am a politician, so I thought I'd act the part and organize a public works project." Tsukasa drew his phone as he spoke and dialed Aoi Ichijou.

A little while later, Aoi came running over to the meeting spot—the point on the river's edge where the people of Elm bathed.

"I apologize for keeping you waiting, Tsukasa, m'lord. What is this request you would make of me?"

"I was thinking of building a public bathhouse here, and I was hoping you'd help."

"A—a public bathhouse?!"

"That's right. It's gotten cold recently, hasn't it? The people from this village may be acclimated to it, but the weather we're used to is much warmer. At this rate, some of us might even fall ill. I want to make sure that doesn't happen. And the people of Elm will probably be just as excited at the prospect of a nice, warm bath. Think of it. Remember the last time you had a hot bath on a freezing winter night? Remember how nice that felt?"

"Oh, I do…"

The memory brought a warm glow to her face. Her body was practically shaking as she grabbed Tsukasa's hands.

"You have my wholehearted support! Whatever you need, I shall gladly assist! I am certain that the people of Elm will be thrilled, too, that they will!"

"I'm glad to hear you say that. There'll probably be a lot of manual labor, so it's good to have you along."

No sooner had Tsukasa finished securing Aoi's assistance than—

"I'm back!"

Having finished the assignment Tsukasa gave him, Bearabbit returned.

"And I come bearing shovels!"

"Good work."

Bearabbit handed Tsukasa the aluminum shovels he was carrying in his manipulator arms. Tsukasa made sure to thank the AI, then inquired about the matter he'd asked Bearabbit to check on.

"So do we have enough spare materials to make a boiler?"

"We do! Thanks to Masato's hard work, we have an embearassment of riches!"

"Excellent. In that case, I leave manufacturing it to you."

"The task is in good paws!"

Bearabbit was brimming with confidence. Well-warranted confidence, too. His artificial mind had been designed with Ringo's as its base.

As a computer program, he couldn't invent new things on his own, but when it came to devices that already existed, he could produce them to the same degree of quality Ringo could. Building a hot water boiler was child's play to him.

"And where are my talents needed?!"

"Aoi, I need you to bring over enough wood for the roof and the waterways. Then I'll show you how to build them. Twenty trees' worth should do the trick."

"The deed is as good as done!" Aoi's reply was cheerful, and her expression was sunny and full of energy. All she'd wanted was to be helpful, and now she was directly contributing to the village's well-being.

And Bearabbit, who felt indebted to the seven waylaid earthlings, was much the same. It was hard to read his expression, but based on the way his manipulator arms were chugging away, his spirits seemed to have picked up a bit.

Seeing the two of them in such high spirits secretly filled Tsukasa with relief.

While increasing the village's quality of life and protecting the Prodigies' health had certainly been one of the reasons he'd decided to build the bathhouse, he'd also hoped to use its construction as a form of therapy for Aoi and Bearabbit.

The idea was that having tangible proof of their contribution to the group would help alleviate some of their guilt. Based on their expressions, it looked like he'd succeeded on that front.

"You two can go ahead and get started. Oh, and if you have official work you need to do, make sure you prioritize that. We're in no hurry to get this built. We should plan on finishing it gradually over the next couple days."

Now all they needed to do was take it easy and make sure they didn't push themselves. Or so Tsukasa thought.

"Nonsense! It shall be done before nightfall, that it shall!"

"Fur sure! This isn't a job that'll take multiple days! Half a day is plenty; I bearantee it!"

"………"

The other two were getting even more into it than Tsukasa had anticipated. It was possible his plan had worked *too* well. A pang of unease flitted through his mind.

However, as the one who'd suggested the idea in the first place, it wouldn't do for him to dampen their enthusiasm.

"…Sounds like a plan. I'm looking forward to that hot bath, after all. I'll be sure to do my best as well."

Aoi's physical abilities were downright superhuman, and it had taken a superhuman intellect to design Bearabbit and his manipulators. The prospect of having to make sure he didn't slow the two of them down made Tsukasa's head spin, but he was careful not to let it show on his face.

Then, after a few hours of work—

The three of them actually managed to finish the bathhouse before the sun went down.

In the end, Aoi brought five people to the completed bathhouse. Keine Kanzaki and Winona, who'd happened to have been free, were first. Lyrule and Roo, having just finished their spelling lesson, were next. The last of the group was Ringo, who Bearabbit had gone and woken up.

All of them gathered under the structure's triangular, anti-snow roof. Upon seeing the steam rise from the tub Aoi had dug out of the riverbank, they all let out cries of joy.

"Wow! It's so toasty and smoky!" exclaimed Roo.

"Oh my. Now this is a pleasant surprise," remarked Keine.

"Tsukasa…did you all make this?" asked Lyrule.

"That we did. Aoi, Bearabbit, and I."

"Gosh, you kids really are amazing. Is there anything you *can't* do?"

"Right? This is incredible! I never knew you could make your own hot springs…"

Lyrule and Winona, in particular, seemed impressed.

In their eyes, hot springs were a gift from nature.

However, while they'd likely heard rumors about places where hot water bubbled up from the ground, they'd never even considered the possibility of making one themselves.

"Oh? What's that little shed over there?" asked Winona.

"That's the boiler hut. It's where we heat the water befur we send it over here."

"Oh, I see. So it's like a big pot."

"They're furly similar. I'll show you all how to use it later."

"Incidentally," added Aoi, "you cool the water using this channel from the river. When that is no longer necessary, all you need to do is divert the flow."

"Wow. You all really thought of everything."

Evidently pleased at how happy everyone was, Aoi and Bearabbit continued their explanation. However, no description was going to be better than experiencing it firsthand. Tsukasa turned to them and offered a suggestion.

"You know, they say experience is the best teacher. There's still some time before dinner, so why don't you all try it out? You seem excited, and the water's already heated. Besides, Aoi, I'm sure you worked up a fair sweat."

"That I did!"

"Roo wants to try, too!"

"I'm embearassed to say that I'll rust if I try to join you, but I could certainly go for a little back scrub."

"Once you're finished, you should let me know if you have any modifications you'd like us to make. I hope to make this the best bathhouse it can be." Not wanting to keep them waiting now that they'd decided to take their bath, Tsukasa turned to leave. As he did, though, Aoi said something outrageous.

"Hmm? Are you not joining us, Tsukasa, m'lord?"

"What?!" "Hweh?!?!"

Alarmed expressions immediately crossed Ringo's and Lyrule's faces. It was a natural response. The question had been downright absurd.

"…If anything, I'm curious as to why you assumed I would."

"It was your idea to build this bathhouse, was it not? It would be wrong to exclude the man who worked the hardest from its inaugural bath."

"That's right! Labor begets re-mooneration! That's what Teacher said!"

"I have no objections to mixed bathing. I'm certainly used to seeing naked bodies."

Roo and Keine piled on as well. The situation was taking a turn for the worse.

Roo was just being a kid, but Keine was probably doing it on purpose. Ringo and Lyrule were both as red as lobsters and sweating bullets, and Keine was watching them with clear amusement.

However, Tsukasa had no intention of playing along with her game.

"While I'll admit that I was the first to come up with the idea, Aoi and Bearabbit both put in far more work than I did. I'll just take my bath with the other men when they get back, so don't worry about me. I'll see you all later—"

He tried to end the conversation unilaterally and stride off. In his haste to leave, though, he made one big mistake.

He casually waved them good-bye.

"…Ah!"

The moment he did, Lyrule keenly noticed what he'd been hiding and quickly grabbed his hand.

"Tsukasa, your hand...!"

...Oh, now I've done it.

Lyrule's action finally forced Tsukasa to acknowledge how stupid he'd been. In order to keep up with the pace Aoi and Bearabbit were maintaining, he'd pushed himself a good deal too hard. Not only had he blistered his palms, he'd broken the blisters, too.

And now Lyrule knew.

"Oh my. Those certainly look painful."

"I just broke the skin because I wasn't used to the work. It's nothing serious."

"B-but..."

Even though he claimed it wasn't serious, that didn't change the fact that his palms looked like shredded rawhide. It certainly was no surprise that Lyrule's and Ringo's faces clouded over when they saw them. However, that wasn't what Tsukasa wanted at all.

Those weren't the kinds of expressions he'd worked so hard to inspire. Aoi and Bearabbit were probably no different. He racked his brain. How could he lighten the mood? He was still in the middle of thinking, when all of a sudden—

"All right, all right, all right! Cheer up, Lyrule!"

"Yeeeep?!"

Without Tsukasa having to do anything, Winona blew away the heavy pall by reaching out and grabbing Lyrule's ample breasts.

"Why're your boobs the only things that ever get bigger, huh?! You little pip-squeak, you!"

"Winona, wh-wh-what are you doing?!" Startled at the abrupt turn of events, Lyrule's face went red.

Winona laughed in exasperation as she told Lyrule off. "If you keep looking guilty like that, how's Tsukasa gonna feel about all the hard work he put in?"

"...Ah..."

That was right. The reason Tsukasa had built the bathhouse in the first place was to make everyone happy. If all he got were depressed looks, how was that going to make him feel? The fact that Winona had picked up on that really carried home the fact that she was their elder, but she didn't stop there. If only she had. However, she only went further.

"But just like Aoi and Roo said, it wouldn't be fair for all of us to go and have fun without the man we have to thank for all this. But don't worry, I have a great idea!" A mischievous grin unbefitting a woman her age spread across Winona's face. Before she even said what her idea was, Tsukasa could already tell that no good would come of it.

"Ah, I see… I have to hand it to you—that was a good idea." Tsukasa took in the view before him as he soaked in the tub. The women were all wearing bikinis made from leaves layered atop one another.

"I never considered making swimsuits out of leaves. Clever thinking, Winona."

"Heh-heh. Wasn't it just? Go on, praise me more!"

"You're right. It's very like you to come up with an idea that straddles the line so narrowly between genius and stupidity. I could never have come up with something like that, and even if I had, I wouldn't have ever considered actually proposing it. You have my respect."

"…Huh? Wait, is that a compliment or an insult?"

Tsukasa averted his gaze, offering no reply. In truth, half of him was impressed, and the other half was thoroughly vexed.

Possibly the most surprising part, though, was the fact that Winona had gotten all the others to go along with her scheme.

"Ah…"

"Heh. It sounds like you're enjoying yourself, Roo," quipped Keine.

"...Back in Roo's country, it was always toasty warm like this."

"Ah, I see. In that case, you should make sure you bundle up in the coming months. Having your environment change so drastically can be hard on your health."

"Mmm..." Roo submerged herself up to the tip of her nose, blowing bubbles as she gave a vague response. Given her expression, they half expected her to just dissolve straight into the water.

Most of the other women were relaxed and enjoying themselves, too. However, although they'd gotten everyone to go along with Winona's plan, one member of the group had been keeping her back bashfully turned to Tsukasa the whole time.

"...Ringo, if it's too embarrassing, there's no need to force yourself to stay." Tsukasa, reading into her behavior, offered her an out.

She still didn't turn around, but she shook her head vigorously.

"I'm...fine..." Her voice came out quiet and thin. With moist eyes, she shot a fleeting glance over her shoulder. However, when her gaze met Tsukasa's, she immediately looked away. The young man could tell what was going on now.

Odds were that it wasn't that she was ashamed of being seen in her swimsuit, it was that she was ashamed of seeing a guy in his. She didn't seem to dislike it, though. She was definitely interested. Internally, her curiosity and bashfulness were warring it out. In other words, she hadn't joined them because she'd caved into peer pressure. It was probably fine to just leave her to her own devices.

"Man, Tsukasa, do you kids really always have hot baths like this in your world?" asked Winona.

"Not everyone prefers to soak their whole body like this, but we generally don't use cold water, no."

"Wow... That must be a lot of work, gathering all that kindling."

"Hmm-hmm," Keine said, laughing. "In our country, we use gas to heat our water, so we don't have to cut down firewood at all."

"Gas?"

"It's a kind of flammable air."

"Oh, Roo knows about that! Roo had that near her village! The burning air is really dangerous, so the mayor told us not to go near it!"

"You probably lived near a deposit of natural gas, then. In our world, we use it as fuel. We cook food with it, heat our baths...pretty much anything you could think of that needs fire. We generally only use firewood when we go out camping," explained Tsukasa.

"Oh."

"The more I hear about your world, the stranger it sounds... But if it means you get to take nice, warm baths like these every day, then color me jealous. Heh..."

"I'm glad it's to your liking."

Smiling softly at how content everyone looked, Tsukasa submerged himself up to his shoulders. He could feel the leaden fatigue inside him slowly melt away.

As he sat, basking in the satisfaction that all those blisters had been worth it, he heard Lyrule call out to him from above.

"Tsukasa, do you mind if I sit here?"

A little while ago, she'd gone back to the village on her own, saying there was something she wanted to go get.

"Of course not. I'm glad you're back. So what was it you—?"

But the moment he turned around, his voice got caught in his throat. The sight of Lyrule carefully dipping herself into the water feet-first so as not to cause any ripples left him speechless.

Her slender ankles and the way her calves gently arced from them. Her round, soft, feminine buttocks—how her waist accentuated them. The slight forward inclination of her posture made her plump breasts (and the leaf bikini that only barely covered them) jiggle with her slightest movement. And finally, the way the water's warmth made her attractive face soften with pleasure.

He couldn't focus on anything else.

...She's so beautiful.

"Oh...this really is nice, isn't it! I can feel my entire body warming up...? Um, is something the matter?"

She was talking to him, but he wasn't responding. How odd. Lyrule focused her lapis lazuli eyes right on Tsukasa. When he finally replied, his voice was as calm and collected as always.

"Ah, forgive me. I simply found myself captivated by your beauty."

"What?! Hwa-wa-wa?!"

Lyrule's face immediately flushed bright red, and she instinctively covered her chest.

"My oh my, how forward." Winona laughed.

"Is there any reason to beat around the bush when praising someone's looks?"

"Mmm! Oh, really now! That's enough flattery, just... Just give me your hand."

"I can't say that was my intention, but what's this about my hand?"

"Just give it here already!"

What exactly was she planning on doing? Tsukasa was confused, but he offered Lyrule his hand anyway.

When he did, she pried it open with one hand and stuck her other in the small, fist-size pot she'd left on the rim of the large bath's basin. Then she scooped up something white and goopy from within the pot and smeared it across Tsukasa's palm.

"What's this?"

"It's an ointment we make from horse fat. It makes the pain go away and speeds up the healing process."

"Oh, thank you for going out of your way to get it. I apologize for the hassle."

©Sacraneco

"Not at all… It's thanks to you all that we have this lovely bath, so it's the least I can do…" Lyrule continued to gently apply the ointment to his hand as she thanked the young prime minister.

The sensation of her dainty, slime-covered fingers crawling across his raw nerve endings sent pins and needles across his whole body. Tsukasa twitched.

"Oh no, did that hurt?"

"No…it just tickled a little."

"If it hurts, make sure you tell me." Lyrule smiled tenderly and resumed the treatment. This time, her touch was even tenderer than before. It still tickled, but the sensation was by no means unpleasant.

It was comforting…and gentle. Ever since he'd destroyed his family, Tsukasa never had anyone care for him like this. He wanted this peaceful time to go on, even for just a second longer…

But then—

"Th-there's been trouble!!!!"

—a shout, along with the sound of frantic footsteps, brought it to an end.

"Akatsuki?"

When Tsukasa turned around, he saw that Akatsuki had come running over from the village. His expression was frantic.

"Tsukasa! Bad news, you have to— Wait, whaaaaaaaaaaaaaaaaat?! Huh?! What kind of joint are you running, exactly?! When did this place get here?!"

"Enough with the nonsense; what's the matter? It must be serious for you to have run all the way over here."

"Y-yeah, that's right! It is! See, what happened—"

Between gasps of breath, Akatsuki elaborated on what had occurred.

"———?!?!"

They all responded with shock. Winona leaped from the tub, her face drained of color. After all, she'd just learned that her family, Elch and Ulgar, along with the hunters they'd been leading, had been attacked by the massive bear known as the Lord of the Woods.

Winona raced back to the village, not even stopping to get dressed. The women and children had already assembled in the village square. The crowd was gathered around Filippo, one of the men who was supposed to be out hunting. He was sitting on the ground, panting.

"Filippo!"

"Whoa! H-hey, Winona, what's with that sexy getup?!"

"Later!"

"Bweh!"

Masato had been treating the cuts Filippo had gotten on his shoulder when he'd dived through the brush, but Winona flung him aside and pressed Filippo for answers.

"Filippo, is it true?! Did you really run into the Lord of the Woods?!"

"Yeah, we did…! Everyone's still fighting it, but once that thing gets going, it's impossible to escape…! Our only option is to take it down…! That's why I— Ah!"

Suddenly, Filippo's gaze shifted to behind Winona's back.

Tsukasa and the others had followed her back to the village, and Filippo called out to one of them in particular—Aoi Ichijou.

"Aoi!"

"Filippo, m'lord! Are you unharmed?!"

"I'm fine. But the others are in danger. This is no time to be chatting! We need your help! You're the only one in the village who can take on that monster!"

The Lord of the Woods was a vengeful creature. Once it picked a fight with someone, it would follow them to the ends of the earth. If the hunters tried to flee, they'd end up leading it right to the village. And they couldn't let that happen.

So instead, most of them had stayed behind as decoys while Filippo ran back to get Aoi. She was the only person they knew who stood a chance against that sixteen-foot-tall behemoth of a bear.

Aoi instantly agreed to the request.

"My blade is yours! Just lead the way!"

"Of course! I—?!"

But the moment he tried to stand, the man immediately collapsed to the ground.

"Filippo, m'lord?"

"Th-this is nothing. Just give me a second, and—"

"That's quite enough."

The second time he tried to get up, Keine pressed down on the back of his neck.

She was probably squeezing some pressure point needed to move. Even with just a woman's strength, she was able to completely immobilize him.

"Bwuh?! Wh-what are you doing?!"

"No moving, doctor's orders. Your ankle is clearly sprained. Trying to run on it would be an exercise in futility."

"I just twisted it a bit, is all! It'll heal on its own in a min— Mmph?!"

"No, it will not. You've suffered a grade-two sprain to your lateral ligament, as well as a complete grade-three tear of your calcaneofibular ligament… Given how serious they are, it's a wonder you made it all the way back here. Now, do as your doctor says and get some rest."

Filippo had kept thrashing despite her warning, so she covered his mouth with a handkerchief.

"Nnn............"

A moment later, Filippo fainted, his body going limp.

"You anesthetized him?"

"As long as he was conscious, he would've crawled there on his hands and knees."

"But how're we supposed to find them with this guy out cold?" asked Masato.

Tsukasa had an idea. "About that... Ringo?"

"Hweh?!" Ringo clearly hadn't been expected to get called on. She jumped a little as she turned toward Tsukasa.

"Aoi and I are going to go save the mayor and the others. I want you to come along, find where they are with your goggles' infrared thermography, and lead us there. Can you do that for me?"

Now Ringo understood why he'd asked. Her goggles had so many features that they required knowledge and experience to use. There was no time for her to teach someone else. It was a job only she could do. Knowing that, she nodded. She said nothing, but the nod itself was firm.

"In that case, I will bear Ringo upon my back!"

"I'll accompany you, too. There are sure to be people injured over there," Keine added.

"Yeah, please do."

"Prince and I will stay here. I figure we'd just slow you guys down."

"Y-yeah, what he said! It's for the best, I'm sure! I'd love to rush off all gallant-like with you, but I'm way better with indoors-type stuff!"

Masato's statement earned Akatsuki's vigorous endorsement. Tsukasa hadn't had any real plans to bring the two of them along anyway, so he offered no objections. He quietly nodded his assent, then turned to leave with the others.

Before he could go, though, Winona grabbed the hem of his suit.

"...The menfolk of this village are counting on you...!"

"I know. —Let's go!"

As she watched the five of them disappear into the forest, Lyrule said a quiet prayer.

"Everyone, please... Be safe..."

"Hey, Aoi and Keine are on the case. There's no way either of 'em will let anything bad happen. You don't need to look so worried."

Masato placed a hand on her trembling shoulder to cheer her up. Hearing the confidence that bordered on certainty in his voice eased Lyrule's expression.

"...You're right. I should just believe in them."

"Damn straight. For now, though, we should do what we can on our end. First off, we gotta treat this guy. Can't exactly leave him napping out here all day, can we?"

"Bring him around to our place for now. I'll get a bed ready," said Winona.

"I can do that, so please get some clothes on...! Look, here!"

"Oh, you brought 'em for me. Good thinking, Lyrule."

Lyrule handed Winona back her cast-off clothes.

It's now or never; I gotta burn this sight into my eyes...!

As Masato carried Filippo away, he turned his gaze toward Winona in her immodest state of undress. However, Akatsuki slipped right into his line of sight.

"Yo, Prince, get outa the way. You're making me miss the most important moment of my life."

However, Akatsuki paid his objections no heed. His expression grew serious.

"Masato...do you hear that?"

"Hear what?"

Now that Akatsuki pointed it out, though, Masato definitely heard something. His hearing was far superior to most people's, after all.

…What is that? An earthquake? No, I hear metal on metal…and a whole bunch of feet walking. But why—?

Still unsure what was going on, Masato turned to face the direction the sound was coming from, the village entrance.

Then he spotted it.

There was a long mountain path that extended from the village and through the trees. Five soldiers in light armor had just rounded one of the bends in the path.

"Soldiers? What is this, a patrol like last time?" Akatsuki, who'd been present for their last run-in with soldiers, wondered if the same thing might be happening again.

However, it soon became clear that the situation was far grimmer than the previous encounter with armed men. Coming up behind the first five were another ten soldiers, then a second set of ten, then a third. Some of them were even clad head to toe in formidable bronze armor.

Winona stared in shock.

"Those are no underlings! They're the Lord's Order of Guardian Knights…!"

""""…?!""""

The villagers were all visibly shaken. Why was the Lord's Order of Guardian Knights, the domain's main military force, coming to their village?

A violent shout rocked the startled villagers' ears.

"You haughty peasants are in the presence of the captain of Marquis Findolph's Order of Guardian Knights, Silver Knight Inzaghi! Lower your filthy heads!"

"Lyrule!"

"Hwah—"

Winona reacted to the voice faster than anyone else, immediately forcing Lyrule's head down. The feudal lord who ruled their lands was a massive lecher, so the village had been hiding Lyrule from him.

The other villagers followed Winona's lead and prostrated themselves.

"M-Masato, what do we do…?"

"Just go along with it for now."

Masato and Akatsuki, the two who'd stayed behind, did the same. There was little to be gained from being stubborn. Even so, a foreboding inkling crossed Masato's mind.

…I've got a bad feeling about how this is gonna play out…

There was one thing he knew for sure. In life, misfortune and hardship had a way of crashing down on you at once. And sure enough, his hunch was on the mark.

The soldiers moved aside to create a path, and a carriage pulled by a white horse rolled up in front of Masato and the others. Its door opened, revealing a knight garbed in silver armor and adorned with a cloak of deep blue. This was the man who led the soldiers and Bronze Knights of the Findolph domain's Order of Guardian Knights.

Silver Knight Alessio du Inzaghi.

The villagers were prostrating themselves, and Inzaghi's tall figure allowed him to lord over them all the more. He scoffed.

"Hmph. This is my first visit here, but I see I wasn't missing much. The village reeks of wild beast, and most of its inhabitants are defects."

Defect was a slur for *byuma*, people with animal qualities. Just that one phrase was enough to tell Masato what kind of person the man was.

"And what business do you have that you'd need to come to our reeking village yourself, Sir Captain?" Masato lifted his head, every inch of his body on high alert, posing his question to the man called Inzaghi.

The Silver Knight flashed his yellowed teeth as he smiled.

"What business? Ha-ha. I see, I see. You plan to feign innocence to the bitter end. You think you can trick me? …You commoners are all utter fools. Very well, though. Allow me to make my purpose crystal clear: You all are being charged with the grave crime of treason against the state."

"Wh-what?! What kind of sick joke is that?!" In her surprise, Winona looked up and snapped at him. Inzaghi looked down at her with abject disgust, then continued, satisfied with ignoring her outburst.

"As I'm sure you remember, you used unlawful means to amass gold within your lord's domain. We've already conducted a full investigation."

"Wait, hold on a minute!" Masato couldn't help but stand and protest. "Unlawful? Those charges are false. We earned that money through legitimate trade. We got a license from the mayor and everything. Take a look through our ledgers; it's all there."

Inzaghi laughed down Masato's rebuttal. "I don't need to. Those *scraps of paper* mean *nothing.*"

"…What?!"

"You people are lowly peasants who hunt beasts up in the mountains, yet you had the gall to come down and lay your grubby, mud-ridden hands on gold coins with the Dragon Crest of the Freyjagardian imperial family engraved on them. And in doing so, you have enraged your lord. The very act of laying your filthy peasant paws on the Dragon Crest constitutes an act of treason against the state."

"Wait, those charges are *worse* than false…!"

"False? You push your luck, peasant. As nobles, our words hold more weight than your very existences. You live when we tell you to live, and you die when we tell you to die. That is the law of this land, and that is justice. And in following with that law, His Lordship has decreed that every treasonous upstart in this village shall be burned to death!"

"""""_____?!?!"""""

The cruel, arbitrary verdict made the villagers blanch and tremble. Inzaghi, however, had no intention of listening to them beg for their lives. He raised his voice and gave the order.

"Let the judgment commence! Seize everyone in this village, then confiscate every last coin and scrap of food! Feel free to kill any who resist!"

""""Hraaaaaaaah!!!!"""""

❦ Pride and Resolve ❦

The thin-trunked conifers whizzed past. Tsukasa and the others raced along in Ringo's wake, trampling moss and ferns underfoot.

"Ringo, do we keep bearing straight ahead?!"

"That's right…! It's half a mile more this way! Keep going!"

"Understood! You two, I ask that we pick up the pace!"

Aoi glanced over her shoulder at the suit-clad young man and the young woman in a white gown a few paces behind her.

"Sounds like a plan."

"Not to worry. I can still keep up."

"You two are impressively quick, that you are."

"Politicians and doctors both need their stamina, after all."

"He's quite right."

"In that case, I shall refrain from holding back!"

"Fur speed ahead!"

Aoi and Bearabbit kicked off even harder against the ground and barreled through the forest.

A short while later, they reached a clearing. The conifers that had been so plentiful just moments before were nowhere to be seen.

Did we leave the forest?! Did I take a wrong turn, mayhap?! —No, wait!

That wasn't it. It wasn't that they'd left the forest. The forest just wasn't there anymore. Dozens of trunks lay scattered at their feet. All had been ripped up at the roots. A few scant minutes ago, the forest *had* been there. Now, though, it had been completely blown away. The trees had been mowed down by some sort of insane force.

And the one who held that force—

"Aoi! It's right bear!"

—immediately commanded the attention of all present.

It was just past the wasteland of toppled trees. The ursine monstrosity easily towered sixteen feet tall, its shiny obsidian carapace covered in black hair.

"Wh-what is that thing? It's like a cross between an animal and a mineral... That's pawsitively unheard-of!"

"So it was a monster, after all. I figured there was a chance, given that this world has dragons and beastfolk, but— Ah!"

Then Tsukasa and the others spotted Elch and the rest of the hunters by the creature's feet. Their bows and axes were held at the ready, but they were all covered in wounds.

"Everyone...!"

But before she could finish what she'd wanted to say, Aoi realized something. Elch and the others were being pushed toward the sheer drop of a cliff. Instantly realizing how urgent the situation was—

"HYAAAAAAAAAH!!!!"

Until now, she'd been holding back so the others could keep up, but faced with a truly dire imperative, she let loose her full strength. The force of her kick shattered the mossy boulder she'd been standing on as she charged the Lord of the Woods.

She shot forward like a bullet, barreling through the air without decelerating even for a moment. Her speed was utterly inhuman. Such was the power of the High School Prodigy who'd survived countless battles with nothing but a single katana.

However, the Lord of the Woods was perfectly aberrant in its own right.

"GRAAAAAAAAAAAAAAAAAAAH!!!!" It immediately responded to Aoi's attack to its flank.

After dodging with speed anything its size shouldn't rightly have possessed, it thrust forward with rocklike claws. It was intercepting Aoi's charge with a counterattack.

This creature's fast! But...

Aoi's reaction proved faster.

As the bloodstained claws that looked as though they'd been hewn from stone slashed down at her, Aoi gathered power in her whole body. Despite having no footholds, she performed a midair forward roll on muscle strength alone. Then she slammed the heels of her feet onto the oncoming claw and used the force from her toes to pull herself upright.

"Compared to rifle shots, you appear to be standing stock-still, that you do!"

She dashed straight up the arm of the colossal creature, all the way to its head, and—

"ZEYAAAH!!!!"

—as she passed it, the young woman drew her katana and lopped it clean off the monster's shoulders. Its head flew up into the gray sky, higher than the tips of the tallest trees.

Aoi finished her dash by landing next to Elch and the others behind the Lord of the Woods' body. The headless aberration toppled lifelessly to the ground in time with the swordswoman's own landing.

"Everyone! Are you all right?!"

"Aoi! Thank goodness you came! Filippo must have really pulled through!"

"We're fine. You made it just in the nick of time. But…"

The villager's looks of relief quickly turned grim. Behind them lay a massive pool of blood and guts that had spilled from Mayor Ulgar's shredded stomach. Elch was kneeling beside him, sobbing.

"Grandpa…!"

"Mayor Ulgar…m'lord…"

Then Tsukasa and the others finally caught up.

"Elch!"

"Tsukasa… You came to rescue us…," Elch said through sobs.

"Of course, although Aoi did most of the actual saving… What happened to the mayor?"

"He took an attack from the Lord of the Woods to protect me…! He just stopped breathing…"

"I see. Well, that's a relief."

"…Huh?"

Elch and all the other hunters gawked at Tsukasa's unexpected response. Tsukasa grinned a little as he elaborated.

"If he *only just* stopped breathing, then there shouldn't be a problem. Isn't that right, Keine?"

"But of course," Keine Kanzaki answered in agreement and approached what remained of the mayor without delay. She then knelt beside the body and carefully looked it over.

"Left-side ribs five through ten are lost. Abdominal lacerations… Large intestine is torn. Viscera are exposed from the thoracic diaphragm down, and the patient has lost consciousness due to shock from excessive blood loss. Heart's been stopped for less than three minutes, I presume. Heh-heh-heh. Very good, very good. I should be able to make this work with the tools on hand."

"Wh-what are you—?"

"I'm about to begin operating. Please stay back. You'll only get in the way."

Keine got to work.

As she raised her hands into the air, a number of surgical instruments came flying up from beneath her gown. There was a scalpel, a pair of mosquito forceps, a pair of surgical scissors, a pair of tweezers, some medicine, a syringe, gauze, a roll of bandages, and countless others.

And before the unbelieving eyes of the hunters—

""""Wha—?!?!""""

—she began to juggle them.

And that wasn't all.

Still juggling the surgical instruments, she began performing her surgery on Ulgar. She sewed up his ripped organs, mended his shredded blood vessels, and rejoined his broken bones, all while keeping everything sterilized.

By catching whatever tool she needed next at each given moment and manipulating her fingers as deftly as an acrobat, she was able to mend the mayor's body faster than the eye could follow.

"Wh-what's going on?! His wounds are closing up before our eyes…!"

"W-wow…!"

The villagers were a given, but even the normally silent Ringo let out a gasp of admiration. That was just how utterly miraculous a feat it was.

Back on Earth, Keine Kanzaki was the greatest doctor in the world. It wasn't just her knowledge and technique that had earned her the title, however. It was also the mind-boggling speed at which she worked.

Normally, any sort of major surgery like this would need a whole team to perform. The surgeon would be accompanied by an assistant, an anesthesiologist, a clinical engineer, and a surgical tech to lighten their load.

Even with such an assembled team...Keine's blistering speed would have left them all in the dust. After all, how could anyone keep up with someone who worked faster than the eye could perceive? And it was thanks to that speed and skill that she performed every role of a surgical team herself.

By mentally storing the entire procedure from start to finish in her mind, she was able to juggle all the instruments and anesthesia she would need and swap them out as necessary to maintain her super-human levels of speed and precision.

That was the technique that had allowed her to save the tens of thousands of lives, even on battlefields lacking in medicine, tools, and manpower.

As far as she was concerned, it was more efficient to do everything herself than to have to rely on the sluggish help of others. She could save more people that way. And ever since she'd adopted her technique, not a single patient had died under her knife.

In mere moments—

"Ruptured intestine repaired. Surgery complete. Now injecting liquid oxygen and beginning pulmonary resuscitation."

—she completed her extraordinary work and moved on to the final stage of treatment.

It was unclear when she'd cut the incision in the mayor's chest, but she didn't hesitate for a moment before sticking her hand in it and grabbing his stopped heart directly.

"Eek...!"

Not having expected the grisly act, several people screamed. However, Keine's concentration didn't waver in the slightest. She merely applied pressure to the heart with exacting tempo and control. And as the air-rich blood circulated through Ulgar's body—

"Ah... Ack, gack!"

"G-Grandpa?!"

—he suddenly coughed up a tremendous amount of blood.

Now that his cardio-pulmonary function was restored, his body was excising all the blood that had built up in his lungs. After confirming that, Keine swiftly withdrew her hand and stitched up the incision in the same motion. With the procedure finished, the young doctor snatched all her tools out of the air.

"The operation is complete. He should wake up in two or three days' time. I also took the opportunity to treat the stage-one stomach cancer I found, so he should make it another twenty years with ease."

Sweat had begun pouring from Keine's body the moment she finished the surgery, and it soaked her hair as she smiled at Elch.

The mayor didn't seem to have regained consciousness yet, but his chest had started rising and falling. He was breathing again. Elch and the others thanked Keine profusely for the miracle she'd wrought.

"Ohhh! Thank you so much! We're forever in your debt!"

"You saved our lives; I saved his. Please think nothing of it."

Keine stepped aside from Ulgar so his grandson could come closer, then went back over to Tsukasa.

"Thanks for your hard work," Tsukasa said, offering a brief word of gratitude as he handed her a handkerchief.

"Heh. A job like that hardly qualifies as 'hard.'"

Keine took it, then turned back to the villagers as she wiped away her sweat.

"Now, I can see you all have varying degrees of injuries, so please line up over here in front of me."

"Huff…" Ringo let out a long exhale from her spot atop Bearabbit's back.

"Are you all right, Ringo?"

"…I'm so glad…that everyone's okay…"

"Yeah. Me, too. I'm sure it'll come as a great relief to Lyrule and the others."

After Keine had finished giving first aid to the villagers, they all headed back the way they'd come. They'd expected the women of the village to be waiting for their return with bated breath.

Unfortunately…they had no idea what lay in wait for them.

"Hmm?"

The first to realize that something was amiss…was Aoi.

A distinctive smell tickled at her nose. The smell of something burning. The smell of fire…

She looked up and saw a pillar of black smoke rising up to touch the dull, cloudy sky.

"…Tsukasa, m'lord. Is that smoke…coming from the village?"

When she pointed it out, he and the others took note of it, too. The moment he saw the smoke, Tsukasa was seized by an indescribable sense of foreboding.

"We need to hurry," he said, then double-timed it out of the forest.

When they got to the village, the first thing they saw was the mayor's house engulfed in a scarlet blaze.

"Wh-what's going on?!"

"Why's our house on fire…?!"

At first, they assumed it had been some sort of accident.

However, they soon realized that wasn't the case.

"Don't any of you move!!!!"

""""Who—?!?!""""

Five soldiers closed in around the group, swords at the ready.

In his confusion, Elch cried out.

"Wh-what the hell's going on here?!"

"Don't play dumb with us, scum!"

"You filthy peasants amassed wealth, and your lord has come to punish you for your crimes! Shut up and submit!"

""""What?!""""

Elch and the other villagers had no idea what was going on. It was all too sudden. Tsukasa, however, quickly talked them down.

"Don't lose your head, Elch. This is no time be asking random questions. Right now, there's just one thing we need to check... Where did you people take this village's women?"

The soldiers' mouths curled into cruel grins.

"Heh-heh-heh, we didn't take 'em nowhere. They're still right here in the village, enjoying a nice little outdoor cooking. They just happen to be the ones on the grill."

"Wh—?!?!"

"Don't worry, though. Our lord told us to put everyone in the village to death. In other words, you guys get to join 'em on the other side!"

Making no efforts to hide their bloodlust, the soldiers swung their swords to attack.

But as the hunters instinctively braced themselves—

"I see. Now I understand what's going on. Aoi?" Tsukasa, armed with the knowledge that the feudal lord was trying to kill the village, gave Aoi her orders. "We don't need these men anymore. They're eyesores, so would you mind cleaning them up?"

Aoi responded with a sigh, her katana's hilt making a clinging sound as she *stowed it back in its sheath.*

"I wish I could obey, m'lord. But you spoke a moment too late. I've already dealt with the problem, that I have."

"Ah. My apologies for being slow on the uptake."

"What are you peasants babbling...about?"

Suddenly, the soldiers lurched forward and collapsed onto the ground in unison, unconscious. Aoi had struck them down with the flat of her blade.

"""" """"
. . . .

Not another word came from their mouths.

Elch and the others spent a moment impressed at Aoi's nigh-invisible swordsmanship, but they quickly came back to their senses and rushed toward the burning house.

"We have to hurry, dammit! C'mon!"

""""Yeah, let's go!"""""

As they were about to take off, however, Tsukasa brought the group to a halt.

"Stand down, all of you. Running into a burning building like that would be suicide."

"Well, we can't just stand here and watch!"

"Don't worry. I'm sure the house is already empty."

"Huh?"

"One of our members can escape from a coffin after it's been *welded shut*. Getting out of a house full of openings like that would be nothing to him."

Tsukasa took out his modified smartphone and dialed Akatsuki's number.

"Our unpleasant guests are gone, so you can go ahead and come out now."

The moment the words left his mouth...a distant bit of underbrush began to rustle.

"Daddy!"

"Honey!"

The women and children of the village came rushing out. The hunters ran over to them in turn, husbands and wives each rejoicing at discovering that the other was safe. Bringing up the rear were Akatsuki and Masato. Upon seeing them, Elch's shoulders trembled.

Masato was carrying Winona's limp body on his back.

"Mom...?!"

Elch dashed over to them, but Masato was quick to assuage the young man.

"Winona's fine. She was about to pick a fight with the soldiers, so I had to knock her out."

Elch and Tsukasa breathed deep sighs of relief. If she and the rest of the villagers were safe, then everything was all right. At the moment, they could ask for nothing more.

"I'm impressed even you were able to sneak all these people past the lookouts, Akatsuki. Thank goodness you were here. Thanks to you, everyone..."

But then...Tsukasa noticed a conspicuous absence.

"...Wait, where's Lyrule?"

The girl he'd spent the most time with out of anyone in the village was nowhere to be seen.

The carriage rolled away from Elm, back toward the castle. Inside, Inzaghi looked at the young woman at his feet and chuckled to himself.

"Heh-heh-heh. I was just after their gold and goods, but I stumbled onto a jackpot. Today must be my lucky day."

Inzaghi had no interest in peasant women, but the girl's beauty had caught even his eye. Lord Findolph was as lecherous as he was corpulent, so the girl would make an excellent tribute for him.

With an offering like this, his recommendation for a promotion to Gold Knight was all but assured. Having a simpleton for a lord certainly came in handy.

That said, handing her over as is has its dangers.

Once she woke up, she would no doubt hate them for having destroyed her village. She'd probably resist with all her might, bare her fangs like a wild dog. No matter how beautiful she might've been, she was still just a commoner. Inzaghi doubted that she'd act with any shred of civility.

She needs to be collared first.

Fortunately, he already had a collar ready.

"Wake up, you. Are you planning on sleeping all day?"

"Nnh... Huh? Where am...? Ow!"

Inzaghi kicked her, and Lyrule's eyes shot open, horrified to discover her situation.

"Huh?! Wh-why are my hands tied up...?! What are you—?"

Suddenly, she met Inzaghi's gaze as he glowered down at her. Recognizing him as the same man who'd attacked the village, rage flared up inside her.

"It's you...! What happened to everyone in the village?! What did you do to them?!"

Inzaghi gave her a faint sneer. His response was brief.

"I killed them."

"No...!"

The light faded from Lyrule's lapis lazuli eyes, immediately replaced with the darkness of hopelessness. However, that darkness soon gave way to a black flame of fury and loathing. As an orphan, the villagers who raised her were her family. And now they were dead.

"How could you...?! How dare you do that to everyone! To my family...! You won't get away with this!"

"Hmph. I knew you were an uneducated mutt," Inzaghi said,

sighing in exasperation. "Who do you think you're barking at? Know your place."

"Agh! Ah...!"

Inzaghi pressed down on Lyrule's side with his foot, then rescinded his earlier statement.

"Don't worry. When I said I killed them, that was just a little joke."

"...Huh?"

"I bound them all up in a shabby little hut and took a torch to it, but...there was that blond girl with them. When my men were tying her hands behind her back, she *twisted her wrists sideways.*"

"...What does that mean?"

"If you turn your wrists sideways when they're being bound, you can simply twist them back the other way to escape the restraints later. In short, she could have escaped whenever she wanted to. She's probably untying the other villagers and helping them escape as we speak. The village's men are coming back, so I had to leave a few soldiers behind to keep up appearances, but I made sure to leave only the utterly incompetent. They won't stand a chance against hunters tempered by the mountains. Understand what I'm saying? Your precious villagers are still alive."

This was the man who attacked her village. There was no reason she should believe a word he was saying. There was no reason...but given the look in his eyes and his tone, he didn't seem to be lying.

If, indeed, everything he'd said had in fact been true, it only served to further confuse Lyrule.

"But why would you...?"

If he knew about the wrist thing, why hadn't he done anything? Inzaghi was more than happy to tell her.

"In order to make a deal with you."

"A deal?"

"Quite. Right now, we're bound for the lord's castle so that I may offer you to him as a tribute. I'm sure you've heard about his proclivities. You're easy on the eyes, so if I hand you over to him, I'll surely earn his favor. However...he's liable to blame me if you do anything untoward in the bedroom. So I offer you this deal: become his obedient concubine and pleasure him with your body."

"N-no...!"

"Then, as long as you fulfill your role properly, I'll spare the lives of your precious villagers."

"!"

This was the "collar" Inzaghi had prepared.

"In fact, I'll even let you see them sometimes. I can guarantee you that much... Should you refuse, however, I will turn the carriage around this minute, mobilize the Order of Guardian Knights, and slaughter this family of yours. And it won't be anything so lenient as flame this time, either. I will flay the flesh off every woman and child in that village before your eyes... Even an uneducated peasant like you can tell which choice is wiser, right?"

"...Waaah, *hic*, waaah..."

The flames of hatred in Lyrule's eyes lost their intensity. As they vanished, fat tears began spilling out in their place.

At the sight of the girl, Inzaghi merely mused, *How sentimental.*

They had no education, no surnames. They were like beasts crawling on the ground.

People like that could never accomplish anything.

Temporary bouts of rage could make them bare their fangs, but that never lasted.

They have no status or goals. It's impossible for animals solely concerned with how they're going to get through each day to muster any sort of sustained drive. After you get past the moment where their anger peaks, the rest is easy.

The sly knight knew how the minds of the have-nots worked, and just as he'd expected...Lyrule nodded her assent to his arrangement.

—Just by giving up her lowly orphan life, she could protect her whole village. To someone as compassionate as Lyrule, it was her only option.

After Tsukasa and the others drove off the remaining soldiers, Masato told them everything that had gone down after they'd left the village.

"That's horrible...! They stole little Lyrule away?!"

"That perverted bastard...!"

The middle-aged hunters ground their teeth and clenched their fists in frustration.

Lyrule didn't have any blood relatives. However, that was precisely why each and every adult in the village treated her like she was their own flesh and blood. And now she'd been abducted. Their collective fury hung thick in the air.

Elch was the one to rally the other hunters.

"C'mon, everyone, there's no time to waste! We have to storm the castle and get Lyrule back!"

"Yeah! You said it!"

"Lyrule is like a daughter to all of us. We won't just sit by as they snatch her away!"

The hunters all followed him. There was no reason they shouldn't. However—

"Hold it right there."

—Tsukasa moved in front of the group and blocked their path, fixing his heterochromatic eyes on them.

"Don't be idiots," the boy snapped with a voice as sharp as a knife.

"What?!"

"The man you're going up against is the lord of the Findolph domain. This isn't some barroom brawl you're walking into. You're committing an act of war against the entire nation. Even if, by some miracle, you actually managed to rescue Lyrule, the imperial court isn't just going to sit quietly by. They'll retaliate with extreme force. I don't know exactly what the scope of this country's military looks like, but I do know it's not something a single village can hope to withstand."

The hunters winced when faced with the cruel reality of their situation. Yet, even so, they were loath to just abandon Lyrule to her fate. That simply wasn't an option. In other words, if Tsukasa was going to stand in their way—

"B-but then, what do you want us to do...?!"

—Elch interjected, assuming that the young prime minister must have concocted some sort of plan.

Tsukasa gave his reply in the same calm, collected tone as always.

"I'm going to go negotiate with them. In exchange for Lyrule, I'm going to get them to drop the treason charges."

"Wh-what?!"

"How dare you! You're just gonna abandon Lyrule like that?!"

"It's not like I'm happy about sacrificing her, but the fact of the matter is she's the one whose life the lord and his men value. In other words, she's the only one we *can* sacrifice. Fortunately, she's an orphan, so we won't have any problems on that front... What? I can make these negotiations work. I guarantee it."

Flames of rage flared up in the villagers' eyes. Elch grabbed Tsukasa by the collar and shouted at him.

"You sick bastard! You can't possibly mean any of that!"

"YOU THINK I WOULD JOKE ABOUT SOMETHING LIKE THIS?!?!"

* * *

"""".......!"""""

Tsukasa's bellow was loud and forceful enough to drown out all the other angry cries. His eyes burned with rage every bit as fervent as anyone else's. It was clear he was just as repulsed as they were. Yet, even so, he pressed on.

"...It's the only way this gets resolved *peacefully*. And it's not like they're going to kill her. If we can trade her...for the future of everyone in this village, then it's the only sensible option. Think of the village's children. And most importantly...*it's what she herself would want*."

He was right. There was no way Lyrule would want the villagers to start a war and fall into ruin just to save her.

"You all... You all should know that even better than I do."

".........." The villagers hung their heads, silently grinding their teeth. Just as he'd said, they knew that wasn't what Lyrule would want.

And yet—

"True. That probably is what Lyrule would want."

"Mom...!"

Winona, who'd woken up, stood before Tsukasa. She, too, spoke with conviction.

"She would try to protect us, even if it meant giving herself up. That's just how gentle and kind a girl she is. We all know that... But right now, Tsukasa, that isn't what matters."

"What do you mean?"

"You're right. We could follow Lyrule's wishes, send you to negotiate with the lord, and get our peace back... But the moment we abandoned Lyrule, *we wouldn't be ourselves anymore*. If we threw a child of ours to the wolves just to save our own lives, we'd be no better than the beasts crawling on the ground that the nobles think we are."

"...Don't you believe that it's better to be a live dog than a dead lion?"

"Not at all. No matter how much the nobles may consider us beasts, we're still people. We're people, just like they are. And we won't abandon someone in need. No matter how much it costs us, we're always going to go support them. Because that's what it means to be human. We'll hold on to our pride, even if it costs us our lives."

""""_____"""""

The hunters, the women...even the small children—all agreed with her. Their eyes burned with silent, resolved affirmation. As people who lived on the barren mountains, it was their one ironclad rule. No matter how many people called them savages, they refused to relinquish their pride as human beings.

The importance of that rule was etched into their very bones. Their souls screamed out, commanding them never to break it.

"We're going. Not just to save Lyrule... To protect our own humanity." As she spoke, Winona stepped toward Tsukasa...and pried open his hands.

""""Ah...!"""""

A stir ran through the villagers.

The flesh on Tsukasa's palms had been gouged, and his raw blisters were bleeding. That was how hard he'd been clenching his fists.

"Well, that's a shame. You just got those treated, too."

"...I'm not some unfeeling monster, you know."

"No, you aren't. In fact, you're just as kind as Lyrule."

Winona took Tsukasa's bloody palms and gently placed her hands atop them.

"...Tsukasa, if you're that worried about us, won't you lend us your strength? We know just how incredible you all are. We can't do this on our own, but with all of you on our side...I'm sure we can save Lyrule...! I'm begging you...! *Please help us...!*" The woman looked straight into Tsukasa's eyes as she made her plea.

Her words moved the boy's heart. He wanted to protect people's smiles. He wanted to be able to lend them a hand. It was an almost childish wish, but it was that ideal that had inspired Tsukasa to become a politician in the first place. It was an ideal he'd clung to every day.

He might end up having to sacrifice everything else. But despite it all, he couldn't just pretend he hadn't heard Winona's plea. He couldn't just pretend he hadn't seen the villagers' eyes.

"...Like I said, what you're trying to do amounts to a declaration of war against the entire Freyjagard Empire. Once it starts, saving Lyrule won't end it. The war will be long and arduous. Corpses will pile up like mountains, and enough blood will spill to fill the sea. You'll experience unthinkable hardships, and you'll know that they could have all been avoided if you'd just stayed servile to the nobles... Is protecting your dignity really worth all that?"

"_____"

The people of Elm didn't reply. Their expressions said that the answer was so obvious they didn't need to. After confirming their resolve...Tsukasa steeled his heart in turn.

"Understood. If you're prepared to go that far, then as a *politician who upholds democracy*, I lend you my aid. I'll join your war—your People's Revolution."

At Tsukasa's verdict, Winona and the others bowed deeply.

"You don't need to thank me," Tsukasa said. He then turned to the other High School Prodigies. "You know the score. I would ask you all to join me in this battle. The situation being what it is, though, I certainly won't force you..."

"We're way past that, Boss," Masato said with a laugh. "We already agreed that you'd be the one calling the shots. You won't hear any complaints from my end. Besides, abandoning Lyrule like this would leave a shitty taste in my mouth."

"It goes without saying that I shall accompany you, too, m'lord.

Yet, had you not gone, I would have fought on behalf of my friends all the same, that I would."

"I suspect my talents will be called for as well. There's no shortage of patients on a battlefield, after all."

"………"

"Ringo's saying that she'll do her best fur Lyrule's sake, too!"

"O-of course I'm gonna come fight t-to help out my friends! Wh-what kind of guy wouldn't?!"

"Prince, dude, your legs are shaking like crazy."

"Shut up! I'm just, uh, ex-ex-ex-excited, that's all!"

Akatsuki protested Masato's assertion while practically on the verge of tears.

However…not even he made to leave. He loved the people of this village just as much as the others did.

"Yo, Tsukasa. You should probably warn 'em first, right?"

"…True. Too true."

Tsukasa turned back toward the people of Elm. No, not just him. The entire group from Earth turned to the villagers in unison. Faint smiles played at their mouths as Tsukasa gave the people of this world his speech.

"Friends, while we're willing to help you, it means we'll be putting our lives on the line. And that means we aren't going to be able to hold back.

"In short, we're likely to end up accelerating your world's culture by a factor of at least five hundred years.

"Your government, your economy, your value systems—they'll all be drastically changed.

"In other words, what I'm trying to say is this:

"Given that we're liable to destroy the world as you know it, is it still all right to give this everything we've got?"

*　*　*

To the people of Elm, no words could have made them happier.

⚜ The People's Revolution and the High School Prodigies ⚜

"Oh-ho! Oh-ho-hyo-ho!!!!"

It was nightfall, and the sound of creepily high-pitched laughter echoed through the lord's castle. The voice belonged to a middle-aged man as round as a barrel. His clothes were adorned with fine gold and silver thread. This man was the owner of the castle, Edwart von Findolph.

His brow gushed sweat, his nose went flush with excitement, and his eyes glimmered with delight as he looked the girl over. On Inzaghi's orders, Lyrule had been neatly groomed and made to wear a white dress that showed off ample portions of her bosom.

"Oh, this one's a real beauty! Oh-ho!" The man's fleshy jaw quivered.

He was the spitting image of a bulldog in heat.

"Her blond hair is as fine as silk threads, and it glimmers like gold dust! And her skin, as white as freshly driven snow…! It's so unbelievably smooth!"

"………"

The feeling of his fat, swollen fingers caressing her hair, cheeks, and neck filled Lyrule with so much disgust, she wanted to scream.

However, she desperately choked down that reaction. So long as she was submissive to Findolph, the villagers were safe. Inzaghi's collar had bound the girl's willpower itself.

Beside her, the man who'd so effectively shackled her bowed respectfully to his lord as he upsold his meritorious deed.

"I found her in the village you ordered me to torch. Because of her

©Sacraneco

beauty, I took it upon myself to spare her life and bring her to you as tribute. I apologize if I've acted out of turn."

"Not at all! You've shown amazing judgment, Inzaghi! It's no wonder you're the strongest knight in my domain! I promise your armor will be sparkling gold in no time!"

"You are most gracious, my lord…"

"Bwuh-hyo-hyo-hyo. Still, she really is something. What's your name, girl?"

"…I-it's Lyrule."

"Lyrule, is it? Well, rejoice, Lyrule! I've decided to accept you as my concubine. You will belong to me, a noble in the service of our exalted emperor himself. How do you like that? Wonderful, isn't it?"

It was anything but. There was no way she could ever come to love a man so clearly only interested in her body. The thought made goose bumps run across her flesh. She forced a smile nonetheless.

"Oh, very. Thank you so much…my lord…"

"Bwuh-hyo-hyo-hyo. Now then, you know what to do, don't you?"

Lord Findolph slid one hand down to her shoulder, began kneading her breast with the other, and puckered up his lips.

Nonononono…

Lyrule had never been with a man. The only time she'd even touched lips with one was when she was nursing Tsukasa back to health. She was utterly inexperienced, and the man before her was viscerally repulsive.

But…if her sacrifice was enough to save her beloved family—

"Yes…master…"

It was painful how strong she was.

Lyrule stifled her emotions, plastered on a fake smile, and braced herself to accept Lord Findolph's kiss.

But before their lips met—

"Gyah?!?!"

"Eeeeek!"

—a burst of blue lightning flashed between their bodies and forcibly blasted them apart.

"Ugh…"

As a result, Lyrule slammed her head into the wall behind her and passed out on the spot. There was no such solid mass behind Lord Findolph; he instead merely collapsed backward onto the bed. However…

"Ahhhhh! Owwwww! M-my lips got singed! Gaaaah!"

The barrel man writhed around. It must have been some sort of lightning attack, as some of the flesh on his lips had been seared clean off.

Inzaghi's eyes went wide at the unexpected sight.

"Magic…?! Th-that girl's a mage…?!"

Inzaghi had seen magic firsthand on the battlefield a few times, so he could tell immediately. What Lyrule had just used had unmistakably been magic.

She didn't show any signs of it when we captured her… Could she really have just awakened?! What awful timing…! If I'm not careful, Lord Findolph will end up blaming me for this…! Dammit!

Realizing the threat the girl now posed to him, Inzaghi ground his teeth and rushed over to Lord Findolph's side.

"My lord! Are you all right?!"

Lord Findolph snapped back at him, enraged.

"INZAAAAAAGHI!!!!"

"Urk…!"

"Cast this swine into the dungeon at once! How dare a commoner like her wound my noble personage…! She needs to pay for this! Make her regret having ever been born!"

"A-at once!"

Every conceivable savage emotion flashed across Lord Findolph's bloodshot eyes as he turned them on Lyrule's collapsed form.

At times like these, it was best to not give excuses and just follow orders. Inzaghi's years of experience in service of Findolph had taught him that. He turned toward Lyrule.

However, his hand never reached her.

The girl's friends had finished the necessary preparations to save her, and it was in that moment that they made their presence known.

"Anchors set. Stand fixed."

Bearabbit reached the top of a knoll overlooking the side of the lord's castle. Ringo's hastily built cylindrical machine was mounted atop his back. After having shot anchor bolts out of his six legs to lock himself in place, he wirelessly contacted Masato.

"Preparations complete! Teddy when you are!"

"We're in position, too. When Ringo does the thing, *that'll be our signal. Their flank's virtually undefended, so let's hit 'em hard!*

"Ringo, they're ready ofur there, too!"

"Got it!"

Ringo was back in the village's power plant, and upon hearing the news, she skillfully tapped away at the laptop hooked up to its generator.

"No abnormalities in the electronic transmission systems. Main inverter connected. Environmental variables analyzed. Angle adjustment locked. Output limiter removed—"

As Ringo typed on her keyboard, the cylinder on Bearabbit's back began to hum. Massive amounts of energy from her pocket nuclear fission reactor flowed up a thick, oxygen-free copper cable and into the cylinder's two long conductor turned electromagnets to create a powerful magnetic field. That was right. The cylinder—

"Seventy-seven-pound depleted uranium shell, fire!"

—was a railgun cannon.

The moment Ringo slammed down the ENTER key, an orange flash exploded from the cannon's barrel. The shell easily surpassed the speed of sound, melting into plasma as it surged through the air.

A lightning-like afterglow followed in its wake as it crashed into the castle ramparts—

—roaring so loudly that Ringo could even hear it in Elm, five mountains away.

That was how tremendous the destructive roar of the cannon was.

Inzaghi and Findolph were close enough to the detonation's epicenter that they experienced it less as a sound and more as a wave of force.

"Pyoooooooooooh?!?!?!"

"Nwah?!"

Glass windows shattered. The ground shook. They both toppled onto their backs.

"Wh-what was that...?!"

"I-Inzaghi!"

"I'm on it!"

Not needing to be told twice, Inzaghi dashed onto the terrace so he could look out over the whole castle.

"What...in the blazes...?!"

The shock was so intense it made his mind go blank for a moment. And it was no wonder. When he made it outside, the first thing he saw was the castle's stone ramparts blown to smithereens.

Up on the knoll, Bearabbit's camera captured the damage as well. When he sent it over to Ringo, she clenched her fist a little.

"The target's been destroyed all right."

The ramparts of the stronghold were worthless now.

There was little nuclear fuel left in the pocket reactor, but it looked like their lack of frugality with it hadn't been in vain.

"The damage is pretty pawful on our end, too, though."

Bearabbit sent over a picture of the railgun cannon.

Unable to withstand the electric heat it had generated, its barrel had melted.

"It couldn't be avoided. We were short on time and materials. I'm glad we were even able to pull off that one shot." As she murmured, Ringo sympathetically stroked the image of the railgun cannon on her display.

"But now the path is open... Good luck, you guys!"

And a moment after Ringo sent her devout cry of support from the village—

"This is it! Everyone, storm the courtyard!"

""""YEAAAAAAAAAAH!!!!""""

Over at the castle, Masato led Aoi, Winona, and twenty-odd hunters out from the woods and toward the massive hole in the ramparts.

The moon was out, so the Order of Guardian Knights spotted them immediately.

"C-Captain Inzaghi! The villagers from earlier are heading toward the opening!"

"So they're the ones behind this?! But how...? No, never mind that!" The moment Inzaghi's wheels started turning, he shook his head.

That's not important right now. I don't know how they managed to destroy the wall, but their goal must be to rescue that girl. That means that cannon fire was no stray shot! The fact that they're sending in infantry is proof enough of that!

"In any case, a few dirty mountain peasants can't possibly pose a threat to us! Give them a taste of our crossbows! Shoot down every fool who dares stand against us!"

Inzaghi's orders were precise, and his men quickly moved to follow them. They rushed from their stations with crossbows in hand to man the battlements. They took aim through the hole in the wall and fired at the rebels.

Bolts whizzed through the air.

Their crossbows were so powerful, they required windlasses just to draw them back. There was no way the destitute rebel villagers had any equipment capable of defending against something like that. Countless uprisings had fallen in the face of such firepower.

Yet—

Clang!!!!

—sparks and the sound of metal filled the air as the villagers deflected every last bolt.

"Whaaat?!"

Impossible. The soldiers' eyes went wide. How could this be?

After all, you'd need an iron shield to block—

"W-wait, what're those...?!"

"Shields?! And they ain't wood, either. That's metal! They've got iron shields!"

"Say what?!"

Inzaghi leaned over the balcony in disbelief and stared at his onrushing foes.

Not only did they have shields, they were even big enough to hide one's whole body behind.

And although he couldn't quite make them out in the darkness, the way they caught the moonlight meant they were definitely metal...!

B-but how?! How could mountain brutes get equipment like that...?!

Not even a Silver Knight like him was issued a shield large enough
to hide behind. Come to think of it, something like that should have
been too heavy to even wield.

Yet the Elm hunters carried them in one hand while running at
full speed. The fact that poor villagers had gotten their hands on iron
shields was uncanny enough, but that they held them single-handed
was just downright baffling. However, what Inzaghi found so hard to
understand was actually quite simple.

The truth was, the shields weren't made of iron at all.

"Damn, these things really can deflect crossbow bolts! They're so
strong!"

"And they're still light enough for us to carry them in one hand!
I've never seen metal like this before!"

"You guys really made this amazing metal from the red clay over
in the valley?!"

The hunters were all amazed by the hitherto unseen material.
Masato let out a booming laugh at the incredulous reactions of the
vanguard.

"You'd better believe it. Nice, ain't it? This stuff completely
changed the course of history back on our world!"

Was it aluminum? Not quite. After all, aluminum on its own
wasn't nearly that strong.

Not only was aluminum not strong enough to repel crossbow
bolts…it wasn't even sturdy enough to make the shovels Tsukasa had
used to dig out the riverbank. In other words, what Ringo had been
cooking up in that lab of hers wasn't ordinary aluminum.

Instead, she'd taken the aluminum she extracted from the bauxite
and refined it with magnesium and a number of other metals. It was
devastatingly cheap, seemed to defy every law of mass, and had once

single-handedly accelerated Earth civilization by centuries and quite literally changed the course of history. It was a *superalloy* in every sense of the word.

"We call it duralumin, and compared to the rest of the stuff in this world, it's basically a Dreadnought-class overpowered item! Arrows, crossbow bolts, guns, I mean, bring it on!"

Masato and the others made their way toward the castle, effortlessly repelling the crossbow bolts without pause. The Order of Guardian Knights began to panic.

"Dammit, hurry it up with that windlass! At this rate, they're actually gonna make it inside!"

Desperate to stop the enemy's charge, the rampart-encamped crossbow archers continued firing. However, the man who'd devised the villagers' invasion wasn't so kind as to let that go on forever.

"Gweh?!"

"Huh…?! A-an arrow?! They've got sni— Glurk!"

"Gah!"

The crossbow unit let out strange screams as they toppled one after another off the ramparts to the courtyard sixty feet below.

"Wh-what's going on?! What's happening?!"

As Inzaghi floundered, one of his men called out to him.

"C-Captain! They're sniping us! With metal arrows! They're metal all the way from the arrowheads down!"

"More metal arms?!"

It was true. Elm had a sniper. The bow's wielder was none other than the greatest archer in the village, Elch.

He was standing atop a tree over six hundred feet from the castle, sniping the crossbow unit from well outside the range of a traditional arrow.

"Damn, this thing is nice," he said, glancing at the metal bow he wielded while marveling at its capabilities.

Ringo had made him a recurve bow with an aluminum alloy handle and a carbon rim.

"It shoots about four times farther than our wooden bows, and its arrows are made of this crazy-light metal. Almost feels bad, sharpshooting this good... It feels like I couldn't miss if I tried. I bet I could even nail a rabbit right between the eyes!"

Elch nocked another arrow and loosed it at his foes. It cast a high arc through the air and whizzed straight toward Inzaghi's forehead.

"Hyah!"

However, he wasn't the captain of the Order of Guardian Knights for nothing. Sensing the projectile bearing down on him, he promptly swatted the arrow down with his sword. The steel blade crushed the alloy-shaft arrow and sent it tumbling to the ground.

"Where's that sniper, dammit?!"

"W-we don't know! All the trees in shooting range of the castle were felled, but we can't spot them anywhere...! There's nowhere for them to hide, bu— GAAAAAAAAAH!!!!"

Another soldier toppled from the ramparts, a duralumin arrow piercing through both his helmet and skull.

Inzaghi clenched his jaw in frustration.

Tch! Does that mean they have a bow that can shoot from impossible ranges?! Where are these filthy mountain hunters getting such things?! Dammit! Dammit! How is this happening?!

It defied all logic.

And with logic yet defied—

"Captain Inzaghi! They've made it to the courtyard!"

—the situation just kept getting worse and worse.

As he broke out into a cold sweat, Inzaghi strained his voice and barked orders to his men.

"We're sitting ducks up here! Grab your swords and meet them in the courtyard! There are only a few dozen of them and almost two hundred of us! We'll crush them with superior numbers!"

Despite all the confusion, Inzaghi was still a skilled enough man to be able to make wise decisions in battle.

He made a good point, too. In combat, the side with more numbers had an advantage, and that advantage was only compounded when it came to close-quarters combat. In other words, his forces had every reason to make full use of that, head down to the courtyard, and engage their foes in melee combat. It was a smart, logical decision. In fact, given his situation, it was probably the best play he could make.

Halberds in hand, the fully armored Bronze Knights charged at Masato and the other intruders.

"Commoner scum! You've brought chaos and violence into our great lord's castle!"

"You'll pay dearly for that crime!"

However—

"Well, in that case…I shall bring you the payment you so desire with my sword, that I shall!"

—there was one swordswoman present who had fought on the bullet-filled battlefields of the future and was said to be a match for *a thousand men*. A tenfold numbers advantage was nothing before her.

As though to prove that, she swung her blade faster than a gale-force wind and lopped the heads off the two Bronze Knights charging at her *through their helmets*.

"My ferocious secret technique—Iron-Cleaving Flash!"

"H-how can this be?!"

As the other soldiers stopped and gawked at her in horror, she closed in on them before they could blink.

"For your affronts, I strike you down."

""""AAAAAARGH!!!!"""""

With just one slash, she bisected three foes.

"I would not normally pursue those who flee, but our numbers today are far too few. Forgive me, but know that all within reach of my sword shall be cut down without mercy!"

She was, in every way, a samurai dominating the battlefield. Spurts of blood gushed through the air in her wake. The soldiers quivered in fear, then began screaming and ran for their lives.

"Sh-she's a monster!"

However, they found themselves crashing into the soldiers who'd just fled from the other side.

"Agh!"

"D-dumbasses, don't come this way! Ah—"

The anonymous soldier breathed his last. A chestnut-haired wolf with a grass sickle in each hand had sliced open his throat.

"Heh-heh. It's been a while since my blood *boiled* like this."

Amid the melee, Winona was fighting just as hard as Aoi.

"I thought my wild days were over once I got hitched, but this is for my daughter. Now you boys are gonna see exactly what Elm's top hunter is capable of!"

The way she dropped low to the ground and ran—she was the spitting image of an actual wolf. Time and time again, her sickles found thighs and tendons, slicing them open and rendering the soldiers powerless.

Earlier that day, she'd been ready to take on Inzaghi's whole unit by herself until Masato knocked her out from behind. If he hadn't been there, though, she probably would have taken at least ten of them down with her. That was just how strong she was.

"Hey! Move aside, you useless lumps!"

"Agh!"

"Gah!"

Eventually realizing that the soldiers were helpless to stop her

©Sacraneco

rampage, a Bronze Knight swept his men aside and brandished his halberd.

"A knight'll be the one to take you down, impudent beast!"

He stabbed forward over and over, the tip of his halberd audibly slicing through the air each time. Unlike the soldiers' inexperienced thrusts, his had the kind of speed that only came with practiced technique. Yet to her, even that speed seemed glacial.

Winona dodged each attack with the smallest movements possible, then chose one—

"Too slow!"

—and used its timing to stomp the halberd into the ground.

"Wh—?!"

Then, with the weapon still embedded in the dirt, she ran up its long grip, leaped into the air, and planted her butt right on the Bronze Knight's face.

"Hraaagh!"

Though it was protected by chainmail and a helmet, the force of the impact snapped the Bronze Knight's neck anyway.

Seeing him crumple to the ground in a cloud of dust, Aoi offered words of praise.

"Good work, Winona, m'lady! Childbirth seemed not to have tarnished your figure, so I suspected that you were practiced, but I never expected it to be to such a degree! I thought myself the only one here capable of felling the Bronze Knights, that I did!"

"What, you thought I'd let you hog all the glory?"

And Winona wasn't the only combat-capable villager in the fray.

The duralumin shield–equipped hunters weren't quite on par with the Bronze Knights, but they completely outclassed the rank-and-file soldiers. Their enemies' numbers advantage dwindled before their eyes.

Even the Bronze Knights who'd made their way down to the

courtyard went shivering in their boots as they witnessed Elm's unwavering advance.

"Dammit, they're too strong! This shit ain't normal!"

Up in the northern sticks, the soldiers got little to no actual combat experience. In contrast, Elm's hunters spent their days running around the mountains. The difference in their base physiques was considerable. Coupled with Elm's overpowered equipment, the soldiers of the castle hardly stood a chance.

"C'mon, surround them! We gotta all charge at once!"

One of Bronze Knights called out, knowing that they were doomed if they stayed scattered like they were.

The soldiers did as instructed and moved to surround Elm's hunters.

Damn. Looks like one of them was able to keep his head. Masato clicked his tongue.

Aoi would be fine, of course, but anyone else would be in trouble if they got rushed by ten people at once. It was time for Masato to play his trump card.

"We can't let them regroup! I'm counting on you—Prince!"

And not a moment later...

"BWA-HA-HA-HA-HA!!!!"

Laughter boomed down from above, and a dark shadow eclipsed the light of the moon. The soldiers couldn't help but look up at the sight.

"Wh-who's thaaaaaat?!?!"

"Th-there's someone flying up there! They've got a mage!"

"N-no way...! What's a mage doing in a grubby little mountain village...?!"

The mysterious figure was wrapped in a dark cloak and hovering up in the air with the moon at his back. There was only one person who could pull off a stunt like that—Prince Akatsuki, the greatest magician on Earth.

"Quake with *fear*! Cower in *terror*! For you stand before a grand and powerful *mage*!"

Akatsuki feigned an overly inflected voice as he focused the attention of the soldiers on himself.

In contrast to his imposing tone and countenance, however—

Please don't shoot me please don't shoot me please don't shoot meeeeee!!!!

—his internal monologue was a terrified scream.

Of all the people there, Akatsuki was the only one with zero experience facing down death.

The hunters' experience was obvious; they put their lives on the line every day they went out hunting. Masato, for his part, lived much like Tsukasa—fending off assassins year-round. Plus, not only was he well acclimated to attempts on his life, but business in and of itself was akin to war. Masato couldn't even remember how many people he'd sent to their ruin on his path to controlling 30 percent of Earth's wealth. Even Ringo, who wasn't there in person, was no stranger to peril. Her intellect was vast enough that it could influence entire nations. Every country in the world wanted her for themselves. Two hands' worth of fingers weren't enough to count the number of times she'd nearly been kidnapped. That was precisely why she chose to live in low orbit. Her mere presence on Earth was enough to spark conflict.

And as for Aoi and Keine, they hardly needed to be mentioned. They spent their whole lives on the battlefield.

But Akatsuki was different.

True, he was blessed with skills that went beyond the pale…but he'd never been in a situation where it was kill or be killed. As successful as he was, he was still just a normal person. The world he lived in was bound by laws and common sense. And because of that, seeing the all-too-real battle playing out below him shook the boy to his core.

People were dying one after another. The green lawn was being stained with dark-red blood. It was a world completely removed from the one in which he normally spent his days.

Tsukasa, being cognizant of all that, had called Akatsuki over before they'd all gone in.

"There's no need for you to force yourself to take part in this battle," he'd said. *"You have an important task that comes after this, so there's no shame in staying back."*

Despite the prime minister's warnings…Akatsuki had come anyway. He knew full well how badly it would shock their foes to see a mage. Him being there would meaningfully increase their chances. With that in mind, there was no way he could just take it easy somewhere safe and wait for his friends to return.

I'm…a man, too, you know…!

He quashed his fear. He suppressed his trembling. Akatsuki was used to performing on big stages, and no entertainer worth his salt ever let the audience see him whine or panic!

"Now take *this*! My secret recipe, mandrake poison *gas bombs!*" With a shout, Akatsuki did as Tsukasa had instructed and hurled a bunch of colorful Ping-Pong-size spheres onto the battlefield. Were they really mandrake poison gas bombs? …Well, no.

Akatsuki had had neither the time nor the knowledge to make anything nearly that exciting. What he'd thrown were the smoke bombs he used in his performances. Like his outfit, they were part of his magician's tools he'd had on him when he'd gotten dropped into that world.

When the smoke bombs hit the ground, huge swaths of colorful green, pink, and blue fumes began billowing from them.

"Ahhh! He's throwing something at us!"

"What's with this weird colored smoke?!"

When Masato saw the dense fumes fill the battlefield, he made his move.

"AAAAARGH! IT BURNS! THIS STUFF'S POISON!" he shouted. He'd had to take control of more than his fair share of discussions turned screaming matches in the past, so the young businessman was more than experienced in making his voice carry. Hearing him immediately sent the soldiers into a panic.

"S-someone's screaming?!"

"Guys, make sure you don't breathe the smoke in!"

"Eeeeeek!"

"Screw this, man! They've got shields I ain't never seen before, they can cut through armor, and now they're throwing poison from the sky? I don't wanna fight these guys anymore!"

"We surrender, we surrender! Just let us live!"

Seeing a mage fly through the sky, watching him fill the air with strange, poisonous-looking smoke, and hearing Masato's scream had dealt a heavy blow to the soldiers' spirits. They'd been trying to surround the Elm hunters, but now their leadership had been routed. Their people were panicking, and more and more of them were losing their will to fight. Any sort of cohesion they may have had as a group was gone.

In contrast, the Elm side had been told ahead of time that it was just colored smoke, so they pressed the assault and broke through the opposing line in no time.

Aoi, who'd previously been prioritizing thinning the enemy's ranks, switched to using nonlethal blows. The battle had already been decided. Most of the soldiers were throwing down their weapons and cowering on the ground. The courtyard was already lost. There was no need for her to take any more lives.

"What just happened...?"

Inzaghi had been watching the whole thing play out from the terrace. A tremble began overtaking him.

This is bad. At this rate...

...the peasants were actually going to make it through.

Even if he was able to withdraw those of his men still willing to fight and redeploy them inside the castle, it would just be a repeat of what had played out in the courtyard. The difference in individual strength between each side was simply too great.

Especially that girl with the long, tied-up hair...

Aoi Ichijou was too powerful for him to deal with. In fact, she was so strong that she could probably have taken the castle on her own. The only person who could stand up to her...would be a mage, but...

"...!"

Inzaghi went pale.

Now that he thought about it, where was that First-Class Mage who'd been stationed at the castle these past few months? Why hadn't he joined the battle? Where or what was he—?

It was then that the true worst-case possibility became apparent to the Silver Knight. What if it wasn't that he *hadn't* joined but that he *couldn't?*

"Was that flashy battle all just a diversion...?!"

Abandoning his men, Inzaghi rushed back toward his lord. He needed to take Lord Findolph and flee the castle.

Down on the battlefield, out of the corner of his eye, Masato watched Inzaghi beat feet.

Looks like the hotshot finally figured it out. But he's too late...!

Certain of their victory down in the courtyard, Masato trusted his hopes for the plan's final steps in their two missing members.

Tsukasa, Shinobu! The rest is on you guys!

Inzaghi's hunch had been right on the mark. Tsukasa had called Shinobu back earlier, and while Masato and the others were invading the courtyard, the two of them had been infiltrating the castle.

The soldiers had all been occupied by the chaos over on the grounds, so the hallways were empty as they quietly slipped through them. With Shinobu's guidance, the two were able to make their way straight to the lord's chambers.

"This has been on my mind for a while now, but I'm constantly amazed at your ability to gather intel. Finding out about the secret passage is one thing, but when could you have possibly had time to learn the castle's entire layout?"

"Nya-ha-ha. There ain't no secret safe from me! I'm the world's greatest journalist, remember? Anyway, back when I first heard what a jerk the lord was, I figured we might have to take drastic measures at some point!"

"Ah. How prudent."

"Weren't you against starting this fight, though?"

"…War carries a toll of blood. Without fail. I'm in no position to bear responsibility for the lives of this world's people. And for a politician, wars should only be started as an absolute last resort. That's what I believe, at least. Lives once lost can never be recovered."

However—

"However, I also know that there are moments where people have no choice but to put their lives on the line and fight. For Winona and the others, that time is now. I can't do much, but I aim to help them however I can."

"Well, that's very 'you,' all right. You sure it's okay for you to be away from Japan for so long, though?"

"Our country isn't fragile enough that it'd just collapse in my absence. Besides…this won't take long. I've got six of Japan's brightest stars with me. Given all our talents, waging this war while searching for a way home at the same time will be easy. That's what I'm counting on, anyway."

"What are you, some sorta slave driver…?"

"Worse. A politician."

"I dunno if that's something to sound so proud about, Tsukes." Shinobu let out a chuckle and looked at the approaching corner. "When we turn this bend, there'll be a staircase! Head up that, and we'll be smack-dab in front of the lord's chambers!"

But as she was about to lean into the turn, she saw something. Just beyond the corner, at the other end of the hallway leading to the stairs, was a man dressed in a blue robe.

"———! Tsukes!"

"Huh?!"

Shinobu suddenly forced her body back, slamming herself into Tsukasa, who was about to round the corner after her. Not a moment later, a loud *bang* rang out, and a large crack appeared in the stone brickwork wall where Tsukasa's head would have been.

"What the…?!"

"My, my. Inzaghi's incompetence runs deep, it seems. I was not counting on having to get involved with a puny little twenty-man uprising, yet the worms have already managed to squirm their way this far." From beneath the blue robe, a male voice echoed through the dark corridor at the two intruders.

"The battle on the surface was a diversion, was it? A clever plan, for a bunch of uncivilized savages. But I'm afraid your luck ran out the moment you met me. I am Gale el Stafford, First-Class Imperial Mage. I'll cut off your rebellious little heads and offer them to the lord as tribute!"

"If he's a mage, then that must have been magic."

Shinobu, who'd learned a thing or two about magic, nodded.

"Yup. A simple wind spell called Wind Edge. It shoots a vacuum blade at the speed of a pistol shot. You saw for yourself how effective it is."

"Well, this is a problem. Is there another path we can take?"

Shinobu shook her head.

"It'd take too long; we don't have the time. It's okay, though, we'll just go through him. Leave it to me!"

"…Are you sure?"

"Thanks for looking out for me, but I got this. I'm not some delicate princess like Lyrule, I'm a lady ninja, a modern-day *kunoichi*. And protecting political leaders is a ninja's job. That means this is my time to shine!" Her declaration made, Shinobu dashed around the corner alone.

The mage wasn't about to let the opportunity that represented slip by.

"Fool! You're just rushing to your death! Wind Edge!"

He swung the baton-like stick he was carrying in a diagonal line and cast his spell. An invisible blade rushed through the air, straight toward Shinobu. And yet—

Shinobu stepped toward the wall, practically hurling herself at it. The attack missed.

"Tch, a lucky guess! In that case, how do you like *this*?!"

Gale clicked his tongue, then waved his wand around and loosed several more Wind Edge spells.

They shot down the narrow corridor, each one flying at a different angle without nary so much as a pause in between.

However, the magical barrage did little to slow Shinobu's advance. She ran toward Gale, weaving her way between the miniscule gaps in the attacks without stopping for a moment. The mage made no efforts to hide his shock.

"B-but how?! Can you see my invisible blades somehow?!"

Shinobu responded with a smirk as she leaped over the blade of wind speeding toward her stomach like she was in a hurdle race.

"Oh, I don't need to. Wind Edge flies fast and is fast to cast, but the trade-off is that you can't really control it. It always just shoots as *an extension of the line you draw with your wand.*"

"How?! No commoner should have such knowledge of magic…!"

"How? Why, you're the one who taught me. Don't you remember…*Mr. Good Lookin'*?"

"Huh?"

Gale suddenly remembered that pet name and seductive tone of voice. A week ago, when he was out drinking in town, he'd chatted up a cute girl who'd sounded just like that.

"Whaaaaat?! Y-you're Sasha?!"

Shinobu wasn't about to let the opportunity his shock presented slip by.

"Yep!"

"Argh!!"

Shinobu's shuriken sank into the back of the mage's hand. The pain forced him to drop his wand. He immediately leaned down to pick it up, but Shinobu got to him faster.

"Whoop!"

"GYAAAARGH?!?!"

When she did, her special stun gun knocked him clean out. She'd modified it to increase the voltage.

"Ninja Art: Bolt Release—or y'know, something like that."

"That was impressive. Now that I think about it, I do remember you mentioning that you were able to make an appointment with a mage. Is that when you learned the castle layout, too?"

"Bingo! Mr. Good Lookin' was surprisingly forthcoming."

"Loose lips sink ships... Although, here it was a ship we wanted sunk, so—?!"

Though the mage had been rendered harmless, apparently, they'd let him shoot off a few too many spells. The sound of the wind blades colliding with the walls had echoed through the castle, and soldiers were starting to gather on their position.

"Intruders! We've got intruders this deep into the castle!"

"Kill them! Don't let them reach our lord!"

Three bronze-clad knights charged toward them from down the hall.

"They must've heard the battle."

As Tsukasa clicked his tongue, Shinobu moved into position to cover for him.

"Tsukes, go! I'll hold them off!"

If he went now, he could make it to the stairs before the enemy reinforcements did.

Tsukasa was pretty sure Shinobu could hold her own, no matter how many knights they threw at her. And so—

"—Okay. I'm counting on you!"

—he left her side and headed for the lord's chambers alone.

Meanwhile, Inzaghi had only just made it back to the lord's chambers himself.

"I-Inzaghi! Wh-what's going on out there?!"

Lyrule was the last thing on Lord Findolph's mind now. The rotund man was covered in blankets and curled up into a ball as though instinctively trying to protect himself. The abnormally loud commotion outside was impossible to ignore and must have clued the lord into the danger he was in. Inzaghi knelt before him and delivered a status report.

"I'm afraid to say that the commoners have formed a mob and are on the verge of taking the castle."

Lord Findolph's eyes went wide in shock.

"What?! C-commoners?! Commoners, you say?! You're a Silver Knight, and you're losing to mere commoners?"

"Regretfully so. But there's nothing common about them. The insurgents all have equipment made from an unknown metal. One of them wields a weapon called a katana and is clearly an experienced warrior. Between their weapons and their skills, they're no mere mob! They're as formidable as any military unit...!"

"......!"

"We're in danger here. Let's prepare to evacuate so we can—"

But he was too late.

"That won't be necessary."

"_____?!"

Both of them looked in the direction of the sudden voice. Someone was standing in the doorway, blocking their exit.

"Whatever you're planning, it's too late."

It was Tsukasa Mikogami, his red eye burning hot and his blue eye ice-cold.

When Tsukasa entered the room, his gaze immediately shifted to the floor, where Lyrule was sprawled. Her shoulders rose and fell; she was breathing.

Well…it looks like we dodged the worst-case scenario.

Tsukasa had been worried that Lyrule, thinking that the villagers had died, would lash out—and that Findolph would kill her in retribution. Fortunately, that appeared not to have been the case. Now all he needed to do was get her out of there.

"I'll be taking her back now."

Tsukasa drew the extendable baton from his suit and charged into the room.

"I-I-Inzaaaaaaghiiiiii!" Lord Findolph screeched.

"Hyah!"

Inzaghi promptly moved to intercept the attack. His sword cleaved a silver arc through the darkness—right into Tsukasa's path.

Tsukasa quickly blocked it, but the impact sent a sharp sting through his bandaged hand.

Ow…!

That single exchange was more than enough to tell him how powerful the foe before him was. Armed with the knowledge of Inzaghi's strength, Tsukasa realized this wasn't someone he could just bulldoze his way through. He turned his gaze away from Lord Findolph, focused all his attention on the Silver Knight, blocking the man's the follow-up attack.

Inzaghi cast a rage-filled glare at him. "Your moves are clearly practiced. You're no amateur. And you're no peasant, either, are you?"

"I do have something of a handle on the basics."

"…There was that woman outside, too. There's no way a commoner could be that strong or skilled. I get it now… So you people gave the peasants knowledge and arms, then riled them up, is that it?!"

"They started this fight, not us. We lent them our strength, but we certainly didn't rile them up. You turned your backs on them, and this battle is their retribution."

"Nonsense!" Inzaghi pushed Tsukasa back farther and farther

using the secret sword techniques only taught to Imperial Knights. He wasn't on Aoi's level, but that didn't mean the man wasn't a skilled swordsman.

Furthermore, Tsukasa's hands were covered in raw blisters, and his extendable baton had a short reach compared to a sword. The deck was stacked against him.

"This won't end well for you, you know! This castle and domain were entrusted to Marquis Findolph by His Majesty, Emperor Freyjagard! Breaking in and raising your swords against the marquis is akin to raising your swords against the emperor himself! His Majesty won't let this stand. He'll kill you, each and every last one of you!"

Inzaghi attacked again and again, his rage growing with each strike. Little by little, he was pushing Tsukasa back. However—

"Then I suppose we'll just have to take your emperor's head before he takes ours."

—Tsukasa's emotions remained unwavering.

His eyes were filled with a fierce light, and they were fixed not just on the enemy before him but on the one behind Inzaghi that the prime minister knew he'd inevitably need to slay.

"Like I said, it's too late. The times have begun changing in accordance with the will of the people. Commoners are just as human as you nobles, and their pride will go on to move the hearts of others in turn. Right now, it's just a backwoods revolt, but just like in our world, it won't be long before the uprising sweeps over all of Freyjagard. It'll be like a wildfire. And the wheels of change stop for no man, so there's only one thing the people like you, the people who ran the old regime, can do when faced with the tides of history—*perish*."

"Silence, you little malcontent!"

As a Silver Knight who served the empire, Inzaghi couldn't let an affront like that stand. The emperor's absolute inviolability was the foundation that provided the basis for the nobility's worth. Yet this upstart boy made light of that. Inzaghi leveled slash after slash at him, seething like a raging fire. Each attack was stronger and deadlier than the last. Tsukasa defended himself laudably, but—

"Agh...!"

—eventually, one of Inzaghi's slashes knocked his baton out of his hand.

Its handle was wet and sticky with Tsukasa's blood, and their repeated exchanges had sapped his grip of strength.

Inzaghi wasn't one to miss an opportunity like that. He brought his sword crashing down toward Tsukasa's head, ready to split him in two.

"Taaaaaake—that?!"

All of a sudden, though, the weapon slammed into something and stopped in midair. However, Tsukasa shouldn't have had anything to defend himself with. But then, how?

The truth lay in the fact that they'd made their way back to the room's entrance. The blade had gotten wedged in the post at the top of the doorway.

"Ah, da..." Damn. He'd noticed it too late.

Having been handed a decisive opening, Tsukasa charged in point-blank. Seeing Tsukasa's collected expression, Inzaghi finally realized *he'd been had.*

This brat used his own wound as a trick...?!

"Hrah!" Tsukasa drove the heel of his palm into Inzaghi's jaw at a harsh angle. The Silver Knight's body flew through the air and toppled onto the bed. He didn't stand back up. The attack had rattled his brain, knocking him clean out.

Now nothing was left in Tsukasa's way. All he had to do was go grab Lyrule—or so he thought.

"—Ah...!"

A roar like a thunderclap echoed through the room. Tsukasa was from Earth. He knew that sound well.

It was the sound of a gunshot.

A searing pain shot through his chest. When he looked, he saw Lord Findolph pointing what looked like a smoking pistol right at him.

"Hya-ha-ha-ha! I shot you! I struck you down!" As Findolph watched Tsukasa drop to one knee, he let out a shrill laugh.

Tsukasa glanced at what the man was holding and clicked his tongue. "...A flintlock pistol? I anticipated the existence of firearms but didn't expect any of them to be small enough to hide in a pocket..."

"You didn't expect it? But of course! This miniature flintlock pistol is the newest technology from Freyjagard's imperial workshops! Only a handful of nobles are entrusted with them. There's no way a peasant like you could have known about it!"

The bullet had struck Tsukasa square in the heart. He couldn't have had much life left in him. Confident of that fact, Findolph flaunted his pistol and crowed victoriously.

"The times are changing? What a joke! We nobles have the technology, the knowledge, and the military! You people have nothing! You're the ruled, and we're the rulers! That will never change!" Findolph cast aside his now-empty pistol, drew forth a knife, and moved in for the kill, a confident expression of superiority on his face all the while.

It wasn't because his bullet had hit its mark. It was more fundamental than that. He was simply sure that a noble like him could never lose to a commoner. He had been special since the day he was born, and the commoners were his possessions, no more than slaves.

Nothing could possibly topple that hierarchy. That was what he'd believed all forty years of his life. Yet all his confidence was built upon castles of sand.

"—Then we will bridge that gap."

"Wh…?"

Suddenly, the young man who should have been on death's door rose to his feet as if nothing had happened.

"H-how are you still standing?! My bullet hit you; I saw it…!" But right as Findolph was about to let out another cry of disbelief, he heard something small and hard hit the floor. The bullet that should have been lodged in Tsukasa's chest rolled back on to him.

"What…?"

"This suit is made of bulletproof aramid fiber. A gun without rifling can't hope to penetrate it. And also…you seem quite proud of that flintlock, but I've got something similar." Tsukasa reached into his suit and drew a gleaming-silver automatic pistol.

Findolph gawked at it in disbelief. As far as he knew, the empire had only just developed small firearms. There was no way a peasant could have gotten their hands on one.

"No way; h-how…?! Y-you must be bluffing—"

To dispel the man's doubts, Tsukasa pulled the trigger and shot the knife right out of the lord's hand.

"Eeeeeeeeeeeeeeek?!?!"

"As you can see, this is no bluff. And this gun…has another six rounds loaded. Do you understand what that means? I could kill you six times over."

"E-eeeeeep?!?!" The young man's words sent Findolph into a panic. Why did a commoner have a gun superior to the best the empire could manufacture? It defied explanation. Who was this kid? Who were these people?

The cold reality of a barrel leveled at his forehead wiped away all of the lord's confusions. In their place surged his primal fear of death.

"Let's… Let's not do anything rash here! Y-you want the girl, right?! You can have her! Just take her and leave! A-and if that's not enough, I'll give you money! As much as you want! I'll exempt you from taxes! S-so let's just put that away!"

Tsukasa quietly shook his head.

"I'm sorry, but I can't do that. It would have been one thing before we started a war, but given the display of force we just put on, making a deal with you won't stop the empire. In their eyes, we're beyond forgiveness. It's how they've maintained control for as long as they have… In other words, there's no turning back for us. We'll take you down; we'll take your allies down; we'll mow down anything that stands in our way. And we'll keep going until this People's Revolution achieves its goal—building a nation by the people, of the people."

"Of the people…?"

"A land where everyone is equal—and where anyone can become the nation's representative. Every citizen will have a chance to participate in government and take responsibility for their own lives."

Upon hearing that, Findolph's jaw dropped for a moment. "Ha… ha-ha-ha! Do you have any idea how foolish you sound?!" Tsukasa's gun was still trained on him, but he couldn't contain himself.

"Commoners representing themselves?! A bunch of uneducated, powerless slobs who can't even survive without us holding their leashes building a nation?! Ha! Ah-ha-ha-ha!" His face still frozen in fear, he began laughing like a man possessed.

They were going to make a country with no kings or nobles, just 'people'? Edwart von Findolph had never heard anything so ridiculous in his life. The world would never accept such radical values. As far as he was concerned, the whole thing was like one big joke.

"Don't be absurd, now. His Majesty will never put up with such nonsense. Society won't put up with such nonsense...! Spreading this nonsense is akin to challenging the world itself...! You people think you can change the world?!" Findolph's mockery wasn't completely without merit.

The strong rule the weak. That was a fundamental rule of nature. Trying to sing equality's praises flew in the face of that. It was like trying to paint over the whole world's value system. None would call it an exaggeration to say that such a feat was beyond the reach of humankind. And yet—

"I know we can...if it's what the people want." Tsukasa's answer was plain and confident. For he knew that the seeds of change had already begun taking root in this world. The young man was confident they wouldn't be so easily ripped up.

The world changes in accordance with the will of the people. That was why—

"That's what politicians like me exist for."

With that, Tsukasa pulled the trigger.

There was a flash and a bang. Findolph's body crumpled to the floor. Yet, somehow...there was no blood. Tsukasa's gun was loaded with rubber bullets designed for riot control. Findolph wasn't dead. Tsukasa had decided he might still find a use for the unscrupulous lord.

In any case, the battle's over.

The battle of this eve, anyway. Tsukasa let out a long breath and dashed to Lyrule's side. "Lyrule! Are you all right?!"

He lifted her into his arms from the rug and lightly tapped her cheek. The moment he did, her long lashes trembled, and her eyelids opened to stare at her savior—

—with eyes glowing jade green.

That wasn't the color her eyes were supposed to be. And it wasn't just the irises that were off, either. Tsukasa could make out snowflake-like patterns of light gleaming in her pupils, too.

"Ly... Lyrule?"

"Thank...goodness... You made it...in time..."

A chill ran through Tsukasa's body. The girl he was holding was without a doubt Lyrule, and yet—

That's not Lyrule's voice...

"Who exactly...?" Tsukasa froze. He didn't understand what was going on. What could only be called Lyrule—and yet not Lyrule—reached up and cradled his cheek in her hand. Her petite lips moved as the strange voice spoke to him.

"There's...no ✖...left anymore. This world...is being engulf✖■ed... in a massive, e▲vil dragon's maw... If you don't hurry ●✕✕✕✕ will ✕✕—"

Her speech was intermittent, like a broken radio, but it seemed to be asking him to do something. Try as he might, Tsukasa couldn't tell what it was, though.

What was Lyrule...or rather, "she" trying to tell him? Who even was she?

But a moment later—

*　　*　　*

"I beg of　, o Seven He oes, you ust　 this world."

"_____!"

—all his questions were blown away.

Choppy as it was, he'd definitely heard her say *Seven Heroes.*

"Wait, was it you?! *Were you the one who summoned us here?!*"

The voice speaking through Lyrule's body grew faint, and Tsukasa grabbed the girl by her shoulders as if to plead for an answer. But then—

"H-huh…? Tsu…kasa…?"

"L-Lyrule?"

The mysterious green glow had vanished from her eyes. They were back to their normal shade of lapis lazuli. After getting a good eyeful of Tsukasa, the blond girl leaped up.

"Tsukasa…wait, wh-wh-wh-wh-what?! Wh-wh-wh-what are you doing here?! I'm… Wait…what's going on? The last thing I remember, there was a flash of light, and I passed out. Hmm? Lord Findolph is… Wait, what? What happened here?!" She looked around the room, but doing so only served to amplify her confusion.

Tsukasa choked back the hundreds of questions he wanted to ask her. He still didn't understand how it all worked, but it was clear that this Lyrule wasn't the same person as the one a moment ago. In other words, hounding her for answers wasn't going to get him anywhere.

Besides…right now, there was something more important he needed to do. After shifting mental gears, he laid his hand back atop Lyrule's shoulder.

"Are you injured at all?"

"Hmm…? Oh no. I hit my head a little, but it's just a small bump."

"Well, that's a big relief."

243

"But…what are you doing here, Tsukasa?"

"I came to rescue you. Not just me. We all came to save you."

"E-everyone…?!"

"Yup. We all worked together to storm the lord's castle and take it over."

"Hwa-wa-wa-wa?!" Lyrule's eyes went wide upon hearing the news…and anguish washed over her face. Her friends and family had started a war against the lord on her behalf. She knew all too well what the empire would do to them.

But the biggest source of her distress wasn't what was to come—

"I'm just the worst…! You all did something so crazy…and yet, I'm still so happy that you all came for me…!"

—it was guilt. Even though she'd made up her mind to sacrifice herself for the village, she was still happy they had sacrificed themselves for her. And she hated herself for being so selfish.

However, her guilt was misplaced. The people of Elm had picked this fight of their own volition. It was the future they'd chosen. There was no reason for Lyrule to feel guilty about that. As her shoulders trembled with anguish, Tsukasa pulled them toward himself and hugged her tight.

"Eh? Tsu…kasa…?"

"You're right. We did something crazy. And things are only going to get crazier from here. We're past the point of no return, and there are mountains of things we need to do and plan for. But we can leave that all for later."

For the moment, Tsukasa felt—

"I'm just glad you're safe." He whispered the words in her ear and squeezed her a little tighter. He wanted to convey to her just how much he and the others cared about her. The fact that they'd saved her was well worth celebrating.

When she realized just how thoughtful he was, the feelings of indebtedness inside her began fading away.

"Mmmmmmmmmm!" A choked sob slipped from her mouth. Contained in it was all the fear and despair she'd been stifling, as well as her relief at having been freed. Her heart was too full, and all her emotions were gushing out.

Tsukasa said nothing. He merely held Lyrule close until she finished wringing herself dry of all the emotions that were too heavy to keep carrying around inside.

Normally, now was when he should've been heading back to the others and letting them know that Lyrule was safe. Instead, he took comfort knowing they were a reliable bunch. His friends could certainly hold out long enough for Lyrule to at least settle down.

Lyrule finished sobbing far faster than Tsukasa had expected. Figuring she'd calmed herself, he let go of her, but the young woman grabbed his hands. The wounds on his palms had gotten so much worse that they were bleeding through his bandages.

Lyrule looked down at them. When she spoke, her voice was still a little nasal, but she sounded surprisingly collected.

"Sniff… You need more ointment, I see."

Tsukasa was a little taken aback.

"You just got saved, and you're already worrying about others? Well, I suppose that's just the way you are."

"You're certainly one to talk."

"…If you're feeling well enough to get snarky with me, I suppose that's all I can ask for."

If her mood had softened, there was no reason for the two of them to stay there. Tsukasa took Lyrule's hand.

"Come on, let's go. Everyone's waiting to see you safe and sound."

"…Okay!"

*   *   *

Tsukasa and Lyrule headed over to the terrace overlooking the courtyard and drew a curtain on the battle by announcing that Lord Edwart von Findolph had been defeated. The hunters of Elm cheered for their victory and the safe return of Lyrule.

It was no normal cry of victory.

It was the cheer that heralded the beginnings of freedom and equality in the Freyjagard Empire.

EPILOGUE

🎇 Revolution's Start and Shifting Shadows 🎇

After taking the castle, tying Lord Findolph up, and giving a big victory cheer, Tsukasa and the others got to work treating the wounded.

That said, most of the people in the courtyard who ended up needing Keine's help were from the opposing side.

None of the Elm villagers had anything worse than minor scratches, so after some basic first aid, they were free to enjoy their reunion with Lyrule. Tsukasa watched them for a bit, then called out to Masato, who was resting against the courtyard wall.

"Good work, Merchant. That was some splendid commanding you did."

"It was lucky we were able to pull off a surprise attack like that. I think the whole thing rattled Prince pretty bad, though. He's been puking his guts up over there in the corner since the battle ended. Shinobu had to go look after him."

"He might not look it, but he's got a strong heart. I'm sure he'll be fine before long."

"Man, I hope you're right. But hey, we got Lyrule back. All's well that ends well."

"This isn't over, and you know it. The real battle hasn't even started yet."

"Yeah, yeah, I know," Masato said, sighing. "You got a plan for what to do next?"

Tsukasa gave him a curt nod. "At a minimum, our goal is to form an internationally recognized independent nation. Merely having the nobles and the commoners reach some sort of compromise...would be pointless, I suspect. At the moment, though, we don't come anywhere close to qualifying as a nation."

"Yeah, true. We couldn't even take over a single castle right," Masato replied cynically. He glanced over at the massive hole they'd blown in the ramparts.

Most of the enemy soldiers had already fled through the aperture. Given the current strength of Tsukasa and the others, even so much as holding the domain wasn't particularly realistic.

"Our first order of business needs to be gathering allies, either by negotiation or by force. Don't worry, though. I have an idea."

"Classic Tsukasa, always on the ball. Whatever your plan is, I'm sure it's a good one."

Masato then clearly motioned to change the topic. His expression went serious, and he followed up on what Tsukasa had told him when they'd met up to cart off Findolph's unconscious body.

It was about what had happened to Lyrule.

"So about that, uh...trance thing Lyrule went into. Does that mean she's the one who summoned us here?"

Tsukasa shook his head.

"...No, I don't think so. The Lyrule with us right now probably doesn't know anything about that. But...that doesn't mean she bears no connection to why we're in this world. Once the mayor wakes up, I'll need to ask him more about her heritage. Also, I think we were right. The Seven Heroes definitely have something to do with us."

"They saved the continent from an evil dragon, right? ...I wonder what happened to them at the end of Winona's husband's story."

"I don't know. We can speculate all we want, but as far as we know, they vanished without a trace."

"...Man, that sounds like something straight out of a JRPG."

"Well, if this were a video game, I suppose that would make this 'evil dragon' or what have you the end boss we need to beat."

"It sounds simple when you put it like that, but...it might not be a literal dragon we're talking about."

"What do you mean?"

"Take a look."

Masato turned toward Tsukasa and flipped something his way.

Tsukasa caught it and laid it flat atop his palm. It was one of the gold coins of this world, emblazoned with the Freyjagard Empire's Dragon Crest.

"...Ah. You're right, that's definitely a possibility," Tsukasa muttered in agreement as he pocketed the coin.

Masato cried, "Hey, give that back!" but Tsukasa ignored him.

"Either way, we're not going to find any answers just thinking about it. We're missing too many pieces of the puzzle. Right now, the best we can do is just deal with each problem as it comes up. With any luck, that'll lead us toward the road back to Earth at some point. In the meantime, though, I've got a job for *him*." Tsukasa looked toward the still-unconscious Lord Findolph.

"Oh, speaking of jobs, you told Prince you had one for him back before the battle, right?"

"I did. What about it?"

"What're you gonna make him do?"

Tsukasa leaned in a little closer.

"Oh, it's simple, really. I'm going to have Akatsuki...become a god."

"...Say what?"

A few days after Tsukasa and co had taken over the Findolph domain, Alessio du Inzaghi seized an opening to flee the castle and made his way to the largest military power in northern Freyjagard: the Gustav domain.

His aim was to seek the help of Duke Gustav in retaking Findolph. Gustav held both the highest knighthood rank, Platinum Knight, and the title of Imperial Prime Mage.

Now, however, Inzaghi's freshly severed head was rolling over to Gustav's feet with his face frozen in an expression of agony.

"One of the empire's prized Silver Knights shamelessly abandoning the domain he protects and the men he commands in order to survive—how wretched. How utterly inexcusable." Gustav's voice dripped with loathing. He hurled aside the sword he'd used to behead Inzaghi, wiped the splash of blood from his face with a silk handkerchief, and cast off his bloodstained jacket. Then he called over a maid.

"Burn everything in this chamber and have the flooring replaced."

"Yes, my lord."

The one-eared maid bowed deeply. Gustav had found the mole on her right earlobe unseemly, so he'd lopped the whole ear clean off.

This country was His Majesty, the Emperor's garden. And a garden must be pruned to maintain its beauty. Nothing ugly could be allowed to exist in it, not even for a moment.

Such was the ideology Gustav lived by. In his eyes, rebels were akin to weeds polluting that garden. To state it flatly, theirs was an existence he would not abide.

"Filthy weeds. I, Oslo el Gustav, shall burn them to the ground."

AFTERWORD

Hello. I'm Riku Misora, the author.

Thank you all for buying *High School Prodigies Have It Easy Even in Another World!*

It's a story with seven protagonists, so it was something of a challenge to write.

You know, I've never had to juggle quite so many characters before. I've always respected Minoru Kawakami, but this is the first time I ever realized just how amazing he really is. In the end, though, I feel like the book came together nicely, and I was able to give every member of the cast a chance to shine.

Did you all enjoy it? If you did, be sure to look forward to Volume 2. Prince Akatsuki is going to become God Akatsuki!

Now I'd like to hijack this space for a bit and thank all the people who helped make this book a reality.

First, to my editor, K: Thank you for all the great revisions you made to the manuscript. You never faltered, even when by some inexplicable turn of events the first draft's 230 pages ballooned to 350.

Next, to Sacraneco, the book's illustrator: Thank you for all the wonderful art and for putting up with all my nonsense, like when I asked that the cover have a big blue sky and a hazard symbol on it.

And last but not least, I'd like to extend a huge thank-you to all of you lovely people who read the book to its end.

Finally, I'd like to touch on a different work for a moment— *Chivalry of a Failed Knight¸* another series I'm publishing with GA Bunko. It's getting an anime this October! I would be so thrilled if you all checked it out. And if you end up liking it, I would love it if you gave the books a try, too.

Anyway, that's all from me. I hope to see you again in book two!